Ciao Don Camillo

Giovannino Guareschi, known as Giovanni to his millions of English-speaking readers, was born at Fontanelle di Roccabianca in la Bassa parmense, the lowland plain on the banks of the Po River in northern Italy, on the 1st of May, 1908. He found his vocation after a package containing cartoons, jokes, prose and proposals was sent to the Milan-based publisher Angelo Rizzoli, who was planning a new satirical magazine, to be called *Bertoldo*.

For two years during the war, Guareschi was incarcerated in one prison-of-war camp after another in Poland and Germany, where he was reduced to a state of despair. Out of it he brought himself to the polemic that would underwrite all his work post-war.

Shortly after he was liberated by the English and returned home in September 1945, he was commissioned by Rizzoli to found *Candido*, the satirical magazine in which Don Camillo, Peppone and the speaking Christ first appeared in December 1946.

So effective was *Candido* in its satirical swipe at life in post-war Italy, where the communist party formed the most effective opposition to Christian Democracy, that the hugely popular *Life* magazine, published by Time Inc., reported that the 1948 elections had effectively been won by Alcide de Gasperi, leader of the Christian Democrats, and Guareschi together.

In 1952 the first of seven films was made, based on the Don Camillo stories, helping eventually to take book sales to more than twenty-three million copies worldwide. In the same year, Guareschi moved back to la Bassa, bought some land at Roncole Verdi, where the composer Giuseppe Verdi had been born in 1813, and built the house he had been dreaming on for years.

Since 2013 Pilot Productions has, in collaboration with the Estate of Guareschi, published eleven collections of the Don Camillo stories, bringing the translations more faithfully in line with the author's original manuscripts and a great many of them to the English reader for the first time.

Titles in the Series

The Little World of Don Camillo
Book 1, in which Guareschi introduces readers to the Little World of the village priest, Don Camillo, and his adversary, Peppone, the communist mayor. A fresh translation of the classic bestseller, with 19 stories available in English for the first time. E-book: ASIN: B00HAMIVUC. Paperback ISBN: 9781900064071. Audiobook: ASIN: B07CZPFQDT.

Don Camillo and His Flock
Book 2, in which the people of the Little World again show their passion for politics, culminating in the battling priest's exile to the mountains. E-book: ASIN: B013TFT1YS. Paperback ISBN: 9781900064187.

Don Camillo and Peppone
Book 3, in which politics and prejudice remain to the fore, but the wit and wisdom of *Il Cristo* help bring Don Camillo home to the Lower Plain. E-book: ASIN: B01CIWE1T8. Paperback ISBN 9781900064262.

Comrade Don Camillo
In Book 4, set against the background of the Cold War, Don Camillo steals a march on Peppone over a matter of conscience and is transported incognito to Khrushchev's Russia. E-book: ASIN: B0722G6GY4. Paperback ISBN 9781900064330.

Don Camillo and Company
Book 5: a unique treasure trove of Guareschi's enchanting, bittersweet stories, made available in English by the Guareschi Estate for the first time in 2018. E-book: ASIN: B07DKBHFJH. Paperback ISBN 9781900064408.

Don Camillo's Dilemma
Book 6: the local elections are upon us once more, a storm breaks and the village priest finds that the last straw can break even a Camillo's back. E-book: ASIN: B08KJ6GT7W. Paperback ISBN 9781900064477.

Don Camillo Takes the Devil by the Tail
Book 7. Taking a serpent by the tail is never a good idea, but in the Little World of Don Camillo, hilarious and unearthly things can happen to draw the poison from its bite. E-book: ASIN: B089KLX8KK. Paperback ISBN 9781900064514.

Don Camillo and Don Chichi
Book 8: it is 1966. In the face of huge changes in the Little World, Don Camillo digs in and finds a surprise ally in Peppone as he fights to save the 3-metre high crucifix through which he conducts his famous Conversations with God. E-book: ISBN: 9781900064552. Paperback ISBN 9781900064569.

Merry Christmas Don Camillo
Book 9 publishes the Christmas stories alongside the author's desperate experiences as a prisoner-of-war which refined his natural humour into a satirical weapon and made his vision of a deeper reality – the voice of *il Cristo* – available to all. E-book: ISBN: 9781900064644. Paperback ISBN 9781900064590.

Don Camillo of la Bassa
Book 10 marks the author's return to the land of his birth and to the characters it continues to inspire. E-book: ISBN: 9781900064668. Paperback ISBN 9781900064651.

CIAO DON CAMILLO

CAMILLO

GIOVANNI GUARESCHI

EDITED BY
Piers Dudgeon

PILOT PRODUCTIONS

Published by Pilot Productions in 2024
Grove Farm Sawdon, North Yorkshire YO13 9DY

A catalogue record for this book is available
from the British Library

Paperback ISBN 978-1-900064-67-5
Ebook ISBN 978-1-900064-68-2

Cover design by BerniStevensdesign.com
Typesetting and e-book production by
epubknowhow.co.uk
Printed and bound in Great Britain by
Clays Ltd, Elcograf S. p. A.

Contents

Titles in the Series	ii
Editor's Preface	9

Post-war

All-out War (1947)	14
A Matter of Conscience (1948)	22
The Sun Rises Again (1948)	28
The Irregulars (1948)	35
The Prodigal Son (1949)	42
The *Polare* Pact (1949)	45
The Petition (1949)	52
Out of the Night (1950)	57
War of Secession (1950)	63
Hand of God (1950)	76

Tales of la Bassa

The Girl with Red Hair (1950)	85
Giacomone (1952)	92
Something from 1922 (1952)	98
Thicker than Water (1952)	109
The Treasure (1957)	118
The Return of St Anthony (1957)	128
An Arrival from the City (1958)	138
An Unnecessary Detour (1960)	149
Il Terrone (1960)	158
The Second Prize (1961)	169

People of la Bassa

The Young Master (1951)   179
The Doctor (1952)   187
Christ in the Dresser (1958)   201
The Sins of our Fathers (1960)   207
Public Opinion (1960)   215
The Vendetta (1961)   224

Editor's Preface

THESE STORIES GO back to 1947, almost to the beginning of the Don Camillo era, and continue right through to 1961, the year in which Guareschi called time as a contributor to *Candido*, the principal vehicle for his satire.[1]

Here are colourful observations of life in Italy's widest and yet most secluded plain, stories so authentic and telling that time and again they reverberate with insights relevant not only locally but also internationally, not only to the era that produced them, but also to our lives today.

Most are available in English for the first time.

The first are set in the immediate post-war period following the defeat of Nazi Germany and the execution of the fascist dictator Mussolini by the Italian Resistance, a force made up of diverse groups united in their shared anti-fascist stance. Now that the battle against fascism has been won, and vengeance wrought on fascist sympathisers close to home, various of these Resistance groups re-emerge as national political parties, with the Italian Communist Party (the PCI) the main antagonist of the Christian Democrats (*Democrazia Cristiana*), which became the ruling party after the 1948 election and with which Don Camillo is associated.

As the title of the first story suggests, the post-war period brought not peace but *guerra a oltranza* – 'all-out war' – particularly so in la Bassa, which played host to the new torchbearers for totalitarianism – the communists, answerable only to Joseph Stalin in Moscow. More members of the PCI resided in la Bassa at this time than anywhere in Italy and conflict spelled tragedy at the family level, as Guareschi shows in his second story, 'A Matter of Conscience'.

---

[1] 'Ciao' is used in the Italian language for both 'hello' and 'goodbye'.

Don Camillo and Peppone had fought side-by-side in the Resistance during the war, the communist Peppone once even acting as Don Camillo's 'altar boy' in the field, as we learn in 'The Vendetta'. Now, the very real fear of *la seconda ondata*, literally 'the second wave', an anticipated communist takeover in Europe, is driving the politics.

The situation attracts the U.S. Secretary of State George Marshall's billion-dollar aid package designed to bind Europe into a strategy to prevent the spread of communism. Being a political gesture, this becomes a battleground in the village, with Peppone refusing Party members the right to handouts from America, while Don Camillo looks to exact political capital out of a situation where capitalism appears in a good light.

In the same year, 1949, the Vatican Decree excommunicating all communist sympathisers from the Catholic Church juices up village conflict further. And the founding of NATO does little to relax tensions. Peppone's view of 'the damnable Atlantic Pact' as an aggressive move by the West finds resonance with Putin's reaction today to Ukraine's would-be NATO membership: 'We need to invade,' Peppone concludes, 'occupy something important! Make a big strike!'

In the Don Camillo stories people kill and are killed because they cling too tightly to their beliefs and ideologies. What is required, Guareschi suggests, is a new way of thinking, involving empathy and imagination rather than the analysis and judgment of politics.

Don Camillo and Peppone, each as weighed down as the other with the ideological and doctrinal baggage they drag around with them, believe that they have a monopoly on the truth. They resist at all costs seeing the true values in the other's tradition.

Guareschi's position on this, hard won in the depths of despair as a prisoner in a German concentration camp during the war[2], is that we have to take into any meaningful dialogue the possibility of making a change within ourselves.

The onus of this he projects upon the crucified Christ, the 3-metre-high figure above the High Altar in the village church. In more than half the Don Camillo stories, *Il Cristo*, who doesn't

---

[2] See 'My Thoughts Turn Inwards' in *Merry Christmas Don Camillo.*

'do' politics, counsels the village priest with wisdom, compassion and gentle humour, exposing and undermining his prejudices and suggesting solutions to his battles with Peppone so simple that they are beyond the reach of political minds clouded with ideology and the need to win.

When the sensory powers are withdrawn from their preoccupations with the outside world and are turned inward, then in the silence and darkness our inner voice is heard. That this faculty is innate, Guareschi confirms in 'Christ in the Dresser' and 'Out of the Night', where even Peppone and his lieutenant, Smilzo, show that, in *extremis*, their natural default is to a higher order of counsel than the adversarial political ideology to which they have long been enslaved. But the search for it has to be undertaken, and is by Peppone, instinctively, when the darkness of death descends.

Guareschi emerged from the war ever the child of la Bassa, which he saw as a palimpsest (or manuscript) on which successive generations have scored their stories. It is a landscape redolent of history and regularly yields an unearthing, be it treasure or the debris of war or some crazy diverting ancient ruse that finds its way into the present. Often there is much honest atonement required, as in 'The Sins of our Fathers', where Italy's alignment with Mussolini and Hitler is examined and agrarians are held to account as the godfathers of fascism. Guareschi is not on the side of 'those who would keep historical truth hidden from children so as not to offend the susceptibilities of their fathers'.

In the deepest sense, he shares the spirit of la Bassa through the characters who spring from these pages into our lap and make us laugh, but they also make us think. As in every good parable, there is always a message underlying his imaginative snapshots of village life. In 'Hand of God', such weighty matters as the interdependence of all facets of reality through time and space, free will and divine intervention are all dealt with by *il Cristo* in a matter of a few pages.

But, in the end, what probably captivates us most is the sense that la Bassa seems to lie on an unmarked frontier between our material world and that other, formless universe where space and time, the great limiters of our finite lives, do not exist.

It is a place in a special relationship with the author's imagination, as he confirms when enjoying a typical August afternoon in his beloved homeland:

'There, in the middle of the deserted fields, in full sun, everything smells of a fairytale and if the Devil should appear scarlet and grinning in the middle of a plain of burnt stubble the apparition would seem like the most natural thing in the world.'

Piers Dudgeon, August 2024

The author in 1945

Post-war

All-out War (1947)

DON CAMILLO HAD what felt like a nail planted in his brain, the sharp end of which turned on the implausibility of the notorious 'legend of the living corpse'.

The story began one day when Don Camillo became convinced he'd seen a young member of the Resistance walking in the city, fit as a fiddle after he'd supposedly been killed in action while fighting alongside Peppone and his men, before being interred by Don Camillo himself with great ceremony in the village cemetery.

Subsequently, information had reached Don Camillo that the young partisan's coffin had contained not a body, but ten million lire's worth of silverware, gold, weaponry, etc, liberated by Peppone and his men from the Germans and used to finance the construction of the People's Palace after the war, which Don Camillo had then been tricked into giving his blessing. The fake burial had been the only way to get the stuff out of the Villa Docchi, previously the German HQ, without anyone knowing.

However, while Peppone's trickery would, at the time, have had devastating consequences for the Mayor had it been made public, Don Camillo had waived political advantage in favour of persuading him into donating part of the illegal haul to realising a dream he had for a playroom and garden with a merry-go-round and swings for use by the village children.

Life in the village had gone on to everyone's advantage, but Don Camillo's conscience would not let him free from the idea that, whatever his good intentions regarding the affair, he had made himself complicit in its murkier aspects. His focus now was on how Peppone's men had managed to dig the coffin out of the village cemetery without anyone noticing and specifically on what else Peppone had been up to in this resting place of the village dead. It was this that was burning a hole in the priest's brain, and he was determined to lay it to rest.

The aforesaid cemetery served the entire municipality. It was vast and stood just outside the village. Built according to the usual plan, it comprised a large rectangle of land enclosed within four buildings which – with the exception of a gatehouse – were plain and unadorned on the outside while, on the inside, they incorporated a series of arches with burial niches in multiple tiers.[3]

To find a solution to what was so niggling him, Don Camillo went to the scene of the crime, slipping into a role inspired by the exploits of the famous detective, Nat Pinkerton[4]. Halfway along the left-hand arcade of arches, along the second tier, he came upon the burial niche he sought, faced, as it was, with a beautiful marble gravestone carrying the fake name of the fake dead soldier.

Standing in front of it, Don Camillo made a sudden about-turn and walked straight across a field of crosses until he reached the central arcade. Here he turned towards the exit and began walking more slowly, all the time counting his steps.

The next day he took the path that ran along the left wall outside the cemetery, again counting his steps, and when he had counted enough to get to the precise location of the partisan's burial niche he came to a halt and ignited his Tuscan vehicle.

The wall was covered with tangled vines, but if anyone were to look carefully he would notice that about a metre from the ground, at the point corresponding to the grave of the fake dead man, there was a square of plaster lighter than the rest. Don Camillo did indeed look very carefully.

---

[3] Designed with more than a nod to the traditional catacomb scheme, but above ground.

[4] The eponymous detective featured in the German dime novel *Nat Pinkerton, der König der Detectivs*, very popular in Europe in the 1910s and '20s and clearly charmed Don Camillo's childhood.

'The coffin will have come out here,' he muttered, adding, 'and where stuff comes out, other stuff can go in... Holes are blessed affairs, they offer two-way communication.'

Continuing his walk, passing in front of the police station, he stopped to have a chat with the Marshal.

So it happened that under cover of that same night, with great caution, a group of *carabinieri* made a hole in the cemetery wall where Don Camillo had noticed the lighter plaster and took out thirty-eight machine guns, twenty-three pistols and a heavy machine gun from the young man's burial niche, all in perfect order – greased, lubricated and shiny – enough to kick-start the Second Wave[5].

The story broke and kicked off a hell of a fuss; even the national newspapers covered it, but no one showed up to claim the weapons as theirs, and the matter got bogged down because Don Camillo was careful not to mention, even vaguely, the previous treasure haul, which had been of benefit to his pastoral work.

'When God offers you a finger, don't take his hand!' he advised the Marshal after he insisted on delving deeper into the mystery. 'Be satisfied with these weapons!'

'How can I be?' protested the Marshal. 'Now that I have found the weapons I must also find the dead man for whom these weapons were substituted.'

'I understand, but don't worry too much, Marshal,' advised Don Camillo. 'The important thing is to have discovered the machine guns, because it's the machine guns that shoot, not the absent dead.'

Peppone, of course, didn't say a word, but he was as calm as someone who'd swallowed a live cat.

'It had to have been *him*!' he shouted with Brusco. 'No one would have thought of making a hole in a dead person's grave if they hadn't been sure that the dead person was not inside the tomb. Whoever it is will have to pay for this!'

---

[5] The second communist revolution, anticipated post-war, which, in spite of the heavy population of communists in Italy, never took off.

'Him', of course, was Don Camillo, who, however, behaved with great discretion regarding the whole affair and limited himself to printing some forty small posters and sticking them on the walls of the People's Palace and Peppone's workshop. They read:

FOUND
The stillborn Second Wave was washed up near
the Municipal Cemetery. All interested
parties apply to the Police Station.

Five days later the village woke up with its walls plastered with large yellow posters printed in huge letters:

LOST
Six hundred pounds of edible products and
various canned goods delivered by the
Regional Welfare Committee ten days ago
to Archpriest Don Camillo for distribution
to the poor have gone missing. If Don Camillo
has found the stuff will he straightway
distribute it to the rightful beneficiaries.

Signed: *The poor of the countryside.*
Death to all thieves!

Don Camillo rushed screaming to the Marshal. 'I'm reporting them!' he shouted. 'I'm reporting them all! This is an outrage!'

'Who are you reporting?' the Marshal inquired. 'The poster is signed, "The poor of the countryside".'

'What poor people in the countryside! It's the countryside scoundrels who did this! It's Peppone and his gang.'

'It may well be: but up to now it is only you who is saying so. Whatever you believe to be the case, report it and then we can start an official investigation.'

Don Camillo returned home and, passing through the square, threw himself at the first poster that came into his sight and began to tear it up in anger.

Someone passed by on a bicycle.

'Tear it, tear them all up if you will,' the someone shouted at him, 'but truth always triumphs in the end!'

'I now know why he's so fat, too,' added a dishevelled woman nearby. 'He makes his living stealing from the poor!'

Don Camillo resumed his journey and, shortly afterwards, came upon Filotti.

'Have you seen what they're up to, Signor Filotti?' Don Camillo exclaimed.

'I have, yes,' Filotti replied calmly. 'But you don't have to worry: for sure you will have what it takes to see them off. If I were you, I would post your original receipts for the goods and a list of the beneficiaries.'

'What receipts? What goods?'

'Those of the Regional Welfare Committee.'

'But I haven't received anything!' shouted Don Camillo. 'I don't even know if such a committee exists!'

'Oh! Can it possibly be?'

'Not only is it possible, it's the unadulterated truth! I haven't received anything – now or ever!'

'This surely cannot be! It seems incredible that someone would invent something like this. But if you say so, it must be...'

Don Camillo continued on his way and met Signor Borghetti, who, with his pince-nez perched on his nose, was reading the famous poster.

'Eh, the world is rotten, Don Camillo!' said Borghetti, shaking his head.

Farther on, old Barchini, the printer, was standing at the door of his shop.

'I didn't print it,' he declared instantly. 'If I had, I would have come to tell you. What *is* this about, Don Camillo? Is it perhaps the shipment the Bishop was supposed to send...?'

Peppone's truck then came trundling by with Smilzo at the wheel:

'*Bon appetit*, Reverendo!' he shouted.

And all the people laughed.

*

Don Camillo missed breakfast: at three he was still lying on his bed looking at the rafters in the ceiling. At four o'clock a hellish ruckus arose in the square and he went to the window. The churchyard was full of people and, in the front row, women were screaming furiously. None of the faces were familiar to him. He thought of the truck with Smilzo at the wheel.

'They've gone and picked up the poor in all the hamlets,' Don Camillo mused. 'They've organised it well…'

'We want our stuff! Down with the exploiters of the people!' the women and their children shouted.

Don Camillo looked out of the window and shouted back:

'I have nothing to give to anyone! Because no one gave me anything! It's an infamous slander!'

They told him to go and tell that to the parish priest of San Quentin.

'We want to take a look!' one woman demanded, shaking her fists at him. 'If you don't have something hidden away, show us!'

The crowd threw themselves against the door of the presbytery and Don Camillo retreated and took down his shotgun from the wall. Then he looked at the gun and threw it on the bed and looked out of the window again. The Marshal had arrived with all six *carabinieri* and taken up a position in front of the presbytery door. But the people continued to scream, clamouring now to get in at all costs. Then Peppone stepped forward.

'Pause!' he screamed. 'Now let me speak.'

The people fell silent and Peppone looked up at Don Camillo.

'Don Camillo,' he said, 'I speak to you as Mayor. I don't intend to argue about the truth of what is printed on the poster. I simply say that the people today feel deceived and are rightly exasperated. So, if we want to avoid bloodshed, you must allow a commission into the presbytery. I will be on the commission and the entire council will be there with me, and, naturally, the Marshal and his *carabinieri* will also be there in the front row.'

'*Bene!*' the crowd chorused.

Don Camillo shook his head.

'There is nothing to see here! This is my home and no one will invade it. What the poster says is all a foul invention. I am ready to swear as much on the Gospels!'

'Swear it on the cupboard where the 600 pounds of our stuff is!' the crowd insisted. 'Don't you fool us!'

Don Camillo shrugged his shoulders and was about to retreat, but the mad crowd threw itself at the six *carabinieri* who were quickly overwhelmed. The Marshal, however, was not to be defeated and, grabbing his machine gun, fired a volley into the air. This was enough to make the people take a few steps back and allow the *carabinieri* to regroup and take up a defensive position.

'Stop or you will force me to use our weapons!' shouted the Marshal.

The crowd hesitated for a moment, then advanced slowly and decisively. The *carabinieri* turned pale and, with jaws clenched, chambered their cartridges.

Things were about to turn tragic and Don Camillo raised his hand.

'Stop!' he shouted. 'I will come down and open the door.'

When the door opened the commission was all ready drawn up in formation before him: thirty people, including Peppone and his general staff and the Marshal and four of the *carabinieri*.

There ensued a ruthless search of the presbytery: they opened all the drawers, all the doors, all the chests. They banged on the walls, on the floors. They left not a square centimetre unexplored in the attic or in the cellar. They searched inside the demijohns and barrels, up the chimneys, in the woodshed and in the stable. If there had been a needle to find, they would have found it. Instead of food they found in the cupboard only a loaf of bread, three eggs and a crust of cheese. And, in the cellar, two salamis and two lard bladders hanging from the ceiling.

Don Camillo, with his arms folded, watched silently and indifferently. When they had also felt the mattresses, they said that they wanted to look in the bell tower too and in the church, and the Marshal turned pale. Don Camillo set off: they looked in the confessionals, under the altar, in the sacristy. They didn't touch anything, they made Don Camillo do it, but they wanted to see everything. They even searched the garden.

And found nothing. In the end they came out heads down. They talked for a while with the crowd in the churchyard, after which the assembly broke up in silence.

*

Don Camillo didn't even eat that evening. He remained lying on his bed looking at the rafters in the ceiling. Then, when he had collected himself, he went into the church and came to a standstill in front of the altar.

'Thank you,' he whispered.

But, from the Christ, there came no response.

Don Camillo returned to his bedroom, which had one window overlooking the churchyard and one overlooking the fields and the vegetable garden. The window overlooking the garden was wide open and since that afternoon a wool blanket had been spread from the windowsill down the outside wall, airing. He pulled back the blanket and, under the sill, were three nails and on each nail was hung a machine gun. He retrieved the guns and bagged them. Then he went down to the cellar and removed the two lard bladders and the two salamis hanging from the ceiling. In reality only one of the salamis contained pork, the other and the two bladders were fat with yellow fat impregnated with machine gun bullets. He threw the fake salami and the two bladders of fake lard into the bag. Then he climbed over the garden hedge and, walking through the fields, reached the embankment and the river. There, he got into a boat, rowed through the flood plain to the famous site of a submerged church and threw the sack into the water.

He then returned home and knelt once more in front of the High Altar.

'Thank you,' Don Camillo whispered. 'Thank you for not letting them find the stuff I threw away. It was what they were looking for. They wanted to make a scandal out of it. I thank you not for me, but because it would have hurt the Church.'

'Very well, Don Camillo. But I have told you many times to throw your weaponry away.'

Don Camillo sighed.

'And now here I am, with nothing left, just an old hunting rifle good for nothing but scaring owls. Who will defend me now?'

'Your honesty, Don Camillo.'

'It appears not,' replied Don Camillo. 'You saw it today: my honesty certainly did not defend me. Peppone and his gangsters knew what they were looking for, but as for the others a slanderous poster was enough to convince them that I was a scoundrel. My honesty did not protect me. And it won't protect me now because they don't know that I no longer have weapons, they are sure that I do still have them and, full of anger at not having been able to find them and shame me, they will continue their all-out war against me. But I...!'

Don Camillo puffed out his chest and clenched his enormous fists. Then he let go, lowered his head and bowed low.

'I have nothing left,' he sighed. 'The slander has been spread: I am he who grows fat on the food of the poor...'

He walked away and went to the presbytery.

The good salami was still hanging from the cellar ceiling: he tore it off to cut a few slices, but the knife met something hard.

'I threw away the good salami and kept the one full of bullets,' he muttered, smiling sadly. He went to throw the minced salami into the cesspit of the stable, tried to gnaw on a cheese rind, then went to bed and thought with no little regret that the next day he would have to start living all over again.

Meanwhile, Peppone looked into the darkness of his bedroom and thought of Don Camillo's cupboard in which they'd found only three eggs, a loaf of bread and a crust of cheese. He tossed and turned in bed for a long time, but then remembered the two salamis from the cellar.

'At least he'll cut himself a few slices of salami,' he muttered and fell asleep with a clear conscience.

A Matter of Conscience (1948)

PEPPONE HAD BEEN hammering on the anvil furiously for some time, but no matter how much he hammered like a man possessed, he couldn't get the thought that was haunting him out of his brain.

'What a cretin!' he muttered to himself. 'Look at the mess he's making.'

The post-war aid tap from America was now flowing freely.[6] Don Camillo was jubilant, because the food parcels were plentiful and well filled and people were happy to get them. The Reds, on the other hand, were under strict orders not to apply to Don Camillo for any form of capitalist welfare, and Peppone's most loyal follower, Stràziami, has fallen to temptation. Desperate for food for his frail son, he has erred and been disciplined and his son has been terrified by Peppone and a heartless party Inspector. But that is not the end of it.

At that moment, Peppone raised his eyes to see that the idiot was there, in front of the anvil.

'You scared my boy,' said Stràziami darkly. 'He's been raving all night and now he's in bed with a fever.'

Peppone continued to hammer.

'It's your fault,' he replied without looking at him.

'Poverty is to blame,' replied Stràziami.

'We gave you an order and the Party's orders must be obeyed without question.'

'The hunger of children is a higher priority than the Party.'

'No: the Party must come before everything else.'

Stràziami took a card out of his pocket, which he placed on the anvil and Peppone stopped his hammering.

'I'm returning my card,' said Stràziami. 'This is no longer a party card but a special surveillance card.'

'You speak unwisely, Stràziami.'

'I speak well. I paid for my freedom by risking my skin in the war. I'm not willing to give it up now.'

---

[6] Following the signing of the Economic Recovery Act of 1948 by US President Truman in April, 1948, America's $13-billion foreign aid project known as the Marshall Plan (named after Secretary of State George Marshall) was designed to rebuild war-devastated Europe, at the same time, thereby, binding post-war Europe into America's urgent strategy to prevent the spread of communism.

Peppone put down the hammer and wiped his forehead with the back of his hand. Stràziami was one of the few very loyal ones; he had fought alongside him, he had shared hunger, desperation and hope with him.

'You betrayed the cause,' stated Peppone.

'The cause is freedom. If I gave up my freedom, then, yes, I would be betraying the cause.'

'Think about it, we'll have to kick you out: you know you can't resign. Anyone who resigns is expelled.'

'Yes, I know. And those who do something really bad are expelled three months before they do it. And we say that our enemies are hypocrites! Goodbye, Peppone. I'm sorry for you that, from now on, you will be obliged to consider me your enemy, while I will continue to consider you my friend.'

Peppone watched Stràziami go away: then he roused himself, threw the hammer into a corner with a curse and went outside to sit at the bottom of the garden. He couldn't believe that Stràziami, of all his men, could be expelled from the ranks of the Party: in the end he jumped up.

'It's all the fault of that damned bastard,' he concluded. 'Now is the time to put things right for good and all.'

The 'damned bastard' was leafing through some papers in the presbytery when Peppone appeared before him.

'You'll be happy now!' exclaimed Peppone angrily. 'You finally managed to get to some of our people!'

Don Camillo looked at him curiously.

'Have the elections gone to your head?' he enquired.

'Nice move! Ruin the reputation of a poor wretch who has had nothing but pain from your dirty capitalist society.'

'I remain mystified, Comrade Mayor.'

'You'll understand when I tell you that Stràziami is to be expelled from the Party because of you. Yes, it's your fault! You took advantage of his misery, you picked him out, you gave him one of your dirty American packages, so the Party Inspector found out last night, he went to catch Stràziami at his house, he threw all his stuff out the window and then he slapped him.'

Peppone had become very agitated.

'Calm down,' Don Camillo countered.

'Calm down, no way! If you'd seen the eyes of that boy when he watched the food snatched from the dinner table in the tablecloth and chucked out of the window and when he saw his father get slapped, you wouldn't be so calm, even if you had only the tiniest bit of feeling!'

The blood draining from his face, Don Camillo stood up and made Peppone repeat what the Inspector had done, then pointed a finger at his chest.

'You rogue! he exclaimed.'

Peppone was furious: 'You scoundrels who exploit the hunger of the poor for electoral purposes!'

Don Camillo grabbed an iron poker from the corner of the fireplace.

'If you open your mouth again I'll slaughter you!' he shouted. 'I have not exploited anyone's hunger, I have parcels here for all the poor and I do not deny the parcel to any poor person. I am interested in the hunger of the poor, not their political ideas. You scoundrel, who, unable to give any help to those who are hungry because you only have printed paper with lies in stock, can expect no one to benefit. When someone does give food and clothing to people in need you accuse him of wanting to buy votes, and you prevent the men of your own party from accepting aid parcels. Then, if one of yours does accept aid, you treat him as a traitor to the people. You betray the people, because you take away from them what others give them. Politics? Propaganda? Stràziami's son, the children of your other poor comrades who, out of fear of you, don't come to collect the package, don't even know that the package is sent to them by America.

'Many of them don't even know that America exists. For them it is simply something to eat, nourishment that you steal from them. You are such a scoundrel because you admit that if a man sees his son suffering from hunger he can steal the bread that is necessary for the boy's life, but you will not admit that a man can accept that same bread if America offers it to him. Because this would be to Russia's moral disadvantage! What did Stràziami's son know about America and Russia? He was finally about to feed himself for once, and you snatched the food from his mouth. You are the scoundrel, not me!'

Peppone shook his head. 'I didn't do or say anything.'

'You allowed a rogue Inspector not only to do this, but to commit the most infamous abuse in the world: that of hitting a father in front of his child. The child always has immense trust in his father, and always esteems him the strongest of all, judges him to be untouchable in this regard, and you allowed a jumped-up ideologue to destroy this illusion – the only good that fate had bestowed on the most wretched of children. What would you say if I entered your house this evening and, in front of your son, slapped your face?'

Peppone shrugged his shoulders. 'Well, you could try.'

'I can do it!' shouted Don Camillo who was in a full flood of fury. 'I can do it!' he screamed again. And, grabbing the big iron bar in his hands at both ends, he gritted his teeth and, roaring like a tiger, bent it into a U.

'I'll tie a tie for you and Stalin and then I'll tie a knot too!' he shouted.

Peppone looked at him a little worried, but made no comment. Don Camillo opened a cupboard and took out a package which he handed to Peppone.

'Take this to him, if you are not the worst of imbeciles! This is not sent by America or England or Portugal: it is sent by Divine Providence, which needs no votes to remain in charge of the universe. You can send for the rest of the packages too and have them distributed yourself.'

'Okay, I'll send Smilzo with the van,' muttered Peppone, hiding the package under his cloak. When he reached the door, he turned, placed the package on a chair, picked up the U-shaped iron bar and tried to straighten it.

'If you manage it, I'll vote for the Popular Democratic Front,' Don Camillo sneered.

Peppone turned red as a cinnabar-chanterelle from the effort. Then he threw the bar on the ground, which hadn't bent an inch.

'We don't need your vote to win,' said Peppone, picking up the food parcel and leaving.

*

Stràziami was reading a newspaper sitting in front of the fire and his boy was curled up next to him. Peppone entered and, placing the package on the table, broke the string and untied the wrapping.

'Here,' he said to the boy. 'This is for you. The Eternal Father sends it directly.'

Then he handed something to Stràziami.

'And this is for you, you left it on my anvil.'

Stràziami took the card and put it in his wallet. 'Does the Eternal Father also sends this directly?' he asked.

'Everything comes to us from the Eternal Father,' muttered Peppone. 'Everything: the good and the bad. It depends whose turn it is. It fell to us…'

The boy had jumped up and was happily looking at all the goodies displayed on the table.

'Don't worry, this time no one will take it away from you,' Peppone reassured him.

*

Smilzo arrived at the presbytery in the afternoon.

'The boss sent me to collect the goods in the van,' he said to Don Camillo. And Don Camillo pointed out the packages piled up in the hallway.

On his last journey to the van, when Smilzo was on the threshold loaded down with parcels, Don Camillo gave him a two-ton kick up the backside, which sent all the parcels and half of Smilzo into the body of the van.

'Put that in your report too,' explained Don Camillo, 'along with the names you gave yesterday to the Party Inspector.'

'We'll deal with you on April 18th,' replied Smilzo, getting out of the van. 'Your name is at the top of another of our lists.' [7]

'Good, do you need anything else?'

'No, I'm fine; I've already taken orders from all three of you: from Peppone, from Stràziami and from you. So why do I end up in a situation like this? Because I follow an order.'

'Orders cannot be followed willy-nilly,' warned Don Camillo.

'Right: the difficult thing is to know beforehand when orders are no good,' Smilzo sighed.

---

[7] General elections were held in Italy on 18 April 1948 to elect the first Parliament of the Italian Republic. The communists did not fare well, thanks in no small way to Guareschi's tales of Don Camillo and Peppone, so popular at the time.

The Sun Rises Again (1948)

ONE AFTERNOON OLD Signora Bacchini came to the confessional to confess her sins and, as usual, Don Camillo listened to her calmly until suddenly, after a moment's hesitation, the old woman said something that made him jump out of his skin:

'Reverend, I intend to vote for Garibaldi.'[8]

Don Camillo left the confessional, drew back the curtain and said: 'Come to the presbytery, we should talk.'

And when they were in her study, he asked whether she had lost her mind. 'I think I've explained how things are more than once!' he exclaimed. 'Clearly, you haven't understood a word I said.'

---

[8] In December 1947 a coalition, known as the Popular Democratic Front, was formed between the Italian Socialist Party (PSI) and the Communist Party (PCI) to contest the first Parliament of the Italian Republic, following the dissolution of the monarchy in 1946. Heavily backed by Soviet Russia, the coalition's symbol was a green star surmounted by an image of Giuseppe Garibaldi, a national hero who had played a critical part in the unification of Italy and died in 1882. Garibaldi was not a communist even ideologically, but during World War II there had been an important connection between the Garibaldi Brigades and the communists brought about by a common repugnance for the fascist forces of Hitler and Mussolini. The Garibaldi Brigades aligned with the Italian Communist Party and made up more than 40% of the Resistance movement. The communists were now looking to exploit that wartime alignment in the Italian Republic's first general election.

'I understand well enough,' replied the old woman. 'I am ready to do all the penance you want, I am ready to fast, to go on a pilgrimage. But I will vote for Garibaldi.'

'There's no point in my explaining again what you already know,' Don Camillo concluded abruptly. 'If you vote for those people I cannot give you absolution.'

Old Bacchini opened her arms wide.

'God will forgive me. I will accept the sentence that will be served upon me. The important thing is that my boy can be returned from Russia. When it comes to it,' she sighed, 'we mothers must always sacrifice ourselves for our children.'

Don Camillo looked at her perplexed and asked what her son had to do with it.

'Two ladies from the City Committee came round the other day,' explained the old woman in a low voice, 'and they guaranteed that if Garibaldi's List win in the elections, my son will be returned from Russia. Those on Garibaldi's List are very good friends of the Russians and, if they win, they will return all the prisoners. They took my name and surname and put my young boy among the first to be released. I also gave them a photograph.

'I understand, Father, that you have a thousand reasons not to absolve me, but my duty is precisely the duty of all mothers: to suffer for the good of their children.'[9]

Don Camillo shook his head.

'Yeah,' he muttered. 'But you should be sure that your son *will* return.'

'I no longer had any hope: now they have given me some. When one is about to drown one clings to anything.'

'Yes,' muttered Don Camillo again. 'But what if the communists don't win?'

---

[9] Between 1941 and 1943 in Mussolini's Italy many young men were dispatched to fight against the Allies on the Eastern Front in Russia. Many were killed and those taken prisoner not returned, old Bacchini's boy among them. However, an ancestor of hers, one Bacchi Luigi, heads the B's on the famous Garibaldi List (or *Ruolo*, as it was known), a list of those who fought in Garbibaldi's army. The local communist office has told her that if she votes communist they will return her son home.

'Patience,' sighed the old woman. 'I must do everything I can to get the boy back. They put his name on their list among the first, they showed me when they wrote it in the register. They are serious people, educated people, very good.[10] They said too that they know how things are, that a mother must do everything possible to get her child back. I *have* to vote for Garibaldi.'

Don Camillo stood up and made a cross in the air.

'*Ego te absolvo*,' he said. 'Four Pater, Hail and Gloria for penance. God be praised.'

Then, when from the window he saw the old woman pass by, as she came out of the church, he presented himself before the crucified Christ above the High Altar.

*

'Jesus,' he said, commandeering reason as his partner, 'if a mother, in the hope of saving her child, is willing to pay personally, whatever the cost, is it not my duty not to take away that mother's hope that she can save her child? By denying her absolution I would, in effect, have said to this poor woman: yes, you are willing to sacrifice yourself because you hope to save your son, but God is not on your side in this!

'And that would have been an ungodly thing, because hope, even if it apparently originates from earthly needs or desires, is surely ultimately of divine origin. You, in your divine wisdom, have turned evil means to a good end. You have spoken through sacrilegious mouths to restore hope to a desperate mother's heart. And I couldn't go against you by denying old Bacchini absolution and therefore riddling her with guilt in hoping for the return of her son!'

Christ smiled.

'Don Camillo,' he said. 'Where do you wish to go with this? Do you want to convince me to vote for the Popular Front?'

---

[10] Garibaldi's army were famously 'serious people, educated people' and apparently the tradition was maintained. Known as 'the redshirts', his army was originally 1,000-strong, the majority from northern Italy. It numbered among its ranks teachers, writers, lawyers, students, doctors, engineers, pharmacists, a group of painters and sculptors, three priests, thirty naval officers and even one woman.

'I simply want to explain to you why I absolved old Bacchini even though she decided to vote for the communists.'

'But why so, Don Camillo? Did I ask you to explain and justify yourself? Is it not enough for *you* to feel that your conscience is clear?'

'The trouble is that I *don't* feel at ease with my conscience. Jesus, it was my duty to deny your enemies that vote which they stole from that poor mother by deceiving her.'

'So, what has become hope in the poor mother's heart is an illusion. Yet hope is a divine gift, Don Camillo – you yourself said it.'

Don Camillo passed his large hands over his face.

'That's true too,' he admitted. 'So ... what is to be done?'

'I do not know, Don Camillo,' Christ replied, smiling. 'I do not do politics.'

*

Peppone, in his workshop, was busy repainting one of the mudguards on his truck, and Don Camillo immediately got to the point.

'Some of those dirty propaganda people of yours are going around the countryside telling poor people who have relatives imprisoned in Russia that if they vote for Garibaldi, Russia will send them all back.'

'Bullshit,' muttered Peppone. 'Name one!'

'I cannot violate the Seal of the Confessional. But I promise you it is true.'

Peppone shrugged his shoulders.

'They're not my people who are doing this, it's stuff that comes out of the city,' he replied. 'On the other hand we are at war and in war everyone defends themselves as best they can...'

'Yes,' said Don Camillo darkly.

'In any case, you always have the knife by the handle because, if someone votes for us, you can deny them absolution.'

'I have not denied absolution to the poor people who want to vote for Garibaldi because your lot convinced them that, by so doing, they will get their children back. I have absolved them and I will continue to absolve them. But God will never absolve you or your accursed flesh.'

Don Camillo had spoken extremely calmly and left immediately afterwards and Peppone remained watching him with his mouth open. He had never heard Don Camillo speak in that cold and distant tone of voice, as if he came from another world. He thought about it a lot, even the following day. Then he didn't have time to think about it anymore because the posters for a Unità Socialista[11] rally had to be posted on the walls throughout the municipality. And after that he could only think about organising the counter-demonstration, as prescribed in his Party's instructions sheet.

That Sunday the town was packed with people.

'Pack the first row in front of the stage with our comrades from Molinetto and Torricella,' were Ppepone's instructions to his men. 'As soon as the speaker slips a little, they will spring into action. They know what they have to do. Comrades from our village will go to Molinetto and Torricella and upset the rallies of *DC* and *Blocco Nazionale*.[12]

'Me, Brusco and the other managers are to be kept out of sight in the Town Hall. We are to intervene only if something goes wrong.'

The speaker was a Saragattian Socialist[13], around thirty-five, a distinguished type who spoke well. But as soon as Peppone heard his voice, he jumped out of his chair and went to peek out of the window.

'It's *him!*' he stammered. And Brusco and Bigio and Smilzo and all the others who were with him agreed that it really was him, and then said nothing more.

A few minutes later, the disturbance teams went into action.

---

[11] *Unità Socialista*, the Socialist Unity Party, a social-democratic alliance in opposition to the two main parties, the Communist Party and the Christian Democracy Party in the 1948 election.

[12] 'DC' refers to *Democrazia Cristiana*, the Catholic-inspired, centrist Christian Democracy Party, whose main opposition was the Communist Party at this time. *Blocco Nazionale* was a right-wing alliance vying with *Unità Socialista* for third place (as it turned out). Peppone was under orders to obstruct all three alternatives to the PSI, the Italian Communist Party.

[13] A follower of Giuseppe Saragat, founder of the Socialist Party of Italian Workers, which was in coalition with the Christian Democracy Party.

The speaker countered the insults and accusations with great energy, but the hecklers became more and more enraged until, at a certain point, they erupted onto the stage and threw themselves upon the man.

Peppone and his general staff rushed down into the square, but it was too late.

The people were now crowding in front of a house where the speaker's supporters had taken the Saragattian. Peppone and his staff threw themselves headlong among them and managed to reach the door with creditable ease.

The speaker was sitting on a sofa while a woman was bandaging his hand. He had blood on his face because someone had hit him in the forehead with a wrench. Peppone stared at him with his mouth open. The wounded man raised his head towards him:

'Hello, Peppone,' he said smiling. 'Did you organise this little party?'

Peppone didn't answer and the wounded man smiled again.

'Ah: and here are Brusco, Bigio, Smilzo, Stràziami and Lungo. And I am here too: the old squad is complete: only Giacomino and Rosso are missing and they will never leave our mountain home. Who would have thought that my good friend Peppone would have organised this reception … for his old commander...'

Peppone spread his arms.

'Chief,' he stammered… 'I didn't know…'

'For the love of God,' interrupted the wounded man, 'don't apologise. We are at war and every man defends himself as best he can. I understand you perfectly.'

His hand bandaged, the wounded man stood up.

'Goodbye, Comrade Peppone,' he said, smiling. 'We resisted the Germans, let's hope we now resist the communists too. Lucky Giacomino and Rosso, who will never leave the mountains to be a part of it.'

The speaker went out and got into a car waiting outside the door.

Peppone heard the screams and whistles that greeted his departure.

Even the voice of the 'Chief' when he said, 'Lucky Giacomino and Rosso, who will never leave the mountains…' was cold and distant as if it came from another world, like that of Don Camillo when he had said: 'God will not absolve you or your accursed flesh.'

In the evening the leaders of the teams that had gone to work in Molinetto and Torricella came to make their reports: in Molinetto the Christian Democrat speaker had had to stop halfway, without serious incident. In Torricella the Bloc speaker had been slapped.

Peppone knew them both; the first was an old university professor, the second a veteran from the German prison camps.

'In the city,' explained the commander of Molinetto's squad, 'there was quite a stir: our comrades beat up the students and even a sergeant from the *Celere* took a beating on the head.'

'Good,' replied Peppone, getting up and leaving.

The sun was setting and Peppone slowly walked along the road that led to the river. On the bank stood someone smoking a Tuscan and looking at the water. It was Don Camillo.

The two men were silent for some time, before Peppone remarked that it was a beautiful evening.

'Really beautiful evening,' echoed Don Camillo.

Peppone lit a half Tuscan, took a few puffs, then turned it off by rubbing it under the sole of his shoe. Finally, he spat angrily on the ground.

'Everyone is against us,' he said grimly. 'Everyone, even my old partisan commander. Everyone's against us, even *God*!'

Don Camillo continued to smoke calmly.

'It is not that everyone is against you: but that you are against everyone, including God.'

Peppone crossed his arms over his chest.

'Why did you tell me that I am accursed flesh? Maybe because old Bacchini will vote for us?'

'Old Bacchini? What about her?'

'Yesterday I visited all the families with missing persons in Russia, and old Bacchini told me that two women had come to her because of the Front. I told her that they're a couple of rogues and even if she votes for the Popular Front, her son will not be returned!'

Don Camillo threw his cigar away.

'And she, what did she say?'

'She asked me who she should vote for then, so that her son is returned. And I told her that I don't know, and the old woman said that if there is no party that will bring back her son, it is pointless to go and vote.'

Don Camillo looked at him.

'You are an idiot,' he said.

He said it in a solemn voice, no longer the voice that he had used to damn Peppone's 'accursed flesh' and Peppone felt comforted. Thinking of the blood-filled face of his former commander, and of the veteran beaten in Molinetto and the old professor booed in Torricella, he felt like crying. But he roused himself and shouted ferociously:

'But we will win!'

'No,' Don Camillo replied calmly, with total confidence.

Meanwhile, the river was still the same as it was one hundred thousand years ago. The sun ditto: it was setting in the west, but the next day it would rise again on the opposite side.

Peppone (who can say why?) found himself thinking about this extraordinary fact and concluded that in the end – let's be honest – God is someone who knows what's what.

The Irregulars (1948)

THE TIME HAS come to talk of Smilzo, municipal 'officer' and head of the local communist section's 'Proletarian Flying Squad'. And, in particular, it is time to define him as he really is: totally immoral.

Or, more to the point, to define him as a man who knows no shame. For what sort of fellow is it who cares nothing for the village scandal he causes by co-habiting with his lover?

Just as bad, Moretta, the unfortunate woman who shares his bed, is as shameless as he. People call her 'Smilzo's kept woman', but in truth she keeps herself very well on her own. A fulsome lady, she works with the horse-power of many a man and works well and to such a degree that she is entrusted with a tractor in the ploughing season, and with Censetti's Lancia Ro (l.c. o) bus[14], which she drives as confidently as Peppone. And although the women of the village denounce her, there isn't a man who, having made a play for her, hasn't received a slap of the sort that makes a man forget his home address.

For all this, and more, Moretta was at the centre of village gossip alongside that other wretch, Smilzo, who referred to her as 'my partner' and took her around the place on the back of his bicycle, when it wasn't he who was sitting on the back with the brazen hussy astride his saddle.

Incited by all the gossip, Don Camillo himself had oft spoken of 'certain loose women who go around the village on their racing bicycles, exposing their bottoms as it were their faces.' And, as a result, Comrade Moretta had taken to wearing one-piece overalls – blue – with a red handkerchief around her neck. This had become her uniform, and given rise to yet more furious scandal.

On one occasion, when Don Camillo managed to grab hold of Smilzo, he had tried to convince him to clean up his act – to 'regularise his position', as he put it. But Smilzo had laughed in his face.

'There's nothing to regularise! We do no more nor less than what the fools who get married do.'

'Respectable people, if you please, not fools!' retorted Don Camillo.

'The fools, I say, who ruin the beauty of a union of two soul mates by putting between them a mameluke of a mayor and a smoking tobacco shop of an archpriest!'

---

[14] The Lancia Ro was a single-decker bus with 32 seats, produced from 1952 to 1955 to transport people over long distances.

'*Il tabaccone*' assimilated the insult and pressed his case further, but Smilzo only laughed in his face again:

'If the Eternal Father had intended men and women to unite through marriage, he would have placed a priest in the earthly Paradise between Adam and Eve. Love was born free and free it should remain! The day will come when people understand that marriage is a prison sentence and they will no longer need priests to marry them. And then we will have lots of dance parties in church!'

Don Camillo found only a brick at hand, but threw it nevertheless. However, Smilzo was so famously fast a mover that it was said that he could dodge between the bullets from a burst of machine gun fire. It was a wasted brick.

Don Camillo did not lose heart and one day he managed to tie Moretta down when she appeared at the presbytery in customary blue overalls and with a red handkerchief around her neck. At the archpriest's invitation, down she sat and lit a cigarette.

Don Camillo neither slapped nor roared at her. On the contrary, he spoke softly.

'You are a hard-working girl,' he began, 'I know that you keep your house clean, that you don't squander your money, that you don't gossip behind people's backs. I also know that you love your husband...'

'I don't have a husband: I have a partner,' interrupted Moretta.

'I know you love your partner,' Don Camillo continued patiently. 'So, although you never wanted to come to confession, I believe you are an honest woman. Why then do you behave in such a way that people label you a fallen woman?'

'Stuff the people,' retorted Moretta just as calmly, tapping the back pocket of her overalls with the palm of her right hand.

Don Camillo, who was starting to see a little red mist, talked more quickly about the sacrament of matrimony, but Moretta immediately interrupted.

'If the Eternal Father had decreed that men and women should be united through marriage...'

'Thank you,' interrupted Don Camillo, 'I already know the rest.'

'Love was born free and must remain free,' Moretta concluded gravely. 'Marriage is an opiate that deadens love.'

*

The old village gossips wouldn't let the matter rest and even lobbied the Mayor, saying that it was a disgrace for the entire municipality, that he had a duty to champion public morality, and so on.

'For my part I am married,' replied Peppone 'and I can marry anyone who wants to marry, but I cannot force anyone who doesn't want to marry to marry. That is how the law stands. The Pope may see things differently, but he is not the law.'

The old women were not to be put off.

'If you can't do it as mayor, you can do it as head of the local communist section: those shameless people are both members of your party. It is a disgrace to your party too.'

'I will try,' promised Peppone.

And in fact, he did try.

'If you make me get married, I'll join Saragat's party,' was Smilzo's response.

And so Peppone didn't talk about it anymore and some good time passed and the scandal of the shameless couple was submerged by interest in the elections. But one fine day the scandal erupted again, ever more furiously. Moretta hadn't been seen around the place for some time, when suddenly a piece of news ricocheted from mouth to mouth: there were now three comrades in the Smilzo household. According to the midwife, a little girl had come into the world, one so beautiful that those two scoundrels didn't deserve her.

The old gossips didn't mince their words, while the politicians sought advantage in the matter:

'Such is the morality of those communist pigs.'

'Do you want to bet they don't even get her baptised, those godless people?'

Word reached Peppone, who rushed to the home of the two hapless ones.

*

Don Camillo was reading in his study when Smilzo arrived.

'There's someone to be baptised,' he said.

'You are joking,' muttered Don Camillo.

'So, do I now need authorisation from the Honourable Andreotti[15] to bring children into the world?' Smilzo enquired.

'All you need is your murky conscience,' retorted Don Camillo. 'Anyway, that's your business. I warn you that if that wretched companion of yours comes in front of me in overalls I will chase you away and slap you all. Come by in twenty minutes.'

Moretta arrived with a bundle in her arms, together with Smilzo, Peppone and Maria, his wife – all dressed up. Don Camillo stood at the door of the church.

'Put all the red stuff away!' he ordered without even looking to see if they had any red stuff. 'This is the House of God, not the People's Palace.'

'Here the only red is the mist that fills your pumpkin!' Peppone replied darkly.

They trooped in. Don Camillo prepared the font and began performing the baptismal rite.

'What name?' he muttered.

'Rita, Palmira, Valeria,' whispered the mother.[16]

Don Camillo looked at Moretta.

'And why not Colonnella and Donga too?' he asked darkly.

'Rita is my mother, Palmira is his mother and Valeria was my grandmother,' protested Moretta.

'Too bad for them!' replied Don Camillo dryly – Emilia, Rosa, Antonietta.'

Peppone pawed like a horse. Smilzo sighed and shook his head slightly.

When it was over they went to the presbytery to witness the entry in the baptismal register.

'So, with the new government, is it forbidden to be called Palmiro?' Peppone asked sarcastically. But Don Camillo didn't listen to him and signalled instead that he and his wife could leave. Smilzo and Moretto remained in front of the table with the little girl in their arms. Don Camillo went to close the door.

---

[15] The Christian Democrats have won the election, the communists are now the official opposition. Giulio Andreotti is a protégé of Alcide De Gasperi, the leader of the Christian Democrats.

[16] With reference to prominent communists: Palmiro Togliatti, leader of the party in Italy, Rita his first wife, etc.

'*Enciclica rerum novarum*,'[17] Smilzo announced, making the face of a man resigned to his fate.

'No speech,' said Don Camillo in a cold and distant voice, 'just a warning. Even if you don't get married, nothing will change, nothing will collapse. You are simply two cockroaches trying to gnaw on a pillar of St Peter. I'm not interested in you or your "product".'

At that moment something stirred in the bundle and the so-called product opened her eyes wide and smiled at Don Camillo. And it was such a beautiful little face, so fresh and so clean that Don Camillo, after an instant of stifled amazement, felt the blood rise to his head and he lost control.

'Cowards, fearful of commitment!' he roared. 'You have no right to burden this creature with your nonsense! You have no right to defile something so pure and innocent! She will become a beautiful woman and people will envy her and in their envy will call her "the daughter of a kept woman". If you were not two wretched rascals you wouldn't expose your daughter to the malice of hypocritical people jealous of other people's beauty. You couldn't care less what people say about you, but how can you not care about the poison that people, because of you, will cast upon your daughter?'

Don Camillo had raised his fists and puffed out his chest and seemed even taller and more colossal than usual and the two wretches had shrunk into a corner.

'Get married, you scoundrels,' he shouted.

Smilzo was pale and sweating and shook his head desperately.

'No, no, it would be the end of us. We would die of shame!'

The little girl was obviously having fun and started laughing while still waving her little hands: at that point Don Camillo felt utterly dismayed.

'Please,' he begged, 'she is too beautiful!'

Strange things happen in this world: for example, a man takes a crowbar and uses it on a locked door and is unable to move it even

---

[17] An Encyclical of Pope Leo XIII (1891). It supported the right to form unions, but rejected both socialism and unrestricted capitalism, while affirming the right to own private property.

an inch. Then, tired as hell, he wipes away the sweat and hangs his hat on the handle and, all of a sudden, a 'trik' is heard and the door swings open of its own accord.

Moretta was that steel door, but she had her own handle too and so, as soon as Don Camillo stopped acting furious and said, 'Please, she's too beautiful' in that voice that seemed to belong to someone else, Moretta, scared as she was, threw herself down on a chair and began to cry.

'No, no,' she sobbed, 'we cannot be married because we've been married for three years. No one knows – we got married away from here. We didn't say anything to anyone. We've always rooted for free love…'

Smilzo nodded his head: 'Marriage is the deadly opiate of love,' he parroted. 'Love is born free. If the Eternal Father…'

Don Camillo went out for a moment to splash water on his face. Upon his return he found Smilzo and his wife quite calm. The girl handed a piece of paper to Don Camillo, it was their marriage certificate.

'Under the Seal of the Confessional,' Moretta whispered.

Don Camillo nodded in agreement.

'And so in your job you are registered as single and you don't even get family allowances,' said Don Camillo to Smilzo.

'This is true,' he replied. 'For the sake of the Idea one can make this sacrifice and more.'

Don Camillo returned the certificate.

'You're two prize idiots,' he observed very calmly.

Then, since the baby girl smiled at him again, he corrected himself.

'You are two and a half idiots.'

When he reached the door Smilzo turned and saluted with a clenched fist.

'In Piazzale Loreto there is always a place for the people's detractors,' he warned gravely.[18]

---

[18] A major city square in Milan, the scene of the public execution of 15 civilians handpicked by the Gestapo in 1944 as a reprisal for a partisan attack. Mussolini is said to have prophetically remarked 'for the blood of Piazzale Loreto, we shall pay dearly' and he was right. Less than a year later his corpse would be on public display in the square.

'Put your hat on, so they won't need to take your place away.'

'April 18 represents a minor episode of insignificant value in the greater struggle,' Smilzo clarified in a solemn voice[19]. 'We have come very far and we will go much further. See you later, Citizen Priest.'

The Prodigal Son (1949)

IN THE PRESBYTERY Don Camillo found a worried looking Brusco waiting to see him. Brusco was Peppone's deputy and a rag of a man who only spoke when he had important things to say. Which meant he spat out about ten or fifteen words a day.

'Has someone just died?' Don Camillo inquired.

'No,' replied Brusco. 'A misfortune has come upon me.'

'You killed someone.'

'No: it's about my son.'

'Which one? Falchetto[20]?'

'None of the eight. Another. The one who's been in Sicily since 1938.'

Don Camillo remembered that in 1938 a sister of Brusco had turned up in the village: she had married well in Sicily and come into some land. Before going home she had looked at Brusco's nine boys all lined up and said:

'Can I have one?'

'Take whichever one you want,' Brusco had replied.

---

[19] The date in 1948 when the Communist Party lost the election to De Gasperi's Christian Democrats.

[20] A known linchpin of the Red action team.

'I'll take the least dirty,' said the woman. So her choice had fallen on Cecotto, who had just washed his face. Cecotto was only about eight years old at the time, and he had always been somehow different from the others.

'Clear understanding makes for long friendship,' warned the woman. 'This one comes with me; I pick him up and you never see him again.'

Brusco, who had just become a widower, saw one son less as an expression of divine grace – the free and unmerited favour of God – and simply nodded his head. Only when the boy was at the door did he grab his sister by the sleeve.

'Would it be all the same if, instead of Cecotto, I gave you Falchetto?'

'Obviously I don't want *him* at all!' replied his sister, as if Cecotto had been paid for in cash.

Don Camillo did indeed remember the story well.

'So?'

'He's been away for twelve years and in all that time I have never seen him,' Brusco confirmed. 'But he always wrote to me and now he says he's coming to see me.'

Don Camillo looked at him intently.

'Brusco, has the five-year plan gone to your head?[21] Is it a misfortune if your child comes to visit you? Can it be that you are ashamed of your damned "Red" children?'

'I am not even ashamed of Falchetto, who is the most cowardly creature in the world,' Brusco retorted. 'It is my fault if I've made mistakes. That is not the question. They're all damned reactionaries down south: barons, landowners, priests and riff-raff like that. On the other hand, children are still children even if they turn out bad... My problem is that, if Cecotto lands on me here like he threatens to, I'll be dishonoured before the Party, because it is down to me to alert the Party about anything illegal...'

Don Camillo gave up.

---

[21] Peppone had been emulating Stalin's first Five-Year Plan for the Soviet Union, 1928–1932. See 'The Kolkhoz', *Don Camillo and His Flock* (Pilot, 2015).

'Brusco, stop talking in riddles and spill the beans! What has the wretch done?'

Brusco lowered his head.

'They allowed him to study.'

'And you are ashamed because you have a child who studies?'

'Yes, but,' Brusco explained darkly, 'he is studying ... to be a priest.'

Don Camillo began to laugh.

'You have a priest for a son! This is phenomenal! A clerical son!'

'Any moment, yes... But stop it, please.'

It was a voice that Don Camillo had never heard from Brusco and he pulled back.

'If he does come, Peppone will notice and, as soon as he does, he will kill me. And then again, since Cecotto is a priest, I wouldn't want him to know that I'm ... one of the others. Being a priest yourself you'll know what to do: but if you don't sort things out for me, I am ruined. He arrives tomorrow on the eight o'clock train.'

'Okay: let me think about it tonight.'

Brusco had never said thank you to anyone in his life.

'I'll owe you one,' he muttered as he left. When he was at the door he stopped and turned: 'Everything has to happen to me,' he said, sighing. 'With all the various reactionaries around down there, *I* have to have a priest for a son!'

Unperturbed by such insensitivity, Don Camillo countered:

'With so many rogues to choose from, a poor priest has to be lumped with a communist for a father!'

Brusco, shaking his head, took the broader view.

'Everyone has their share of misfortunes in this damn world,' he sighed bitterly.

The Polare Pact (1949)

THOSE WERE THE days when discussion about that great piece of international bureaucratic machinery that the newspapers called the 'Atlantic Pact'[22] was all the rage, its name perhaps pointing to the fact that there is an ocean-sized gap between saying and doing. But when Peppone heard about the treaty, he took it as a personal affront.

So angry was he at what he saw as a threat to post-war peace between East and West that if it had been up to him he would have declared war on America within the blink of an eye.

So, when he saw Don Camillo making his way slowly along the road towards him, intent on reading his Breviary, he stood on the threshold of his workshop with the tranquillity of someone who had eaten a live cat and uttered a hair-raising, blood-curdling blasphemy that brought the priest to a standstill.

'You called?' the priest responded quietly, raising his eyes from his prayers.

'I was talking to God,' Peppone replied threateningly. 'Are you God?'

'No, but since God doesn't have time to listen to you, I'll make the time, if that's what you want.'

Peppone was willing to declare war on America but, for many reasons, not to open hostilities with Don Camillo just now; not least because while America was far away, Don Camillo was nearby

---

[22] The North Atlantic Treaty formed NATO on 4 April 1949, the West mindful of aggression by the Soviet Union.

and had picked up an iron bar and had it held tightly in his hand: and frankly Peppone didn't like being blessed by a priest holding an aspergillum like that.

So, he simply shrugged his shoulders. Then, fortunately, a tractor clattered up and stopped between them in front of Peppone's workshop, and he let Don Camillo go.

'It's not right,' complained the driver as he got out of his tractor. 'It spits, it kicks back, there must be something wrong with the ignition.'

The tractor was a big Fordson; Peppone looked grimly at the machine, then touched the 'Made in USA' mark with the handle of his hammer and shouted:

'Everything is over between me and America! If you want to fix your trap go ask the priest here who's in with the Americans!'

Don Camillo, who had just resumed his journey, stopped and slowly walked back.

When he came to the tractor man, he handed him his hat, Breviary and overcoat. Then he rolled up his sleeves and, lifting the bonnet, began to rummage inside the engine.

'Give me a No. 10 tubular spanner,' he said after a while: and the man from the tractor searched in an iron box for what was needed and handed it to Don Camillo.

The priest worked for a few more minutes, then withdrew.

'Give it a go now.'

The man started the tractor.

'Like clockwork!' he exclaimed cheerfully. 'What do I owe you for your trouble, Reverend?'

'Nothing,' replied Don Camillo. 'It's all in the gift of the Marshall Plan.'

The tractor moved off and away. Peppone remained there with his mouth wide open and Don Camillo placed the open Breviary in front of him and pointing to a place on the page, said:

'Read here and tell me what it says.'

Peppone shrugged his shoulders.

'I don't know a lot about Latin!' he muttered.

'Then you're an ass!' Don Camillo concluded placidly. And he went on his way. With a nose black with oil, but his head held high.

*

This was a cheap little victory, but it was enough to increase Peppone's discontent. That evening, having gathered his general staff into the People's Palace, he began to shout that they had to get busy to demonstrate to the world the popular indignation aroused by the treacherous signing of the damnable Atlantic Pact.

'We need to invade – occupy something important!' he concluded. 'Make a big strike!'

'Boss,' Smilzo reminded him, 'we are already big in the municipality, the People's Palace is ours, our children are in the school, our dead are in the cemetery: all that's left to occupy is the church.'

'All right!' Peppone shouted. 'And when we have occupied the church, what do we do with it? Set up in competition with the Vatican? We must occupy something that represents an effective conquest by the workers. Only in this way can we mount a fitting protest against the Atlantic Pact. Brusco, do we understand each other?'

Brusco immediately understood where Peppone was going.

'Okay,' he replied. 'When is it to be done?'

'Right away. By midnight everyone must be notified. Units made ready to act by two o'clock. The island must be occupied by five o'clock tomorrow morning.'

*

The river widened in front of the village to such an extent that it looked like a sea. Downstream from a sunken church was what was known as the Island. It was really only an island in a manner of speaking. In reality it was a large slice of detached land, a sort of isthmus about fifteen metres from the mainland shore, which ran for 1,000 metres or so parallel to it until, in the end, a thin strip of muddy ground re-attached it to the shore. The island was not cultivated *per se*, maintained but only in the sense that a forest of poplars was allowed to grow there untroubled until Signor Bresca, the landowner, would turn up and mark with a knife a number of trees to be cut down and sold.

Peppone and his gang had long decided that the land was effectively abandoned and could therefore legally be occupied by workers for the creation of an agricultural cooperative. The actual

occupation had, time and again, been postponed, but now its time
had come.

'We will challenge the "Patto Atlantico" with the "Patto
Polare",' concluded Peppone on the evening of the historic
decision. 'Because the word "Polare" derives much more from
the River Po than does the river's older Latin name [*Padus*], the
roots of which lie in the most rotten and putrid reaction.[23] It is
really time to put an end to our obsession with Julius Caesar and
the ancient Romans, who spoke in Latin to pull the wool over the
eyes of the people, just like the Roman Catholic priests do today.'

Peppone oft responded in these terms to those who pointed out
to him, *temporibus illis*, that it was improper to call a newspaper
which purported to be the Voice of the Po, *Squilla Polare*, owing
to its etymology. 'Gone are the days of etymology!' he would
argue. 'Words start again ... as of now!'

Whatever, the '*Polare* Pact' was concluded according to
Peppone's directives and, at seven the following morning,
someone came to warn Don Camillo that the Mayor had occupied
the island with his men. These men, even though they were mostly
women, had worked like hell chopping down poplar trees.

One poplar, the tallest, had been stripped like a plucked
chicken's neck and now served as a flagpole. And the Red Flag
waved gaily in the fresh air of that post-electoral April morning.

'Father,' said a perplexed bearer of the sad news to Don
Camillo, 'this is going to end badly. The *Celere* have been called
out and Peppone has given orders to dig out the strip of land
connecting the island to the shore.[24] The drawbridge is up! If you
don't move, there's going to be an almighty mess.'

Don Camillo immediately donned a pair of moleskin trousers,
climbed into his boots (because the island was an empire of mud),
put on a hunter's jacket and set off towards the Po.

*

[23] The Roman author Pliny wrote of the Padus of his time, but earlier the
river was known as Bodincus by the Ligurians and yet earlier as Eridanus.
Peppone's 'Polare' sings of the Fronte Popolare, the Communist/Socialst
coalition of 1947.

[24] *Celere* units are mobile police units, a ready-to-use resource for riot
control in Italy.

On the island Peppone stood – legs apart – directing the work of segregating the isthmus into various planned areas apposite to its defence. At first he didn't recognise Don Camillo, then he pretended not to recognise him and, in the end, he couldn't stand it anymore and exploded.

'Did you disguise yourself to come and spy on the enemy?'

Don Camillo trundled down the embankment and, sinking half a leg into the mud, crossed the isthmus and came to a halt in front of Peppone.

'Let it go, Peppone,' he said. 'You've stirred up a hornet's nest and swarms of them are coming from the city!'

'They'll find it worth the trip!' replied Peppone. 'If they want to conquer the island they'll have to borrow the United States Navy!'

'Peppone, they'll be only fifteen metres from the island and bullets travel!'

'They'll also find that it's only fifteen metres from us to them and our bullets travel too!' Peppone replied darkly.

In truth it was a bad moment for Peppone, and Don Camillo pulled him aside.

'Look: you have the right to be a scoundrel and to behave like a scoundrel. But you have no right to drag your poor people into this mess. If you feel like going to jail – master of all that you can see – resist and shoot. But you have no right to force others into doing so.'

Peppone thought for a few minutes, then shouted: 'Everyone can do what they want! I'm not forcing anyone. Whoever wants to stay, stay.'

The roar of engines could be heard on the provincial road. The men dredging a channel from the isthmus ceased their digging.

'It's the *Celere* jeeps arriving!' Don Camillo warned. And the men looked to Peppone.

'Do what you want!' he muttered. 'Democracy is beautiful because everyone does what they will. And here on the island we have a wholehearted democracy!'

Smilzo and the others from the general staff appeared on the scene. Smilzo looked inquisitively at Don Camillo:

'So, is the Vatican interfering here too? Haul off, Reverend, things are going to get hot here soon.'

'I'm not afraid of the heat,' Don Camillo replied calmly as, up on the road, along the embankment, a cloud of dust arose.

'They're coming all right,' said the men who were now throwing away their pickaxes and spitting as they crossed the isthmus and waded ashore. Peppone looked at them with contempt. There were six trucks of *Celere* and they came to a halt up on the embankment. The commander stood up, facing down the people who were felling trees on the island:

'Clear off! Move along!'

Some continued to axe the trees and the commander turned to a nearby adjutant:

'Maybe they didn't hear. Play them some music!'

A burst of machine gun fire filled the air and everyone on the island raised their heads.

'Clear off, *now*!' the commander shouted.

Peppone and his staff moved to the far edge of the isthmus: people began to pass by them and, having reached the shore, scattered to right and left, climbing up the embankment away from the trucks. About ten remained on the island and continued to strike the trunks of trees with their axes.

Peppone gathered his staff together, forming a wall that blocked the entire isthmus, and remained there, silent and with arms folded across their chests, waiting.

'Clear out, you lot!' came more shouts from the top of the embankment. Nobody moved and officers of the special unit jumped out of their trucks and descended the bank.

Peppone gritted his teeth and the veins in his neck swelled to bursting.

'The first man who touches me will have his head busted!' he muttered darkly.

Don Camillo had remained where he was, next to Peppone, part of the defensive wall, intending to negotiate a climb-down.

'Peppone,' he said, 'in the name of God, don't do anything crazy.'

'What are you still doing here?'

'I am doing my duty. I am here to remind you that you are a sentient being and must therefore submit to reason. Let's go!'

'You go! I have never run away from anyone and I won't run away now.'

'This is the law!'

'It's not my law, it's yours. You obey it and go.'

The unit had come down the embankment and stopped in front of the narrow strip of muddy, partly dredged land.

'Clear off now!' they repeated.

Don Camillo grabbed Peppone by his sleeve.

'Come on, let's go!'

'I'll not leave even if they kill me!' he replied. 'The first one who touches me I'll bust his head.'

The armed unit repeated the order to evacuate, then moved in through the mud.

They found themselves in front of that wall of men and repeated the order, but no one moved and no one responded.

An officer grabbed Peppone by the jacket and the unfortunate man would have ended his days badly if his target had not found himself trapped in the iron arms of Don Camillo.

'Leave me!' he said through gritted teeth.

Don Camillo, unrecognisable as a priest, dressed as he was like everyone else, with trousers, boots and jacket, took the first blow to the head and gritted his teeth, suppressing a strong desire to drop Peppone, grab two or three of the riot police and throw them into the water. Instead, he took it without batting an eyelid.

More blows landed on his head and began to rain down on Smilzo's head and on those of all Peppone's general staff. But no one uttered a word. They hugged each other and took it in silence.

At length the *Celere* had to roll them out of there as if they were a solid boulder: still, no one had reacted, no one had even opened his mouth, no one had lifted a finger.

'This is a country of total lunatics,' concluded the *Celere* commander. And shortly afterwards the island was no longer occupied, because the few remaining rebels had escaped in little boats.

Finally, the officers of the special unit got back into their trucks and left.

Don Camillo, Peppone and the others remained silent for some time, sitting at the foot of the bank, looking into the water of the river and tat he red flag waving on top of the tallest poplar.

'Reverend,' said Smilzo at last, 'you've got a lump on your forehead the size of a walnut.'

'I don't need you to tell me,' Don Camillo replied harshly. 'I can feel it!'

Then they got up and went back to the village, and that was the end of the *Patto Polare*.

The Petition (1949)

D ON CAMILLO WAS returning to the village along the *Strada Bassa*, his Tuscan vehicle happily idling, when, arriving at the turning to Pioppetto, he found himself confronted by Peppone's gang. There were five of them and Smilzo was in charge.

Don Camillo looked at them with a sort of patronising curiosity.

'Are you going to kill me here or have you a more suitable place in mind?' he enquired.

'Don't push it!' Smilzo replied, taking a piece of paper out of a folder and presenting it to the priest.

'Is the condemned man to choose from among some last requests?' asked Don Camillo.

'It's a petition for signing by everyone who desires peace, and for not signing by those who want war,' explained Peppone's lieutenant. 'It is also a test to see if someone is a good man or a warmonger.'

Don Camillo made some quizzical observations about the dove-of-peace printed at the top of the sheet, then concluded:

'I am a benevolent man, but I do not intend to sign. No-one who wants peace needs to sign anything when there is no war.'

Smilzo turned to Gigò, who was standing next to him.

'He thinks this is a political move,' he said. 'As he sees it, everything we do has a political agenda!'

'Reverend,' began Gigò, turning to Don Camillo, 'this has nothing to do with politics. This is about safeguarding the peace. Peace is good for all political parties. We need signatures to force the withdrawal of the Atlantic Pact, a treaty that binds countries in the West to make war on the Soviet Union. If you don't sign, it'll all happen again – like last time – and we'll be up to our necks in it.'

Don Camillo shook the ash from his cigar.

'You'd better get on with it then,' he advised. 'If I'm not mistaken you have zero signatures so far.'

'Clearly, we have not yet started. We wanted to do you the honour of being first on the list. If a petition is about peace, the first signature should be that of the priest.'

Don Camillo spread his arms:

'But if everyone knows that priests want peace, it's taken for granted that my signature is already there.'

'So, you aren't prepared to sign?'

Don Camillo shook his head and left.

'With a clergy like this we'll have two wars on our hands!' Smilzo concluded bitterly, putting the petition back in its folder.

*

Later, Peppone arrived at the presbytery.

'Politics has nothing to do with my presence here,' he premised. 'I am here as Mayor, as a family man, as a citizen, as a Christian and as a gentleman.'

'Too many people all at once!' observed Don Camillo. 'This is more like a rally: come in here as Peppone and leave the rest outside.'

Peppone sat down.

'We're in trouble,' he began solemnly. 'If good men don't make an alliance, the world will end up bursting like an exploding pumpkin.'

'I'm sorry to hear it,' replied Don Camillo gravely. 'Is there some news of which I am unaware...?'

'The news is that if we don't preserve our peace, war will soon destroy everything. Let's forget about parties and politics and let's all unite for once.'

Don Camillo nodded his head.

'That is an argument I like,' he replied. 'It's about time you dumped those sons of Satan.'

'I said, leave politics out of it!' Peppone retorted. 'It is time to think and act in terms conducive to universal peace.'

Don Camillo looked at him astonished: he had never heard Peppone embrace global, consensual values before.

'Do you want peace, yes or no?' said Peppone, cutting to the chase. 'Do you or do you not agree with Jesus Christ?'

'Certainly I do.'

Peppone took the folder with the petition out from under his jacket and placed it in front of Don Camillo.

'When fighting for the holy cause of peace, the clergy must lead the way!' he urged.

But Don Camillo shook his head.

'Now you've changed your game: we were not to involve politics in our affairs.'

'I am here as a simple citizen,' protested Peppone.

'Good: and I, as citizen to citizen, tell you that I don't care to sign.'

Peppone stood up agitatedly.

'Don't be upset: you know very well that if I sign this paper of yours then you can fill it with other signatures, otherwise you'll only gather those of the Party faithful. And not all of them, either, because a number don't even know how to sign their name. And since I know what you're up to, if you want to stay here with me, put that peace pigeon back in your pocket and take a glass of wine with me. If not, you, pigeon and peace may take your leave.'

Peppone put the paper away.

'So, since you're giving yourself such airs, I'll show you that I can get all the signatures I need without you!'

And Peppone left with his head held high.

Smilzo and the peace squad were outside waiting for him.

'Start collecting immediately. Our lot to be called upon last. *Everyone* must sign. Even peace may be negotiated with a few slaps.'

'And if I end up in jail, Boss,' enquired Smilzo, 'what then?'

'Nothing: keep collecting signatures in prison.'

This didn't sound very reassuring. But Smilzo set off, followed by the rest of the gang including a reinforcement from the People's Palace.

Now, if one owns barns and haystacks and vines and if it is explained that politics is not involved, one is unlikely to say no to someone who asks you to sign a petition for peace. Moreover, in a rural community, the important thing is to get the first five or six to sign. Once they are on board, there is little need for persuasion, except, as it turned out, in the case of Tonini, who, when Smilzo showed him the paper, shook his head.

'Don't you want peace?'

'No I don't,' replied Tonini, who was a handsome Christian man with two big hands that looked like shovels. 'I like war. A lot of scoundrels lose their lives and the air is cleared.'

Smilzo made a sensible observation.

'But as you know, in wars, unfortunately, a lot of those who lose their lives are good men.'

'Good men are worse than scoundrels.'

'What if *you* die?'

'I'd rather get killed than sign anything. At least when one dies, one knows where one will end up: when one signs a piece of paper one never knows where it will lead.'

Peppone's gang made a menacing move forward, but Tonini took up his shotgun, and Smilzo said that he quite understood his point of view and not to bother.

For the rest, everything went smoothly. When Peppone saw the sheets full of signatures in front of him, he slammed his fist on the table so much that it made the whole building tremble. He was thrilled and immediately went to compare the signatures with the municipality address lists. And everybody was accounted for.

Earlier he had spoken with the mayors of other municipalities and all said that they were struggling to get signatures because the general reaction was strongly against disposing of what they saw as a valid defence treaty. In Castellina shots had been fired, in Fossa the punch-ups lasted a whole day. While in Peppone's zone all Smilzo had to do was spend an hour with each of the first five or six signatories – spending an entire evening on it – and thereafter everyone, except Tonini, had signed without any hassle at all.

'It's down to the reputation and influence of the Mayor in this municipality,' Peppone explained and, putting the signed petitions back in the folder, he went to enjoy his victory.

Don Camillo was reading a book when the Mayor appeared before him in the presbytery.

'Father,' Peppone began, 'it is my solemn duty to announce to you the declining importance of the clergy in this village and I thank you on behalf of the democratic peoples for not signing the petition against the Atlantic Pact. If you had signed, maybe I wouldn't have gotten even half of the signatures I did. In all this I feel particularly sorry for the Pope...'

Peppone spread the signed petition papers across the table in front of Don Camillo.

'America is screwed!' he jeered. 'For us the War Pact, as people now call it, is not valid because here every single person is against it. And the same will be true everywhere!'

Don Camillo took the list of signatories and began to scroll through them carefully. Finally, he spread his arms:

'Well, I am sorry: you cannot claim that everyone has signed – Tonini's signature is missing.'

Peppone laughed it off.

'I have the whole place except Tonini. One "against", 800 counts "for" is a lot!'

Don Camillo opened the table drawer, took out some papers and displayed them in front of Peppone.

'You have the signatures against the pact; I have the signatures *for* the pact.'

Peppone opened his eyes wide in amazement.

'Russia is screwed,' continued Don Camillo, 'because I also have Tonini's signature.'

Peppone scratched his giant pear.

'No great mystery,' explained Don Camillo. 'I worked on the people during the day; you worked on them in the evening;. That's why you found no difficulty getting people to sign, for in fact you were doing them a favour: by signing for you they were annulling the signature they'd given to me. The only person who was not very happy was Tonini, because I had to bang him a little against the wall. But I wouldn't pursue him if I were you because he has sworn that rather than sign another piece of paper, he will blast the pollster with his shotgun.'

Peppone took his briefcase and left, and so, all things considered, in Don Camillo's municipality, America won by one-Tonini to zero.

Out of the Night (1950)

APPARENTLY INEXPLICABLY, Don Camillo had, for quite some time, been waking up in the middle of the night.

He would listen for a while but never hear anything untoward: nevertheless, he did feel that something was not quite right.

Finally, his vigilance was rewarded. One night he heard a shuffling outside and, getting out of bed, he glimpsed from the window a shadow moving around by the little door under the bell tower, next to the church.

He must have made a noise because the shadow slipped quickly away: but, from that night on, Don Camillo remained on the alert: he left the window ajar and his shotgun at the ready on the windowsill. Then, as time passed, he had second thoughts:

'If whoever it is wants to get into the church it's not like he wants to kill me,' he reasoned. 'Unless, of course, he intends to plant a bomb somewhere…'

Maybe so, but intentions should never be put to the test, not even in la Bassa. So, the following night, Don Camillo concealed himself inside the church.

For three nights he acted as sentry, and the whole business was beginning to irritate him: then, on the fourth night, he heard someone scratching at the lock of the little door under the bell tower. He didn't breathe a word and the scratching continued until the bolt clicked back and the door slowly opened. There were only two candles lit, it being the second week in Lent, but at least something could be deciphered in the sparse light they cast: what Don Camillo saw was a rather thin young man making his way through the church in an altogether furtive manner.

The trespasser looked around and, chancing upon a ladder, pulled it gracefully up and placed it cautiously against the wall to the right of the High Altar, where little pictures with silver hearts *ex voto suscepto* were hung[25], and Don Camillo realised: 'So that's what you're after!'

He let him climb halfway up the ladder, then darted out of his hiding place.

However, when Don Camillo moved, he had the lightness of a Panzer tank: he made such a frightening noise that the man jumped out of his skin, down upon the ground endeavouring to make his way back through the door once more, but Don Camillo caught him by the scruff of the neck, perfecting the capture by letting the scruff go and hooking him by both arms, lifting them up to check if he had some nasty weapon to hand.

But the man had by this time been reduced to a rag doll and, even if he had had a gun, he would never have found the strength to pull the trigger.

Don Camillo carried him bodily into the sacristy and, turning on the light switch with his teeth, looked his game in the face for

---

[25] Devotional objects, sacred hearts *ex voto suscepto* ('from the vow made') have for centuries been offered and placed, especially in Catholic churches in thanks for wishes granted, prayers answered, or intentions agreed by the grace of God.

the first time. As soon as he saw who it was he dropped the whole bundle onto the floor and sat down beside him.

'Smilzo, even as a thief you're not worth four cents,' said Don Camillo.

And Smilzo shrugged: 'Thieving is not something I do,' he replied. 'I wasn't trying to steal anything.'

Don Camillo grinned.

'But of course! To say the Litany it is good form first to enter the church alone, at night, with a false key and climb a ladder.'

'Everyone has their own system,' agreed Smilzo.:

'I understand, and you will have the opportunity to explain your system to the Marshal.'

On hearing the word 'Marshal', Smilzo jumped up, but Don Camillo slapped him back down with a paw.

'I can't be doing with that sort of trouble,' he exclaimed. 'Here everything becomes a matter of politics and that means a dreadful mess. Nowadays it's fashionable to throw everything into the political pot.'

'Don't worry: we'll keep the matter within the scope of common law. Simple Attempted Theft!'

Don Camillo picked up the bundle of rags and searched his pockets.

'Actually, not so much "attempted" as Theft!' he exclaimed, showing what he had found.

'I've stolen nothing,' protested Smilzo. 'This is my stuff, paid for with my own money.'

It was an *ex-voto*, a little picture with a silver heart inside. It was brand new; but Don Camillo didn't believe Smilzo that it was his and, dragging him behind him, he went to look at the wall by the High Altar where the ladder was leaning. And in fact nothing was missing because the votos formed a complete rectangle and it would have been immediately noticeable had one of them been missing.

Don Camillo looked at the small devotional object found in Smilzo's pocket – it was regular stuff, silver with a hallmark, no jokes, no tricks.

'So?' he asked, 'what's the story behind all this?'

Smilzo shrugged.

'Gratitude is good, politics bad. I'd promised that if a certain matter went well for me, I would give the Eternal Father a thank-you like this. But since relations between the Party and the Vatican are tense, I couldn't show up in broad daylight … precisely to avoid speculation. You clericals are specialists in speculation: we know each other too well. In any case the match is simply postponed, Reverend, you and the warmongering gentlemen…'

Don Camillo interrupted him.

'Forget it: I know all your ranting by heart anyway. Let's get back to the business in hand. If you didn't want to be seen delivering your *ex-voto*, you could have sent someone else. I don't see the need to turn your story into a novel.'

Smilzo stuck out his chest.

'Us ordinary folk are straightforward when it comes to matters of religion. I promised to bring my offering, and I brought it. Now, I deliver it to you.'

In la Bassa, by the Great River, they are all a little cracked. Don Camillo thought about it for a little while, then spread his arms:

'All right,' he said, aiming his boot in Smilzo's direction, here's a receipt, now let's not talk about it anymore.'

Smilzo dodged the kick and ran away; when he was at the door he turned to admonish the Christian Democrats:

'If you manage to go one more year without being hanged in the proletarian revolution that's around the corner, you'll need to offer one of those *ex-votos* three-by-three metres in size.'

Finally Don Camillo was left alone with Smilzo's offering in his hand and showed it to Christ.

'We must understand these people,' said Don Camillo. 'It's much less complicated than one might think. They are primitive creatures and, even if they do something honest, they have to do it violently. We must forgive them many things.'

'Naturally, Don Camillo: we must forgive them many things,' replied Christ, sighing.

Don Camillo was sleepy:

'Now, I'll put this up on the wall beside you and think about it more deeply again tomorrow,' he decided. And, having climbed the ladder, he went to hang the little silver heart beneath the last one in the row.

'In fact,' he muttered, taking out the pin he had stuck in the wall and going to stick it in another place, 'I'll put it next to his wife's. Because God made them and conjoined them and it is right that they are together in the House of God, just as they are in the House of the Devil.'

The last silver heart had been brought three months earlier by Moretta, Smilzo's wife. She had been very ill and, seeing that the Party was unable to raise her from her bed, she had turned to the Eternal Father. And so, once she had recovered – it had been almost a miracle – she had brought the little picture with the silver heart.

Don Camillo stood looking at the two votos, which were precisely identical:

'Two bodies and one soul,' he muttered, shaking his head.

He climbed down the ladder and made as if to go out: but he didn't reach the door. All of a sudden, as if something had come to him, he stopped and walked back to the altar.

'Jesus,' he said, 'someone breaks into a church at two in the morning in order to hang a votive offering on the wall by the High Altar: it's a story that just doesn't ring true!'

He walked up and down the church a little, then went back to climb the ladder once more. Removing the two votos, he brought them down and scrutinised them under a lamp. After a time, he raised his head.

'We must forgive them many things, Don Camillo,' repeated the smiling Christ.

*

The following evening Smilzo arrived at the presbytery.

'I'm here again because of that business,' he explained casually. 'My partner has now got it into her head that she must have two silver flowers added to the voto that she brought in three months ago. If you'd let me have it, I'll bring it back to you straight away tomorrow.'

'Good idea,' replied Don Camillo. 'I have it right here, on hand. Last night, when I was hanging yours next to it, I saw that some dust had gotten under the glass, so I took it apart and cleaned it.'

Don Camillo opened a drawer in the desk and took out the little voto. Then he brought out something else which he showed to Smilzo.

'Actually, between the backboard and the velvet I found this in there. I can't imagine how it ended up there. It is yours?'

It was indeed Smilzo's: his Party card.

Smilzo extended his hand, but Don Camillo was ahead of him and placed the card back in the drawer.

'So?'

'There's little point in beating about the bush,' replied Smilzo. 'My Moretta was sick – terminally, it was thought – and so she made the silver heart voto and I, for my part, vowed that, if she recovered, I would offer my proletarian heart: my communist party membership card... Then she recovered and I put my Party card under her voto. But I didn't have the courage to resign from the Party... And now the boss is on the warpath, because if a member loses his card it's not like you clergy or the bourgeoisie, where everything is settled by crossing a palm here or crossing a palm there with a tip. No, right now I can foresee not a few regrets and big troubles. In short, *I need the card back!*'

Don Camillo turned on his Tuscan.

'Now, everything falls into place: you had the same voto made as your wife and you broke into the church like a thief in the night to replace the original with the new one to get your Party card back.'

Smilzo shrugged.

'What does God want with a communist party card?'

Don Camillo raised his finger solemnly.

'He who makes a vow enters into a contract and has a solemn obligation.'

'I'll pay my debt when the time comes. I can't do it now.'

Smilzo seemed to have reverted to the pathetic bundle of rags of the night before. Don Camillo took the card from the drawer and handed it to him.

'It is better that rubbish like this does not litter a church,' he explained contemptuously.

Smilzo got up and, grabbing the card, carefully placed it in his wallet. Then he said solemnly:

'Render unto Caesar what is Caesar's, render unto God what is God's, render unto the people what is the people's.'

'And render unto Smilzo what is Smilzo's!' Don Camillo shouted, booting his backside.

Smilzo collected the kick with a certain dignity but not the humility or acquired wisdom of the true penitent:

'Whoever raises a provocative hand against a defenceless member of the proletariat,' he said, 'will pay with interest on the Day of Redemption, even if the hand is a foot!'

Afterwards Don Camillo went to re-hang the two votos and, passing in front of Christ, spread his arms in dismay. But Christ smiled: 'We must forgive them many things, Don Camillo. The day they present themselves for Divine Judgment, they will all be without their membership cards.'

Meanwhile, Smilzo was marching proudly towards the People's Palace with his communist membership card in his pocket, feeling perfectly at ease with both God and man. Not because he had his proletarian heart in his wallet, which he did not, but perhaps because the silver heart was now, after all, hanging next to the Crucified Christ on the wall to the right of the High Altar.

War of Secession (1950)

PEPPONE'S SUDDEN ARRIVAL at the presbytery was followed by Smilzo, Bigio, Brusco and Lungo. The matter had all the air of a punitive expedition, and Don Camillo thought immediately of Falchetto, who had withdrawn his party membership in order to marry Rocchi's girl.

'They'll be furious,' the archpriest said to himself, 'because they'll imagine that I had something to do with it.'

But nothing could have been further from the gang's collective mind.

'Neither God nor politics has anything to do with why we are here,' announced Peppone, snorting like the tram as it makes its ascent up the Mulino Nuovo. 'This is about patriotism. I am here as Mayor, and you are here as citizen priest.'

Don Camillo spread his arms:

'Speak up, citizen Mayor. The citizen priest is all ears.'

Peppone took his place in front of the table behind which Don Camillo was sitting; the others remained standing behind their leader: mute, motionless, legs apart, arms crossed on chest.

'Our historical nemesis!' Peppone said in a solemn voice.

Don Camillo looked a little worried.

'Our historical nemesis!' the Mayor repeated. 'And, if that's not enough, also our geographical nemesis!' he continued. 'And if that's still not enough…'

'I think it will be enough,' cut in Don Camillo, who, upon hearing talk of geographical nemesis, immediately calmed down. 'Expound the facts.'

Peppone turned towards his general staff and brought a smile to his phizog that was somewhere between indignant and ironic:

'And now *they* would presume to govern themselves!' he said. 'But they don't even know what's happening a mere fifty metres from home!'

'These are people who have never evolved beyond mediaeval self-absorption!' Smilzo explained no less haughtily. *"Cicero pro domine di lui,"* lest the people die!'[26]

Don Camillo raised his eyes towards heaven and then landed them on Smilzo.

'Do they also teach you lot Latin now?' he enquired.

---

[26] Roughly, 'Let Cicero be our master.' Preposterously, Smilzo evokes the eloquence of Roman orator Marcus Tullius Cicero, pointing in particular, perhaps, to his most famous speech against Catiline – *In Catilinam* – in which he cited a conspiracy to overthrow the Republic and assassinate Cicero himself.

'And why shouldn't they?' retorted Smilzo. 'Do you, pray, have a monopoly on culture?'

Peppone brought the discussion to an end:

'What we are talking about is a band of unpatriotic, misanthropic, outlander scoundrels who want to usurp the sacred rights of their people, inventing infamies in order to establish local autonomy. In short, they are the cowards from Fontanile who want to break away from the municipality and create an independent municipality of their own.

'Therefore, it is incumbent on us immediately to crush the insurrection with a manifesto from A to Z containing an explanation of why it is their historical and geographical nemesis that *we* have the right to be the capital of our municipality, with *them* mere dependants.'

The indication, for the first time, of where Peppone was headed with his allusion to 'historical and geographical nemesis' failed to amuse Don Camillo. He knew la Bassa inside out and also that when two regions go on the alert and begin to look at each other sideways, even if historical and geographical nemesis might have something to do with it, there is absolutely nothing to laugh about.

There was indeed still some unfinished business between the two – stuff from years and years ago which would return to the surface within a matter of a few minutes. Furthermore, the people of Fontanile had always had the idea of becoming a municipality. There was nothing new about it.

They had made the first attempt at independence in 1902: they had come to an agreement with three districts of four houses each, which had found the money to very quietly erect an elegant building with a portico, a staircase and a tower with a clock and lots of coat of arms. It must have been their version of a town hall. Then this created such a ruckus that the police had to intervene and someone even went to jail. They hadn't got any further than that. But the building remained and no one had ever occupied it. They made another move soon after the war, in 1920, and it went badly then too. Now they were up and running with it once more.

Don Camillo enquired cautiously: 'Have you tried talking to them?'

'Have I talked to them?' Peppone shouted. 'The only comms I'll have with them is a burst of machine gun fire.'

'On that basis it seems to me that it will be difficult to open negotiations,' observed Don Camillo.

Peppone seemed to be sweating like a labourer; he was so brim-full of anger.

'We are responding perfectly democratically,' he managed with difficulty. 'We make the manifesto explaining the historical-geographical nemesis and if they understand it, well... and if they don't understand it...'

Peppone left it like that – in the air – and Bigio, who of the whole gang was the most serious and balanced, said in a dark voice:

'If they don't understand it, we'll beat them up!'

When the easy-going Bigio said this it meant that the conflict was already at a very bad stage.

Don Camillo turned the position around.

'If they want to secede and form their own municipality, why do you care?'

'It's not about me!' Peppone shouted. 'Something like this undermines the sovereignty of the people! The municipality is *us* and that's all there is to it! If they take away Fontanile and the three hamlets beyond la Rocchetta, what are we left with? What municipality will ours become? Have you also lost a sense of patriotism?'

Don Camillo sighed.

'Why make a tragedy of it from the start? Haven't the authorities always denied Fontanile the right to form into a municipality? They will continue to deny them. Practically nothing has changed.'

Peppone stood up and pounded the table with his fist.

'So you say!' he screamed. 'That is to ignore the politics of the situation, the fact that our Party has been elected to power, while in Fontanelle they're a lot of reactionaries and maybe the Government will think it is better off creating a new municipality with an administration politically opposite to ours which also takes away half the territory and its people.'

Don Camillo looked at Peppone.

'If you say so, you are the citizen Mayor and you know a thing or two about politics; I am just the poor citizen priest and I know nothing about politics; what do you want me to say about it?'

Smilzo stepped forward and pointed an accusing finger at Don Camillo.

'America's hit man!' he said sharply.

Don Camillo shrugged his shoulders:

'So, what do we do then?'

'First we draw up our manifesto with historical, geographical and economic justifications for our position.'

'And where do I find them?' Don Camillo enquired.

'Make them up! Did they teach you nothing in the seminary except how to make propaganda for America? Then we'll see. If they stop their nonsense, fine, if they don't, we'll send them an *intimatum*![27] Either they give up or the will of the people will prevail!'

'God's will, if I have anything to do with it,' corrected Don Camillo.

'It has already been agreed that politics have no place here,' Peppone insisted. 'In any case, I'll take care of the *intimatum* if it comes to it.'

Don Camillo spent half the night messing about with a poster explaining why it would be appropriate for Fontanile to renounce its independence claim. The difficulty was how to word it in such a way as to save the day without irritating anyone.

The poster was subsequently printed and a team of young men, led by Lungo, pasted it up at dead of night all over Fontanile.

*

At midday Peppone received a small box from the municipality. Opening the box, he found a bundle of posters posted that night. And further investigation revealed the presence of ... a bad thing.

---

[27] Accusative supine of *intimo* (Latin, Italian), rooted in a sense of 'closeness' or 'intimacy', more likely to apply to a friend or even to lingerie than to the final or peremptory demand by one upon another. But then Peppone's malapropisms are famous and his body language rarely leaves anyone in doubt as to what he means.

Peppone rewrapped the paper and ran towards the presbytery. He placed the bundle on the table, before Don Camillo, and carefully spread the wrapping paper open.

'*This*,' he said, 'is Fontanile's answer.'

'I see,' said Don Camillo. 'I was the one who wrote the manifesto, so this is addressed to me. Leave it here and don't you worry about it.'

Peppone shook his head.

He carefully repackaged the bundle and made to leave in silence, until reaching the door, when he turned and said:

'You will soon have a lot of work on your hands, citizen priest.'

Don Camillo remained where he was, stunned, not knowing what to say because Peppone's words had him seriously bothered.

'Jesus,' he said to Christ above the High Altar, 'wasn't the Second War enough, aren't politics enough to fill the hearts of these people with hatred?'

'There is always room for more hatred in the heart of man,' sighed Christ.

*

Throughout the day there was a lot of coming and going at the People's Palace and Don Camillo couldn't understand what the hell everyone was up to across the square from the presbytery, given that nobody knew anything or, if they did know, they didn't want to say anything. Then, around nine in the evening, when he was getting ready for bed, someone knocked on the presbytery window overlooking the churchyard and it was Smilzo.

'You are urgently summoned to the Town Hall,' said the Hermes of the Red Council. 'Get on with it because the people care nothing for the convenience of the clergy.'

Smilzo's tone was rudely peremptory and not only because between him and Don Camillo was the solid grill of the window: that evening he had the tone of a messenger firmly convinced that he was carrying out a mission of the highest importance.

'What kind of "people" are you referring to?' Don Camillo enquired. 'Your type is it?'

'I didn't come here for a political discussion, Reverend. If you're afraid to come out of your den, that's another matter.'

Don Camillo threw on his cloak, took his umbrella because it was raining again that evening (as God determined), and left the presbytery behind him.

'May I know what is going on?' he enquired along the way.

'It is not something to be discussed in the street,' replied Smilzo. 'It would be like me asking you what was written in the latest secret circular you received from the Pope.'

'You'd better leave the Pope out of this or I'll break my umbrella over your head,' retorted Don Camillo. 'The Pope has nothing to do with your nonsense.'

'Whether he had anything to do with it or whether he didn't have anything to do with it will be revealed on the Day of Redemption,' replied Smilzo. 'However, let's forget about it. When you are in the Town Hall you will find out what it's about.'

On the threshold of the People's Palace, Don Camillo and Smilzo were blocked.

'Who goes there,' sounded a voice.

'*Venezia*!' replied Smilzo.

'*Sampierdarena*!' the voice replied.

They were passed through and Don Camillo asked what the password nonsense was about, but Smilzo replied that it wasn't nonsense, and concluded: 'War is war.'

Entering the Council chamber, Don Camillo was astonished to find it was packed with people and they weren't just any people: present were all foremost people at every level of the municipality, people of every political hue: reds, blacks, yellows, greens – right across the board, without exception.

They were waiting evidently for Don Camillo, and in dead silence. When he entered the chamber, the mottled crew parted and made way for him through their midst.

Peppone then stood up, and took stock of the situation.

'Reverend,' he began, 'at this tragic moment when the destiny of our homeland is under threat, you see before you the most representative of all our citizens, irrespective of their politics: landowners, workers, shopkeepers, craftsman, all united by faith in one people, upon whose sacrosanct rights a gang of reckless personages threaten to trespass and whose advance must, at all costs, be arrested. On this, I believe, we agree...'

'*Bene!*' the assembly replied unanimously.

'To remove any political prejudice, any fear of inter-party speculation, the representatives of all ideologies and tendencies here present have agreed to choose one person to give his dispassionate and apolitical opinion on every decision of the Public Safety Committee, a committee that we have established for the defence of the municipality. By a secret vote *you* have been elected and now, having silenced our political differences, we call upon you to be part of the Committee as *neutral observer.*'

Don Camillo looked around him.

'I accept,' he replied. And the assembly gave him a big round of applause. Peppone continued his presentation.

'We note your solidarity with the Committee. The situation is, therefore, as follows: to our manifesto duly approved by you – representative of the Vatican – the population of Fontanile have responded with a provocative, offensive and anti-democratic gesture which shows the shameless character of their challenge to the moral capital!'

A dark murmur swept through the assembly.

'Yes indeed! Our historical, geographical and economic rights authorise us to define ourselves as *the moral capital of the municipality*! A capital which is one and indivisible and can only be one and indivisible!'

'*Bene!*' the assembly shouted.

Peppone had now engaged fourth gear and was proceeding at full speed.

'In this apotheotic climate of harmony and understanding, we tell you that the abuse of power by the autonomists of Fontanile, who seek to split the municipal unit – our homeland – by establishing their independence, will not be tolerated! I therefore propose that an energetic *intimatum* be sent to the managers of Fontanile: either you desist or we'll make you desist. Because democracy is a good thing: but when you come across cowards like those of Fontanile...'

Peppone, swollen with anger, seemed even bigger and more powerful and the assembly looked at him with fascination: unfortunately, when he finally arrived in Fontanile, his dictionary was closed and he had run out of words. So instead he found a large telephone book three fingers thick under his paws: so he grabbed it and, twisting it slowly between his enormous hands, tore it in two.

Arguments of this kind, well known down in la Bassa, are always decisive: the assembly let out an enthusiastic roar and, when Peppone threw the two sections of the book on the table shouting: *'And this is our intimatum!'* the applause almost brought the ceiling down.

Finally, when calm had returned, Peppone turned to Don Camillo:

'Does the neutral observer wish to give us his opinion?'

Don Camillo kept his cool, stood up and said in a loud voice:

'In my opinion you are all crazy.'

His words were like a blast of cold wind, and a heavy silence fell upon the assembly.

'You have lost all sense of reality,' he continued. 'You are building a fifteen-story building on five centimetres of foundation stone. Your argument will collapse upon you, overwhelming all of you. This is not about issuing ultimatums or tearing up telephone directories. It's about deep thinking. Reason tells us that before starting to discuss the matter we need to wait for the authorities to grant Fontanile permission to break away and form an independent municipality.'

'*We* are in authority!' Peppone shouted. 'These are things that concern *us*!'

Don Camillo looked at the assembly and in the front row was old Rocchi.

'Father,' said old Rocchi, 'we agree perfectly that we should not dramatise the situation and remain calm. But if we wait until the authorities give permission, we will no longer be able to oppose it because it would be interpreted as open rebellion against the Government. We must, in appropriate fashion of course, prevent those of Fontanile from submitting their application for independence. In my opinion, the Mayor is wrong when he says we should use violence, but in essence he is absolutely right.'

'*Giusto!*' exclaimed members of the assembly variously: 'In essence the Mayor is right. The Mayor has political ideas many of which we may not share, but it is clear that politics has nothing to do with this move for independence! The interests of the municipality come into play here! In any case, let's be honest: we know the people of Fontanile well enough! This is something we cannot swallow!'

Peppone looked at Don Camillo with an air of triumph and Don Camillo spread his arms:

'It is sad,' he said, 'that men can only agree when it comes to doing something very foolish. In any case, before pushing things to extremes, we need to talk and discuss. Send a commission to speak with Fontanile. This is the first thing to do.'

'Of course, this is the first thing to do,' approved Rocchi. And everyone else nodded their heads.

Peppone didn't have another telephone directory to tear apart, but he had something else in his drawer and he took it out and showed it to the assembly: it was the famous poster with the famous bad thing within:

'How can we go and discuss anything with people who respond like this?' Peppone asked.

The assembly then became restless.

'Rather than sending them an *intimatum*,' shouted the farmer Bacchini, waving his big stick, '*This* is all the *intimatum* those scoundrels deserve!'

Don Camillo felt quite alone.

'I cannot pray to God to enlighten your brains because you have none,' he shouted. 'But I'm telling you, you cannot proceed with what you propose!'

'And who is going to stop us?' Peppone retorted.

'I am!' replied Don Camillo.

He walked resolutely towards the exit and, when he was at the door, he turned and waved his umbrella:

'In the meantime, I'll go and warn the Marshal!' he shouted. 'And while I'm gone, have a good think and get a hold of yourselves.'

From the top of his dais Peppone pointed an accusing finger at the priest.

'You rat!' he shouted.

The crowd formed a wall between the two and Don Camillo made haste to speak with the Marshal.

*

The forces of law and order in this case consisted of four men plus the Marshal. The garrison was split in two: one half were immediately deployed in Fontanile and the other in the moral capital, with the Marshal, who could not be split in two, taking a tour on his bicycle, reinforcing first one and then the other in turn.

Three days passed and nothing at all happened. 'You can see they've thought about it,' the Marshal said confidently to Don Camillo. 'They've calmed down.'

'Let's hope that God has given them brains and enlightened them,' replied Don Camillo, unconvinced.

On the afternoon of the fourth day a bad mess occurred elsewhere: a group of unemployed labourers, who had arrived from who knows where on bicycles had invaded a large farm known as as Case Nuove, demanding to be taken on at once.

Besides anything else, the demand was impossible to fulfil because it had been raining for ten days and the only work that could be done in the fields was to extricate oneself from the mud in which anyone labouring would be stuck up to his butt. Evidently this was one of those political affairs organised by regular agitators and unconnected to the Fontanile breakaway movement. Nevertheless, it meant that the Marshal had to move his men to Case Nuove to prevent the situation there from turning sour.

Towards evening Don Camillo went along to see what was going on: the farm had been cleared and the original, massed group of labourers had been split into many small groups who were wandering around, going their own way.

'If we leave,' the Marshal warned, 'in five minutes they will all come back and the story will start over. And then night will fall, which augurs badly when there's trouble like this going on.'

On his way home, Don Camillo came across one of the deconstructed groups: five men, one of whom Don Camillo recognised immediately as the tailor from Molinetto.

'Have you made a mid-life career change?' Don Camillo asked him. 'Have you become an unemployed labourer?'

'If everyone would mind their own business it would be a better world,' replied the tailor, clearly ruffled.

Don Camillo continued on his way and came across the old village postman on his bicycle with a toolbox slung over his shoulder. The old postman also worked as a lineman repairing overhead electrical lines, telegraph and telephone lines and the overhead network of railways and electric tramways, as he explained to Don Camillo when he expressed himself amazed to see him around at that hour:

'I'm having a look round. With these damned storms something must have gone wrong: nothing works anymore, neither telephone nor telegraph lines.

So Don Camillo, instead of returning to the presbytery, ran to Brellis' place, quickly wrote a letter and gave it to the younger man to deliver:

'Take your motorbike, race to Villetta and deliver this note to the parish priest. It's a matter of life or death!'

Brellis got on his motorbike and sped off like a damned man. Then, after an hour, he returned:

'The priest said that he would telephone immediately.'

*

The river was swollen in those days and the water was pressing against its banks, and all the tributaries that cut across the plain and flowed into the big river were also swollen. These cheap little tributaries normally make you laugh because they run dry or they only carry around four tubs of water and one wonders how people who have their heads on their shoulders could throw away mountains of money to build large embankments along them. But they are potential rivers nonetheless: like men who drink barely a glass a day and then one day they lose their home address and before you know it they're three sheets to the wind. Every now and then these little rivers swell and then they become worse than the Mississippi and fill not only the entire stony bed, but reach halfway up the bank and even farther.

At this precise point in time even the small rivers were frighteningly swollen and people began to wander around the banks measuring the water level with a stick to see if it had risen further. And the water kept rising.

Fontanile was divided from the territory of the moral capital by one of these rivers that ran between two sturdy banks and for at least twenty years the level had never been so high.

By now, evening had fallen, but Don Camillo was nervous and continued to walk up and down the little road at the top of the embankment and his nervousness only abated when he heard the crash of a large vehicle arriving.

The vehicle was full of policemen. Only then did Don Camillo return to the presbytery and reattach his shotgun to the nail on the wall.

After dinner Peppone arrived, looking gloomy.

'You were the one who called the police, right!' he said to Don Camillo.

'Of course: since it was you who organised the antics at Case Nuove to get the police away, thereby freeing your hand. And it was you who cut the telephone and telegraph lines.'

Peppone looked at him with contempt:

'You are a traitor to your country!' he shouted. 'You asked an outsider to intervene. You are beyond disloyal!'

Peppone was coming on so strong that Don Camillo was left speechless.

But Peppone hadn't finished yet.

'You are a godless man!' he screamed again. 'But your police won't accomplish anything because in two minutes time God's own justice will triumph!'

Don Camillo jumped up, but didn't have time to say a word before a distant roar was heard.

'The Fontanile embankment is down!' Peppone explained. 'With a well-hidden wire you can control a small mine remotely. Now they can found the municipality of Venice if they want.'

Don Camillo grabbed Peppone by the throat, but didn't have time to squeeze before another roar was heard, but rather closer. A torrential rush of water followed, pouring into the presbytery. And only when it reached their waists, did the water stop rising.

'Now can you see what murderers they are?' Peppone shouted. 'This is the bad thing they were planning, those ... cowards!'

Don Camillo looked sadly at all that liquid misery, then shook his head and sighed:

'Good God, if this is the beginning of the Universal Flood, blessed be your divine mercy, which frees the world from this poor idiotic humanity.'

But Peppone had a different take on it.

'*Navigare necessariorum est!*' he shouted proudly, starting to splash towards the door. 'Italy's destiny is on the sea!'[28]

In the church there was a good metre of water. The candles on the High Altar were lit and the water flashed with their flames.

'Gesù,' said Don Camillo to the Crucified Christ, 'I would ask your forgiveness, but if I kneel I will be in it up to my neck.'

'At all costs, Don Camillo, stay on your feet,' Christ replied, smiling.

Hand of God (1950)

FOR PEPPONE'S FAMILY, cinema was of particular interest and not unrelated to the fact that – as the old folk remembered well – Peppone's father was the first to bring a threshing machine to the farmyards of la Bassa.

Young people of today would find it amusing to hear people talk about the advent of cinema and the first threshing machine in the same breath: but the young people of today are derisive of how things were in the old days, having been born with the number of their home telephone written on their brains and, in

---

[28] The original line – '*Navigare necesse est, vivere non est necesse*' – was Pompey's when, on the way home, there was a great storm and his captain advised caution, whereupon Pompey took matters into his own hands, proclaiming, 'We have to sail, we do not have to live,' which has a similarly paradoxical, mock-heroic, Marx-Brothers-style charm to Guareschi's own utterance when he was taken prisoner by the Germans in 1943: '*I will not die even if they kill me.*'

matters where sentiment comes into play, being equipped merely with the grace of a sow going for a walk in a corn field.

Way back when, electricity was a luxury reserved for city mamelukes and, since electricity was needed to run a cinema projector, Peppone's father, a passionate fan of the movies, planted a dynamo on the steam engine used to run his thresher-cum-baler and, when he wasn't threshing, he went around the local villages with his steam machine dragged by two oxen to put on a reel-to-reel presentation of the latest films.

Diesel engines are stinky rubbish. They began to arrive on the scene at the end of the Great War. Years have already passed since then and today's young people haven't got a clue about how the oxen-led steamers that roamed the countryside were constructed. They had a high chimney (lowered in transit), were painted green, with magnificent polished brass hoops, and carried a large flywheel. They didn't make any noise: they worked in silence without any stink, and they had a whistle that was nothing short of marvellous.

For Mayor Peppone, cinema was thus an inherited passion and once the People's Palace was built and he found a large meeting room at his disposal, the first thing he thought of was opening a cinema.

And so, one fine morning, the village woke up to posters announcing the inauguration of the first film season at the People's Palace the following Sunday.

It cannot be said of Don Camillo's father that he had ever dreamed of going around the villages showing films: however, the idea of setting up a projection booth in the Parish Hall had always been Don Camillo's obsession and so, when he saw Peppone's posters, he felt like a live cat had been let loose in his stomach.

On the Sunday afternoon he consoled himself (a little only) because a cursed storm broke out and rain produced something akin to a Universal Flood. At ten in the evening he was still up waiting for a report on the inaugural presentation, when Barchini arrived at the presbytery dripping wet but happy:

'There were only four people in total at the People's Palace: the water kept the people of the hamlets away. On top of everything else, electricity fluctuated so badly that at one moment, they had to stop the film altogether. Peppone was furious.'

Don Camillo then went to kneel before the Crucified Christ above the High Altar:

'Jesus, I thank you,' he said.

'For what, Don Camillo?'

'For having caused the storm that damaged the power line...'

Christ sighed.

'Don Camillo, I have nothing to do with electrical failures: you know that I was a carpenter, not an electrician. As for the storm, do you really believe that the Eternal Father enlisted the winds and the clouds and the lightning to prevent Peppone from screening his film?'

Don Camillo bowed his head.

'Not really,' he stammered. 'It is the cursed vice of us poor humans to thank God for the things that serve us well and to believe that that was their purpose.'

*

The storm abated around midnight, but at three in the morning it resumed, more furious than before, and suddenly an infernal roar wakened Don Camillo with a start. Never had he heard a crash so loud and so close: he jumped out of bed, ran to the window to see what on earth had happened and was left speechless. The bell tower spire was no longer there. A bolt of lightning had pulverised it. That was the simple fact of the matter, but for Don Camillo it seemed so incredible that he went forthwith to confide in Christ.

'Jesus,' he said, his voice shaking with emotion, 'the lightning struck the bell tower!'

'I see, Don Camillo,' Christ replied calmly. 'The fact that during a thunderstorm, lightning strikes a building is common.'

'Lightning struck *our* bell tower!' Don Camillo pressed on totally mystified.

'I do understand what you are saying, Don Camillo.'

Don Camillo looked at the Crucified Christ in amazement, then spread his arms:

'Why?' he asked in a voice full of bitter disappointment.

'During a thunderstorm, lightning struck the spire of a bell tower,' said Christ. 'Do you believe it necessary for your God to justify himself to you for this simple fact? A little while ago you thanked him for having caused that storm to break out, which spoiled your neighbour's film night: do you now blame God because the same storm spoiled things for you?'

'It's not that the storm spoiled things for me,' replied Don Camillo. 'It has damaged the House of God!'

'The House of God is infinite and eternal. Even if all the worlds that populate the universe were pulverised, the House of God would remain intact. During a storm, lightning fell on the spire of a bell tower, that's all there is to say or think about it, Don Camillo. The lightning was always going to fall somewhere.'

Don Camillo continued to engage with Christ, but couldn't let go of the thought of his beautiful bell tower.

'That bolt of lightning could very well not have fallen!' he cried.

And Christ took pity on his pain and appealed sweetly to his reason.

'Don Camillo, be calm and think. God created the universe, and the universe is a perfect, harmonious system in which each element is inextricably linked, directly or indirectly, to all the others, and it is therefore systemic that lightning fell where it did and not a thousandth of a millimetre away. And we must thank God for it, just as we must thank the Creator for everything that happens in the universe because everything that happens in the universe is proof of the infallibility of a perfect system. It was not chance, nor was it intentional, but systemically inevitable that the lightning should have fallen there and not a thousandth of a millimetre further away, Don Camillo: the one whom you might point to as making a mistake is the man who built a bell tower in that very spot: he could have built it two metres away.'

Don Camillo in his confusion thought only of his beautiful bell tower lying open to the elements and his heart was full of bitterness.

'If the system is so perfect then the position of the bell tower is as predetermined as where the lightning would strike, it *couldn't* have been built further away. And if that is the case, what of free will? Where does it leave man's freedom to act as he chooses, if it is all preordained!'

'No, it could have been built a few metres away,' Christ replied gently, still smiling. 'But woe to those who, overcome by anger or pain or the exaltation of their senses, forget what deep down we all know: God shows mankind the right path but leaves man the freedom to choose it or not to choose it. Since the goodness of God is infinite, he leaves man the freedom to take the wrong path and to save his soul by recognising, through repentance, that he has taken it.

'In this case, during a thunderstorm, lightning struck the top of a bell tower; the lightning's work was irredeemable, but the man could have built the bell tower elsewhere and the builder should thank God for allowing him the freedom to choose to build it where it was built.'

Don Camillo sighed.

'Jesus, I thank you. However, if with your help I succeed in having the spire rebuilt, I will equip it with a lightning rod.'

'Yes, Don Camillo: if it is established that you put a lightning rod on the top of your bell tower, then you will put a lightning rod on the top of your bell tower.'

Don Camillo bowed. Then, in the first light of dawn, he went to gaze sadly at his poor mutilated bell tower.

'When all's said and done,' he said to himself in the end, 'he did want the bell tower built there.'

*

People soon began to come to the square to see the blasted bell tower and when everyone was there the rain was coming down thick and thin, and they watched in silence and dismay. With the square full, Peppone turned up accompanied by his general staff. He made his way through the crowd and, having reached the front row, looked intently at the ruined bell tower for some time, then, solemnly raising his finger towards the sky, declared:

'Here is the proof of God's wrath! Here is God's response to our excommunication by the Church.[29] Lightning falls where God sends it, and God sends it where it must be sent.'

---

[29] In April 1948 *L'Osservatore Romano* (the unofficial Vatican City newspaper) published a decree to excommunicate those who propagated 'the materialistic and anti-Christian teachings of communism', followed a year later by the Holy Office (of Pope Pius XII) issuing the famous 'Decree against Communism' which excommunicated all Catholics collaborating in communist organisations.

Don Camillo was listening from a window in the presbytery: Peppone saw him and pointed him out to the people.

'The archpriest is silent!' he screamed. 'He is silent because lightning struck his Church. You would hear all about it if the lightning had struck the People's Palace instead!'

Smilzo also looked towards Don Camillo:

'This is God's answer to the warmongerers!' he screamed, with reference to the newly formed NATO.

'Long live Mao Tse-tung!'

'Long live peace and the CGIL plan!' the band chorused.[30]

Don Camillo counted to fifty-two before saying what he wanted to say. Then he didn't say anything: instead, he took a half Tuscan out of his pocket, stuck it in his mouth and calmly set it on fire.

'There you are!' shouted Peppone. 'It's Nero playing the lyre on the ruins of Carthage!'

And with this precious historical reference the Mayor and his general staff left with their noses in the air.

*

Towards evening Don Camillo went to lay his sorrows at the foot of the High Altar.

'Jesus,' he said at last, 'the thing that drives me mad with anger is that this scoundrel talks about divine wrath! I don't even dare to think that I can disturb the harmony of your universe: but if, after the blasphemies that those criminals came up with this morning, lightning were to fall on the People's Palace, it would truly be a magnificent thing! With their sacrilegious words they will surely have provoked divine anger!'

'Don Camillo, now *you* are the agent provocateur,' Christ said, even now still smiling.

'How do you have the face to trouble God, in all his majesty, to blow off a few tiles from the roof of the puny Palace of the People? Respect your God, Don Camillo, please.'

Don Camillo returned to the presbytery and the journey from the church was a short one. Nevertheless, at night, even journeys of a mere twenty steps can lead to shameful encounters. It was still

---

[30] The CGIL, the communist dominated Union, the Italian General Confederation of Labour, was founded in 1944.

raining and, at midnight, the rain increased in intensity. At one o'clock the story of the previous night was repeated: the thunder and lightning began again. At two o'clock a crash was heard which woke up half the village. At ten past two the whole village was awake and word spread that a house in the square was burning – lightning had struck it and set it on fire – and it was indeed the People's Palace.

By the time Don Camillo arrived, the square was full of people and Smilzo and his team had already put out the flames. The roof of the building had fallen in, some of the beams were completely destroyed and the rest of it was reduced to smoking embers.

By chance Don Camillo ended up close to Peppone.

'Neat job,' the priest observed with indifference. 'To be sure, conscience is inherent even in lightning!'

Peppone turned towards him.

'Would you like a half Tuscan?' Don Camillo asked him.

'I don't smoke!' Peppone replied darkly.

'Yes, nor should you: the People's Palace smokes enough for all of you. But I am sorry; for if you don't smoke, how can I say: "Here is Nero playing the lyre on the ruins of Carthage!" Incidentally, it wasn't the burning of Carthage: it was Rome that was burning.'

'My pleasure!' moaned Peppone, 'is that Rome dies with all the priests who inhabit it.'

Don Camillo shook his head and said gravely, but in a loud voice: 'We must not provoke God's anger. Can you now see what your sacrilegious words this morning have achieved?'

Peppone was bursting with anger from every pore.

'Do not be angry,' advised Don Camillo. 'Now the CGIL restoration plan will be activated and put everything back in order.'

Peppone stood in front of Don Camillo, fists clenched.

'In three days the roof will be back on, Signor Reverend! We don't need plans,' he shouted, 'we're in charge here!'

'*Bene*, Signor Mayor,' replied Don Camillo in a low voice. 'So you can kill two birds with one stone. When you submit the cost of replacing the roof of the People's Palace to the Council, you can take advantage of the opportunity to get the cost of replacing the roof of the bell tower also allocated.'

'Over your dead body!' said Peppone. 'Tap America for the money! The People's Palace is a public utility building, the church is a private utility building!'

Don Camillo re-lit his Tuscan vehicle.

'Of course it was a great bolt of lightning,' he observed. 'A much more impressive lightning bolt than mine. It really made a magnificent racket and caused a lot of damage. It would truly be a bolt of lightning to study. I mean to discuss it with the Marshal as soon as he arrives.'

'Mind your own dirty business!' said Peppone.

'Exactly: I'm only interested in having you fix the roof of the bell tower.'

Peppone looked at him darkly.

'All right,' he said through gritted teeth. 'But some day I'll settle with you.'

Don Camillo headed towards the presbytery because now there was nothing interesting left to see or hear or say. His idea was to go straight home, but he knew that Christ was waiting for him.

'Don Camillo,' said Christ sternly when the priest stood before him in the semi-dark church. 'Have you come to thank me because lightning struck the People's Palace?'

'No,' replied Don Camillo with his head down. 'A bolt of lightning is part of the natural order of things, preordained by God. It cannot be presumed that God would inconvenience the wind, clouds, thunder and lightning to blow the roof off so rude a piece of village architecture to please as wretched a country priest as I.'

'Exactly,' said Christ, 'and above all one cannot think that God would take advantage of a storm to throw a grenade onto the roof of a People's Palace either. Only a very wretched country priest could choose to do something like that.'

Don Camillo spread his arms.

'All this is true, Jesus: however, even in this shameful fact, the benevolence of God can be seen because if the very wretched country priest, incited by the Devil, had not thrown the grenade onto the roof of the People's Palace as a reprisal for a devastating bolt of lightning, the ammunition box hidden in the attic of the People's Palace would not have exploded and a serious danger would not have been eliminated. Nor would a poor country priest have been given, thereby, an opportunity to exploit the situation to have the spire of the bell tower, destroyed by a real bolt of lightning, rebuilt. Furthermore, we must consider the fact that anyone who blasphemes the name of God must be punished for his arrogance.'

'Don Camillo,' said Christ, 'are you therefore convinced that you have acted rightly?'

'No,' replied Don Camillo. 'God gives men the opportunity to know what the right path is and to choose the right path: I have chosen the wrong one: I recognise that and I will regret it.'

'Do you not regret it right now?'

'No, Lord,' whispered Don Camillo. 'It's still too early. I request an extension.'

Christ sighed and Don Camillo went to bed and, despite having a horribly dirty conscience, slept soundly and dreamed that they had replaced the felled spire on the bell tower with one made all of gold.

When he woke up, he thought about the dream and felt pleased: then he realised that he had forgotten something very important. So, quickly, he fell asleep again and dreamed that they were placing a wonderful lightning rod on the all-gold spire.

Tales of la Bassa

The Girl With Red Hair (1950)

HE ARRIVED IN a dilapidated caravan dragged by a horse as small as an Albanian Myzeqeja, and came to a halt in the piazza.

Immediately, children appeared from everywhere and crowded around the caravan.

'Stay away from the horse!' shouted the driver, a big man with a forbidding face.

Coming down from the rattle-trap he asked for directions to the Municipal headquarters and set off towards the People's Palace, whereupon a red-haired girl appeared and sat on the short platform at the front of the caravan.

In the atrium of the Town Hall the man met Peppone just as he was leaving.

'I'd like to talk to someone about a permit,' he said. 'Where should I go?'

'If the Mayor is good enough for you, you can remain where you are and speak to me,' replied Peppone, who, when he was able to make direct contact with the people, always felt – even when on foot – like the Roman Emperor Trajan.[31]

The big man doffed his hat.

---

[31] Legend has it that Trajan stopped his horse to talk to the widow of a murdered man and made time to settle her case despite all other calls on his time.

'I'd like a permit to stay here a while to work in the square,' he explained.

'What kind of work do you do?'

'Shooting.'

Peppone pondered the matter for a little while, then asked:

'Do you include in your gallery that device which, when a shot hits the target, makes a charge explode?'

'I do,' replied the big man. 'But if it would disturb the public peace I don't necessarily have to use it. I've got some other cool stuff that makes less fuss.'

'No, no: don't for a moment be tempted to scale down your operation. People around here aren't scared even if a cannon fires. Come by in half an hour and you will find the permit and the designated site where you may set up shop.'

The shooting gallery was allotted a space at the end of the square, on the right, in the free space that separated the People's Palace from the presbytery, and the caravan and horse also fitted very comfortably there. So, in the evening, while Don Camillo was having dinner, a cursed bang shook the presbytery windows. He thought immediately it was a bomb, but of course it was the shooting gallery that was already fully functional.

His initial intention was to go out and start screaming: then he thought better of it and went back to eating his dinner. But at the third spoonful, another damned bang was heard. He resisted for three more explosions because his working principle was that unless something concerned a moral transgression, a parish priest should avoid as much as possible confounding people who are having fun. And target shooting is not something that violates a moral principle. The trouble is that it can violate the nervous system and, if so, a parish priest has the right to intervene to protect his personal rights *as a citizen*.

He left the presbytery and walked resolutely towards the shooting gallery. He had time before arriving to hear another bang, and when it arrived he regretted having left.

There was a large rabble gathering in front of the gallery, and Peppone was in the front row with his entire staff. Just then the red-haired girl was reloading Peppone's rifle, while the big man, having replaced the moveable element of the damnable explosive target back on the top of the iron bar, charged the cup with powder.

'We're all having a go,' Peppone explained to the gang in the meantime. 'Fifteen shots are fired each: whoever scores less than ten hits pays for all the others.'

There were ten of them in the gang: calculating an average of eight hits each, there were eighty explosions to come.

Don Camillo gritted his teeth, especially since his eye had fallen on a sign posted on the front of the shack:

'By order of the Mayor, the use of target shooting during religious functions is prohibited.'

Peppone fired, hit the target and the sixth bang rang out.

By now everyone had noticed Don Camillo's arrival, and Don Camillo, having tamed the internal revolution, managed to assume the expression of someone who is simply there to look around. While the ruckus continued, Don Camillo struck up a conversation with someone nearby.

'I don't understand what fun there is in making all this noise!' a woman had said to him. 'Wouldn't it be the same if they were shooting at chalk pipes?'

The provocation was evident, but Don Camillo did not fall for it.

'No,' he replied. 'For someone who is a hunter or, in any case, who has a passion for firearms, taking a shot without hearing the shot is like a player blowing into the trumpet and, instead of hearing a note, sees it appear written on a musical score.'

He remained there for another half hour then slowly walked towards the presbytery behind the smoke screen of his Tuscan vehicle. He planned to lock himself in the cellar, but the sound of explosions could be heard there too; and there were not eighty, as he had predicted, rather at least a hundred.

The same thing happened the following evening, but this time Don Camillo didn't emerge into the square. Each blow was like a hammer to the head, but his head was as hard as iron and he resisted. And he never gave up, not even on following evenings:

'Jesus,' he said to Christ above the High Altar, 'you know what I am holding within. Keep it in mind for the day I have to account to you for my sins. Those scoundrels provoke me, but I will not go along with their game. Should they fire cannons or explode atomic bombs, my reason will always succeed in overcoming my impulses.'

Christ smiled, while the explosions of the infernal shooting gallery continued to ring out.

This continued on about fifteen evenings. On the sixteenth, the fatal hour came but no explosions were heard.

Don Camillo stuck his nose out the door and saw that the shooting gallery had its tarpaulin down.

He went out into the square and saw that the big man and the red-haired girl were sitting together on the platform of their caravan.

'I'd like to take a couple of shots,' he said, 'taking advantage of the absence of interest you've enjoyed every other evening.'

Indeed, the only people in the square were Don Camillo, the shooting gallery man, the man's daughter and the horse. Four in all if you consider the horse, who is not a person, as a person.

The big man hesitated and repeatedly smoothed his chin with his hand.

'I'd like to take a couple of shots,' Don Camillo repeated, now in a rather abrupt voice.

'I'm going to have a drink,' the big man said to the girl. 'You look after him.'

The red-haired girl went to pull up the tarpaulin of the gallery and turned on the light.

She then asked Don Camillo who was waiting, leaning on the parapet:

'A Flobert gun[32] or spring-powered air rifle?'

'Extended 149 gun!' replied Don Camillo, grabbing one of the rifles and taking aim. He didn't make a mistake and the first explosion reverberated around the deserted, silent square.

'Recharge the gun and be quick about it!' Don Camillo instructed.

---

[32] A gallery gun, developed in 1845, by French inventor Louis-Nicolas Flobert. Don Camillo suggests a heavy howitzer – the 'extended 149 gun', probably the Obice da 149/19 modello 37, which served with Italy during World War II. The author himself served as an artillery officer in the war until the Armistice, when he refused to fight for the Germans and was imprisoned (see *Merry Christmas Don Camillo*, Pilot 2022).

The red-haired girl was quick and Don Camillo was quick to aim: it looked like a carpet bombing. At the tenth shot Smilzo arrived: he came from not far away, because the shooting gallery was but twenty metres from the People's Palace. Nevertheless he was panting as if he'd come from Nicaragua.

When he realised that it was Don Camillo it was too late, he had already shouted: 'Stop now!'

'And why? Is there perhaps some religious function going on?'

'The Provincial Secretary is making a speech in the hall of the People's Palace,' replied Smilzo.

Don Camillo aimed, shot and detonated another mine.

'The Provincial Secretary, you say? I would never even have imagined it,' he said smiling.

Smilzo found himself without any directives on the matter and turned back, reappearing after another fifteen explosions, but paying no attention to Don Camillo. He turned instead to the red-haired girl:

'You, tomorrow morning, pack up and leave,' he said in a harsh voice. 'If you haven't cleared out by nine in the morning, the city police will intervene and arrest you.'

The red-haired girl gaped at him, then she spread her arms and reloaded the infernal machine.

The explosions continued until the people meeting in the People's Palace emptied out into the square. Then Don Camillo stopped shooting, paid what he owed, lit his cigar and repaired slowly to the presbytery.

Peppone watched him, the veins in his neck swollen to bursting, then took it out on the red-haired girl:

'You,' he shouted, leaning inside the gallery, 'be off with you tomorrow morning or I'll throw you into the river with all your merchandise!'

The red-haired girl drew back as if in fear and then, as was natural, she smashed the infernal target which sprang up for action and made the most frightening explosion of the entire evening.

*

At nine o'clock the next morning the municipal guard went to inform Peppone that those of the shooting gallery had not moved, but that he did not feel like having them removed.

Peppone set off at full speed, reached the end of the square where they'd set up shop, violently pushed aside the people who were blocking his passage and found himself in front of the big man and the red-haired girl who, motionless, were leaning against a corner of the gallery, watching like forlorn idiots a large bag of bones abandoned on the ground: their dead horse.

It was such a tragic sight that Peppone's blood for an instant stopped flowing. He threw his hat aside, scratched his head, then turned back.

*

What is a traveller if you take away his horse? He is a castaway washed up on a rock in the middle of an ocean.

The gallery remained where it was and, after a month, people no longer cared one way or the other about it. Every now and then, some kid would come and fire a shot. But cheap stuff. On a Saturday evening a few young men might show up, but if the red-haired girl wasn't around, they'd soon disappear.

Everyone except Diego, the youngest of the Marossi clan.

Diego was his own man: he was about twenty years old, with two strong shoulders, a face that was always frowning and words only in exceptionally serious cases. Every Saturday afternoon Diego arrived at the gallery, took the rifle that the red-haired girl handed him and began breaking plaster pipes.

He'd continue shooting for a couple of hours and his only words were '*buongiorno*' when he arrived, '*quanto?*' when he wanted to pay and '*buona sera*' when he left.

The Marossis were big tenants, serious people and well off: old man Marossi was the one in charge. Every Saturday he gave his children and grandchildren a set amount to spend on entertainment and a good night out. Clothes, linens, shoes, food, etc were bought by the old man in person.

Diego received 500 lire every Saturday and, every Saturday, he went to shoot 500 lire at the shooting gallery. This didn't bother old Marossi either way:

'Everyone must spend his money as he pleases,' he would say. 'If tomorrow someone wants to buy a destroyer, that's his business. Everyone gets their fun in whatever way they want.'

And Diego enjoyed shooting that gallery.

Winter fell suddenly: the red-haired girl's father became ill and Peppone had him admitted to hospital. He stayed there for only a short time because, after a week, he was dead.

The girl was left alone, waiting for her only customer to come.

The customer always came on time because he truly had an extraordinary passion for shooting and didn't care if the air was a little cool. However, when one Saturday buckets of snow began to fall, the red-haired girl didn't even emerge from her caravan, and it looked like she had given up on her last customer. Then, at five in the afternoon, she heard a knock and it was Diego, covered in snow like Mont Blanc.

The girl went out to pull up the tarpaulin of the gallery and handed the rifle to Diego. Then she started crying.

Diego began shooting quickly because the girl was cold, reloading the rifle himself. When he had fired the usual number of shots, he placed his 500 lire note on the railing and left.

The following Saturday it didn't snow, in fact it was a fine day, but Diego didn't show up. At one in the morning, however, someone knocked on the door of the caravan. And it was Diego and he was pulling a horse behind him by the halter.

They dismantled the shooting gallery and fixed it on the side of the caravan. Then they harnessed the horse.

'Hey-up!' Diego said as he climbed onto the short platform of the caravan.

Old Marossi habitually came down each night to check out his animals. That night he came down at one o'clock and found one of his two horses missing.

He went to wake up the four children.

'They stole the mare,' he explained. 'If she's still in the village we will find her. If she's left town she'll have taken the road to the embankment because there's half a foot of snow in the fields and you can't go that way. Two of you take the cart and make your way up the embankment. Mario and Gino take the motorbike and side-car and come with me: we'll cover the road.'

They arrived at the embankment road and the two vehicles went their separate ways. Twenty kilometres later, the old man brought the motorbike to a halt.

'They can't be any further ahead of us,' he said. 'We will return. You can tell they must've gone in the opposite direction.'

They turned around and, after about ten kilometres, their headlight picked up the advancing caravan … which had left the village after them.

The old man immediately recognised his mare.

'We'll turn left, up that little road,' he directed. They stopped, jumped out and, taking up their shotguns, the three of them took up positions at the intersection.

A lantern hung under the little front shelter of the caravan and its light shone directly on Diego, who, sitting on a sack of rags, was holding the reins. The red-haired girl sat beside him. They didn't speak: fixed in position, they wore expressions like hooked cod, looking, as one, up the road ahead.

'Not a word; don't move!' the old man whispered to his two sons, one of them Diego's father.

The caravan passed by and was lost in the darkness.

'Everyone must follow his own destiny,' concluded the old man. 'Start up the engine and let's go back to bed.'

'Everyone must follow his own destiny,' he repeated when he was in the sidecar and the motorbike took the road back to the village. Diego's father who was now driving the motorbike sighed.

'Attend to your driving, you,' the old man ordered. 'Everyone must follow his own destiny. Even in a caravan pulled by my horse.'

Giacomone (1952)

Old Giacomone had a shop in the lower city. A small room with a carpenter's bench, a cast iron stove and a chest.

Inside the chest, Giacomone kept a horsehair mattress, which, in the evening, he took out and laid on the bench: and there he slept. Even eating was not a serious problem for Giacomone because, of a day, he could get by with a piece of bread and a crust of cheese: his problem was drinking. In fact, you could say that Giacomone's stomach was a thing from a bygone age, when many a man managed to find in a pint of wine all the nourishment necessary to live as healthy and adapted as a fish in the sea. Maybe because, back then, they hadn't yet invented calories, proteins, vitamins and the other rubbish that complicates life today.

As a result, Giacomone ended each day drunk. In the summer he slept on the first park bench that he came across, in the winter on his workbench. And, since this was long but narrow and high, Giacomone ran the risk of falling to the ground should he become agitated in his slumbers: and so, before closing his eyes, he would wrap himself up in a cloak, clamping the edges of it between the jaws of a vice. Thus could he turn over without any danger of hitting his pumpkin against the stone slab floor.

Giacomone only accepted conceptual work that would enhance the essential concept or *eidos* or underlying reality of something that already existed. In other words he did repairs of chairs, frames, planters and stuff like that. Heavy-duty joinery didn't interest him. And by heavy-duty he meant any work that involved the use of a plane, a chisel or a saw. He permitted himself only glue, sandpaper, hammer and screwdriver, basically because he didn't own any other tools.

However, Giacomone also dealt in the commercial sector. If someone wanted to get rid of some old furniture, he sent for it. But this generally involved cheap trifles – there was little to get excited about.

One exceptional deal did fall into his hands however, when one day the old woman who lived on the first floor of the house opposite died. She had a house full of well-kept chattels and left all of it to a nephew who, even before looking at what he had inherited, was thinking about where and when he'd be able sell it.

Giacomone took charge of the matter for him and, in a week, had managed to place the merchandise. At length, only a large crucifix of almost one and a half metres in height, embellished with a carved wooden Christ figure, remained.

'Well, what about that?' the heir asked Giacomone, pointing at the crucifix.

'I thought you'd want to keep that,' replied Giacomone.

'I wouldn't know where to put it,' explained the heir. 'And don't you give it away. It seems very ancient, it just might be that it's something of real value.'

Giacomone had seen very few crucifixes in his lifetime: but there was no doubt in his mind that there could be no more ugly a crucifix than this in the universe. He carried the cross away on his shoulder, but no one wanted it.

The following day he tried selling it again and it was the same story. Then he paid the heir a visit and told him that if he wanted to sell the crucifix, he should do so himself.

'Keep it,' replied the heir. 'I don't want to know anything more about it. If you feel like making a gift of it to someone, make a gift of it. If you can sell it, all the better for you: keep what you get for it.'

Giacomone kept the crucifix in his workshop and the first day he found himself in need of money he hooked it over his shoulder and went round the neighbourhood offering it for sale.

He wandered around until late that day and, before returning to his workshop, entered the Moro tavern. Placing the crucifix against the wall he sat down at a table and ordered a glass of red wine.

'Giacomone,' the innkeeper replied, 'you already owe me more than you can afford. Pay what you owe, then I'll bring you some wine.'

'I'll pay for everything tomorrow,' Giacomone promised. 'I'm negotiating with a lady from the old town, from Borgo delle Colonne. This here is a very old Christ – artistic stuff – and it's going to make me big money.'

The innkeeper looked at the crucifix and scratched his pumpkin, perplexed: 'I don't know anything about art,' he muttered, 'but I have an idea that there isn't a Christ more ugly than this one in the entire universe.'

'The uglier, the more beautiful a work of art is, if it's really old,' replied Giacomone. 'You look at the statues of the Baptistery and tell me if they are more beautiful than this Christ.'

The innkeeper brought the wine and then brought more, because Giacomone was so thirsty that he would have drunk a demijohn of Barbera[33].

The tavern filled with people and the poor Christ heard things that would turn an officer of the law's hair curly.

At midnight Giacomone returned to his workshop with Christ on his shoulder and, since two or three times he found himself on the verge of losing his balance and falling flat on the ground, he let rip with endless curses from the depths of his wine-soaked belly. This was repeated on successive days: for every evening Giacomone would stop at one of the many taverns where he was known.

And so it continued until, one night, a police patrol stopped Giacomone with Christ on his shoulder as he was sailing home, rolling like a ship tossed in a storm. They took him to the police station and Christ, leaning against a wall of the guardroom, had an opportunity to listen to the witty stories that usually cheer up police officers on night duty. In the morning, Giacomone was brought before the commissioner, who immediately told him not to be stupid and own up as to where he'd stolen that crucifix.

'I was given it to sell,' Giacomone explained and presented the name and address of the old lady's nephew. The police put him back in the holding room and, towards evening, took him out again.

'The crucifix is yours,' the Inspector told him, 'that's fine. But this nonsense has to stop. When you go to a tavern, leave Christ at home. The first time I catch you up to your tricks again you'll be in the slammer.'

This was a sad evening for Christ, because Giacomone took his fury out on him and gave him hell.

Later, he got drunk without Christ but, at three in the morning, he got up, put Christ on his shoulder and, having reached the outskirts of the town unobserved, by way of dark and secluded snickelways, he set off into open countryside.

---

[33] *Barbera "Umberta"*, a viticultural triumph of northern Italy, indelibly characteristic of the area.

'Now just see if this time I can't get shot of you to some wretched peasant or parish priest!' Giacomone muttered to the Christ.

It was autumn and starting to get cool in the morning: Giacomone had put on his cloak and so, with the hefty crucifix on his shoulder and a tired step, he had the manner and appearance of a pilgrim.

At dawn, he came upon an isolated house: an old woman in the garden, on seeing Giacomone with Christ on his shoulder, crossed herself.

'Pilgrim!' she said, 'would you like a bowl of hot milk?'

Giacomone stopped in his tracks.

'Are you bound for Rome?' the old woman enquired.

Giacomone nodded.

'Where do you come from?'

'Friuli,' said Giacomone.

The old woman opened her arms in dismay and told him again that he must come in and wet his lips with something.

Giacomone went in. The very sight of the milk nauseated him, but when he tasted it, it was good. He then ate half a bite of fresh bread and continued on his way.

Still avoiding the provincial roads, he took shortcuts through the fields and passed other isolated houses.

'I pass by here because the road is full of stones and dust and my feet are bleeding and my eyes are weeping,' Giacomone explained if he was held up crossing a farmyard. 'I vowed to make this journey. I am bound for Rome on a pilgrimage… I come from Friuli.'

No one denied him a bowl of wine and a piece of bread. Giacomone would put the bread in his pocket, drink the wine and resume his journey. At night he'd sleep off his drunkenness under some hut or other in someone's field.

But of late he was getting smarter. He no longer drank the wine when they gave it to him; he poured it into a large two-litre water bottle he'd acquired: 'I'll keep it for tonight, for when I'm cold or weak from walking,' he'd explain to his charitable hosts. Then he'd decant what he'd been given into his bottle.

Everything was geared to having a full water bottle of wine in the evening, when he would drain it and perfect a hangover.

*

The cold began to make itself felt, but, when Giacomone supped his wine, it was as if he had a radiator warming his belly. So off he went again with his poor Christ on his shoulder.

'I'm bound for Rome, I'm from Friuli,' he explained, time and again. And when he was drunk and wobbly, people would say: 'Poor old fella, he's so tired!'

Giacomone had a head on his shoulders. By then he had grown a beard and looked more and more the part. He'd managed to cover large areas beyond the city in his wanderings: but what man proposes, wine disposes and he ended up losing his compass and found himself, one fine day, walking a road that never seemed to cease going up, never to stop getting steeper.

At first his instinct was to turn round and go back down to the plain: but then he thought it would be better to take advantage of what remained of the good weather to cross the mountain ahead. From there he would surely find the sea and however cold it may get it is always warmer by the sea.

He walked from one daily hangover to another, always avoiding roads, seeking out isolated houses for succour, minimising the risk of running into the police.

The final hangover was awesome: he had ended up crashing a wedding feast in a house miles from anywhere and they had stuffed him up to his eyes with food and wine.

That night, at full throttle, he crashed out in a cabin and, the next morning, woke up late, around midday. Looking out of the window it seemed that he'd been transported into the middle of a desert of white sand: half a leg of snow had fallen. And it was falling still.

'If I don't move off now I'll get stuck and die of hunger or cold,' thought Giacomone. So, as ever carrying the Christ on his shoulder, off he set again.

According to his calculations, the nearest village was an hour away. But he still had a cloudy head from the great quantity of wine he'd imbibed the day before, and then of course snow obscures the horizon. By late afternoon he was lost, bound by the snow. And it kept on snowing.

He brought himself up under the shelter of a large rock. His hangover had completely disappeared. His brain had never been so clear, his thinking so pure.

He looked around and there was nothing but snow. Snow on the ground and in the sky and coming down from the sky. Giacomone looked at the Christ leaning on the rock.

'What a mess I've gotten you into, Jesus,' he said. 'And you … you are completely naked…!'

With his handkerchief Giacomone swept away the snow that had collected on *il Cristo Crocifisso*. Then he took off his cloak and covered Christ with it.

The next day saw Giacomone sleeping his eternal sleep, curled up at the feet of Christ. And people couldn't understand why he'd taken off his cloak to cover the figure of Christ on the cross.

The old priest of the village remained for some time transfixed by the whole scene. He arranged for Giacomone to be buried in the small village cemetery and had these words engraved upon his headstone:

> *Here lies a Christian.*
> *We do not know his name,*
> *but God knows it,*
> *for surely it is written*
> *in the Book of the Blessed.*

Something from 1922 (1952)

THE BOY IMMEDIATELY thought that it was one of those damned shoe tacks that lie around on the ground every two or so steps wherever peasants or soldiers pass. But as soon as he jumped from his bicycle the boy realised that someone had played a trick on him by loosening the valve of his back tyre.

Whatever, he was now in a fix for sure because ownership of a bicycle pump was not even a pipedream for this impoverished urban boy. He hurled a never-ending curse at the tyre from somewhere deep in his stomach, even though, in truth, he knew that it would be no less flat for that.

On the plus side, this boy was tough, one of a kind, happy to wend his way on foot under a summer sun so hot that it cracked stones, along a pencil straight road bordered by fields and overlaid with half a hand-span of dust.

For, in these parts, in 1922, asphalt was as yet nowhere to be seen.

The boy pressed on, pushing his bike for a good kilometre and a half without meeting a soul: no one travels along country roads on a hot July afternoon. Rather, they hole up in their houses and practise *riposo*.

In time, the boy came to a bend in the road where he was faced by a house surrounded by a garden of small trees and shrubs. It was an old house, more or less like others round about, but more pretentious due to the little bit of greenery, and above all a little gate, which separated and distinguished it from the rest.

The boy went to look through the gate: the windows and doors of the house were closed, but on a wicker chair in the shade of a magnolia tree, a girl sat reading a book.

'I am stranded and I have to get back to town,' the boy explained. 'I could use a pump.'

The girl hesitated for a moment, then got up and went into the house, returning shortly thereafter with a bicycle pump, which she handed to the boy through the palings of the gate.

The boy grabbed the pump and began to inflate the tyre. When he had done so, he raised his head for a moment and, seeing that the girl had gone back to reading her book, he neatly slipped the pump into the belt of his trousers, jumped into the saddle and set off at full speed, muttering:

'Damn you and all landowners!'

After a kilometre, at the edge of a field, he caught sight of an apple tree and abandoning his bicycle in the ditch, he launched himself into an assault upon the tree, desisting only when he realised that if he continued to stuff apples between his shirt and skinny torso much more, his shirt would part company with his trousers.

Picking up his bicycle, he set off once again and progressed another kilometre before leaving the road for a cart track. Sitting down in the shade of a hedge he began eating his apples.

Poor spoils: hard as wood and bitter as gall! Biting into the first apple, he spat out the cack and threw the rest of it behind him. Then he took a second, spat that out too, and threw it behind him. In this way he continued for some time in the hope of finding at least one apple that was edible. It was, in any case, a way of freshening up his dirt-dry mouth.

As for the discarded apples, once they'd been tasted in this way, they set off in reverse gear, winging their way over the hedge behind which the boy was sitting, and fell with a thud upon that dust bowl of a road.

'Well? What's going on here?' came a voice all of a sudden, just a few steps away.

The boy turned his head sharply.

Someone, evidently passing along the road, had gotten an apple, plonk, on his head, and taken the cart track to see what was going on behind the hedge.

The boy's victim was a friar.

He recognised the fellow. More or less everyone in the area knew him. If you saw him just once, you never forgot him, because he was a friar.

He was carrying a white sack, like a pillowcase, on his shoulders that looked weighty. He placed it on the grass beside him and sat down.

'One doesn't throw away food given by the grace of God,' he said to the boy.

'The apples aren't ripe,' the boy muttered.

'Not so,' replied the friar. 'They are not meant for eating raw; they are cookers.'

The boy made no reply. He had no time for friars, priests, nuns – he didn't like them at all.

He stood up and picked up his bicycle.

'I'm tired,' said the friar. 'I cannot carry this bag any further. Would you be so kind as to carry it into town on your bicycle? You could leave it at the tollhouse. Tell them I'll be along and pick it up later.'

He gave the boy the name he should leave with the toll collector and picking up the pillowcase, the boy placed it on the handlebars of his bicycle.

'Don't drop it, or the sack will break,' the friar cautioned. 'It's flour.'

The boy muttered that he understood and, returning to the road, continued his journey. A sack full of flour is a fair weight, but for a plumber's boy accustomed to carrying loads of the strangest iron gadgets, all sorts of cast iron and lead contrivances, on his handlebars, it was a cinch.

Magrino was indeed a boy – he was all of seventeen – but being small-boned and thin, he barely looked fifteen.

It took him some time to travel the five kilometres to the main road, so unremittingly hot was it, and when he got there, instead of making straightway for the tollhouse, he took his time and paused to eat watermelon at a pop-up canteen some fifty metres distant.

It was a Saturday afternoon: since the previous Monday, he had been working on a water well, leaving the town for the countryside early each morning and returning late in the evening. Not so that day, for, having finished work shortly after midday, he had set off meaning to go home. He'd been given a tip and even though he would still have to fund a week's spending, he had, unusually, a little money to enjoy for its own sake.

He dawdled around a few slices of watermelon for a while, striking up a conversation with one or two other customers, but always keeping an eye on the road to the tollhouse. So it was that one fine moment he caught sight of the friar walking at a camel's pace towards the tollhouse, chatting with the excise officers and, at length, continuing on his way.

Magrino paid for the watermelon and loosened the valve of his bicycle tyre, then set off towards the tollhouse. Once there he explained to the excise officers that a friar had given him a bag of flour to deliver, which he would then stop by the tollhouse to collect. Unfortunately he'd got a flat, so he'd taken longer to get there than anticipated.

The excise chief felt the bag:

'Your friar stopped by two minutes ago,' he explained. 'He left word for you to take the flour to the church. If you hurry, you'll get there ahead of him.'

Magrino set off in the footsteps of the friar, pushing his two-wheel beast-of-burden. After travelling a hundred or so metres he turned right and, pausing in a doorway, took the bicycle pump out of his trousers, re-inflated the sagging tyre, jumped on his bicycle and, in a roundabout way, arrived at the entrance to where he lived.

A woman had a little shop nearby from which she sold fried pastries – *crostoli*, that famous food made of bread dough cut into lozenges, which, when thrown into boiling oil, balloon into large blisters. Magrino explained to the old woman that in the village where he'd been working they'd given him flour as a tip instead of money and he wanted to sell it.

The old woman saw that it was good stuff: they quickly agreed a price and Magrino walked away with her money in his pocket, satisfied.

Except for the business with the apples, everything had worked out well. In addition to the money and the pump purloined from that idiot girl in the garden, there also remained the pillowcase sack which he'd been quick to explain to the old baker woman, had to be returned to the farmer. Il Magrino, waiting to sell the brand new and barely used pillowcase, stuffed it in a tin box and hid it under the stairs of his house, in a hidey-hole only he knew about.

*

In July 1922 life was not easy in this part of the world. Politics were no longer conducted with words, but by raining down cursed blows on your adversaries, or worse. [34] One month on and

---

[34] From 1922 to 1943 Italy was governed by the fascist dictator Benito Mussolini.

barricades would be erected, snipers would appear on towers and tall buildings, and truckloads of armed men pour into towns and cities from all sides.

Magrino was extremely reserved and when it came to his own affairs, like the one involving the friar's flour, he kept his own counsel. But when it came to politics he did what others told him to. That very evening he went to the tavern where leaders of the Reds regularly gathered to hand out directives.

But there was nothing on: no reprisals, no beatings. Absolute lull. Magrino stayed there playing cards and drinking a bottle.

The town, winding and tortuously narrow, opened out onto a ring road and the last of the row of houses on the right stood huddled together at the foot of very tall and squalid prison walls. The tavern was, in fact, one of the last of these houses: and, who knows why, perhaps due to nostalgia, perhaps to some sort of unconscious 'complex', every evening at the tables of that tavern there was someone who had recently been released from prison. As a result, every now and then, prisoners' songs were heard, sung in a way that only those who have been inside can sing.

On that very evening there were two or three who, a few days earlier, had been incarcerated behind those walls, which sentries patrolled.

They talked about the people they'd met there, the life they'd lived there, but, above all, they talked about 'him' – the friar who walked like a camel, the friar who had given the bag of flour to Magrino that afternoon.

He was a truly extraordinary man. He was the prisoners' friar and the prisoners unloaded all their suffering on his shoulders. He was no local – he came from afar – but he had two good shoulders.

Everything seemed to jump out of the sleeves of his cassock, as if he were God's magician.

He might be seen wandering the streets of the town with a faggot on his shoulders, carrying it to warm some prisoner's family. Or with a baby in his arms, loping up and down looking for some woman to breastfeed the poor thing, because of course the natural mother – whether free or in prison – had no milk.

One day, in the main street of the town, the friar had started dancing to the music of a street musician and then collected money for the unfortunate fellow and the two bundles of rags with him – his wife and son. Tales of this friar are the sort of thing you might find written of in books, or, if not yet, surely at some point.

In short, the friar was a legend, and they were talking about him in the tavern that evening. Magrino listened for a while and then left to go home.

He found the village a hubbub of people: women had brought their chairs into the street and in front of every door there was a conference of some sort going on. The girls and young men laughed and shouted to each other in the doorways, or at the street corners. But more often than not they stood on benches along the avenue and laughed and shouted quite a bit.

Magrino was 'difficult' when it came to girls. He had never seriously thought about them. That evening, however, he took care of it while he was returning home. He thought of the pump girl. He remembered that she had looked at him very carefully and, all things considered, he concluded that the girl was much more important than the bicycle pump.

She wasn't at all like the others in the village. As for her beauty, the others easily beat her: but as for all the rest of her, she won. Yes, even if Magro, as he was known because he was so skinny, even if he didn't have the slightest idea of what 'the rest of her' was (since he hadn't heard the girl's voice either).

'And I,' he concluded exasperated, 'I'm going to steal her bicycle pump!'

Then he considered the fact that, at a rough estimate, had he not stolen her pump he wouldn't have gotten a damn thing out of it.

Now, a plumber's boy really isn't made for the type of idiot who reads books in the garden and doesn't even deign to open her mouth when someone speaks to them. But, all things considered, il Magrino was a handsome boy and brushed up well for a party...

'I'll show that one!' he vowed.

*

The next morning he got dressed up, polished himself up, rolled up his trousers to his knees, then, covering the bicycle seat with a handkerchief so as not to shine his suit on the saddle, he set off on his journey. He studied the itinerary and the stops in order to find himself in sight of the clump of trees at the same time as the day before. He then unrolled his trousers, dusted himself off with his handkerchief and, getting back on his bicycle, aimed straight at the target.

He could feel it: all the windows in the house were closed and the girl was reading a book, sitting in her usual place.

Magrino stopped in front of the gate.

'Hey!' he said.

The girl raised her eyes from the book and looked at him.

Magrino showed her the pump. The girl got up and approached. She looked very concerned, but, when she reached the gate, her face brightened.

'Ah!' she exclaimed, 'the pump boy.'

Magrino reached through the bars and the girl accepted the pump.

'Have you finished with it?' she asked. 'If you still need it, take your time…'

'I've finished,' explained Magrino seriously.

'Okay then,' the girl said, standing there with the pump in her hand.

There were a few moments of silence, then Magrino came at her full on.

'Do you work in town?'

'Yes,' the girl replied.

'I thought as much,' he exclaimed. 'So, we could go dancing.'

'I don't think so,' the girl replied calmly. 'I work in the town, but I've never gone dancing.'

'Where do you work?'

'I study,' the girl replied, blushing.

'Studying is not a job, it's a luxury!' Magrino stated sternly.

The girl simply spread her arms. She too must have been around seventeen and was already well developed as a woman, but clearly confused.

Magrino sensed it: he stared at her in a certain way and paid her a deliberately crude compliment.

The girl blushed.

'*Stupido*!' she exclaimed.

Magrino chuckled:

'We'll see if you'll have the nerve to agree to meet me in the town where there won't be this gate between us!'

The girl turned pale.

'Sorry,' she stammered, terrified. 'I just said it... I'm not used to... Here, keep the pump but don't give me any trouble...'

Magrino looked with contempt at the pump the girl held out to him.

'You and I will see each other again ... in town,' he said, getting back on his bike and leaving.

*

It was even hotter than the day before: Magrino, having reached the turning point, took off his jacket, rolled up his trousers and put his handkerchief back on the saddle. He resumed his journey but did not continue pedalling for long: at the first track he left the road and continued through the fields until he found some shade and coolness. Then he took off his trousers, which he folded with extreme care and lay down on the grass.

He began to think about the girl but, soon, he fell fast asleep.

He woke up when the sun was starting to set: he got dressed and slowly retraced his steps up the track. When he was about to turn onto the road he felt oddly out of breath. At that moment, the famous friar was passing along the road; walking with his famous camel step, and carrying a sack on his shoulder.

Their meeting was an extraordinary surprise for both of them, and they stood for a moment looking at each other without speaking.

'Well, what d'you know!' the friar finally exclaimed cheerfully. 'I didn't recognise you. You are yesterday's boy. Why, you look like a m'lord today!'

Magrino wanted to jump on his bicycle and get the hell out. But something kept him rooted to the spot. And perhaps it was the friar's smile.

'It is Divine Providence that sends you!' exclaimed the friar. 'Yesterday, when you were dressed for work, I had a sack of white flour. Now that you're all dressed up and you could get dirty carrying white flour, I have a bag full of wheat. I cannot bear the weight of it anymore. You should carry this for me too, like yesterday.'

Magrino wanted to jump on his bicycle more than ever, but by now the friar had dumped the sack on the handlebars of his bicycle.

They set off together on foot.

'I tell you no lie,' the friar exclaimed after a while. 'Yesterday, after giving you the sack of flour, I thought: "That guy will run off with my sack and get away with it." Then I thought: "Even if someone has a prison face like you do, he can't be such a thief as to rob a friar who goes around finding stuff to help the families of people in prison." You really do have a very brutal face, my boy.'

Il Magrino replied: 'Yours is beautiful!'

'It's worse than yours,' the friar announced calmly, 'but it's not like a prison face. You, on the other hand, do have a prison face. This doesn't mean that you are dishonest: the trouble is that you have a prison face and you will end up in prison even if you are honest. Unfortunately, people set a lot of store by a face. And it seems there is a typical prison face, gentleman's face, bad guy's face, good-natured one and so on. It's a problem because even the most knowledgeable are deceived by the game. "He has a face like a prisoner and he's stealing my sack," I thought yesterday. Then, when I arrived home and found the sack that you had already brought to the church, I asked God for forgiveness for having been so superficial and unjust as to judge a man by his face.'

They walked for a long time, then the friar said:

'It's getting late: jump on your bike and move on. They'll let you pass at the tollhouse.'

Magrino jumped on his bicycle and pedalled like a damned man.

At the customs office he tried to stammer something or other and the boss intervened to say:

'It's the same as yesterday. Let him pass.'

Then he arrived at the church and knocked on the convent door: a young friar came to open it:

'Ah, it's you! Just put the bag there in the corner where you put the one from yesterday. God be with you, brother.'

Magrino marched home with nothing and everything on his mind. Having reached the corner and looked into the little shop where the baker was frying the *crostoli*, he asked the old woman:

'Was the flour okay? Have you tried it?'

The old woman looked at him puzzled:

'Flour? What flour?'

'The sack of it I brought you last night.'

The old woman shook her head:

'Magrino, have you lost it?'

The boy insisted that he was perfectly sane and gave her some details, how much money she had given him and so on.

'I don't remember anything of what you say,' insisted the old woman. Then Magrino ran up to his house and went under the stairs to rummage inside the famous hole.

And found the tin box, but the pillowcase sack was no longer there.

*

This story was told to me many years later by Magrino himself. who had stopped being Magrino some time earlier. I mean he was by then emancipated, an ex-criminal.

I finally asked: 'So, do you believe in miracles?'

'No,' replied Magrino. 'No miracle. In all cases, all coincidences: someone who looked like me brought a sack of flour to the church, the old baker woman no longer remembered or she was wary of causing trouble; someone stole my pillowcase. See, no mystery. Let's not start spreading the word about miracles. Otherwise people will start screaming that we need to make that friar a saint. And, once made a saint, he stops being a man and becomes ... a symbol. And if he becomes a symbol, everyone who remembers him, as I remember him, will feel he's further from their hearts than he once was. Chance, pure chance. Coincidence. Or, perhaps, the whole affair was organised by him for whatever might have been his purpose. I never had the courage to ask...'

'So you saw him again after that Sunday?' I said.

'I saw him again, yes. First on the barricades, then when he visited me in prison. He wasn't wrong when he considered me a prison guy. But, as you can see, all ended well. Everything; and it's only thanks to him.'

'And have you seen the pump girl again in town?'

'Even too much,' he sighed, laughing, that one who was *il Magrino.*

Thicker Than Water (1952)

A T GHIAIE EVERYTHING generally worked fine so long as there was plenty of water. As soon as there was none, everything quickly took a turn for the worse and for Bacchi the problem became intolerable whenever he couldn't buy any in.

Old Bacchi owned a lot of land and had money. He had been the first in the region to think of digging a well and constructing an irrigation system: but, although he'd sunk money and many an iron pipe in the ground, there was no water available. For the well that kept man and beast alive in the height of summer ran dry. And when there was no water in Ghiaie, even the cats were aware of it.

Bacchi, however, was not one to throw in the towel. The irrigation system had become his obsession. As a result, there was a constant coming and going of technicians and water diviners across his land. As soon as he heard tell of some diviner or other, he would send for him immediately, and for some time now it had been said that inch-by-inch every bit of Ghiaie had been tested for an underground water source.

Bacchi spared no expense: he was willing to do anything:

'If they tell me that there is water under the floor of my kitchen or stable, I would not flinch to tear down my house and rebuild it somewhere else!' he pronounced.

But, no danger of that. For at the Ghiaie, there was no water. The most famous diviners – all of whom, without fail, began by saying: 'Water is down here, albeit at many metres below the surface,' concluded, as one, after divining up and down the Ghiaie, that apart from where a thin superficial vein fed the one well, they hadn't felt even the mildest jerk from their rods.

No one had heard anything like it before.

Now one year the drought was truly terrible. Fires combusted the fields and Bacchi, clearly out of God's grace, was beside himself.

So, when someone showed him a newspaper article in which there was talk of an old professor near Rome, who was a master diviner and could find water where no one had ever managed to find it before, he didn't think twice before setting off to find him. What he came upon was a true gentleman in his fifties, very serious, very busy with his studies and his business.

Nevertheless, the determined Bacchi received a polite, but firm, 'No ... too far away, no time to waste.'

The farmer offered the professor good money, but it wasn't a question of money: the master diviner didn't need money and had never accepted any for his divining work.

'When I look for water,' the man explained, 'I do not "do a job". God has provided me with a sixth sense, not so that I can speculate with it, but so that I can use it for the benefit of men who do not possess it. Accepting money would be like I'd happened upon a country of blind people and taken advantage of the fact that I have good eyes in order to make money out of their misfortune in not being able to use their eyes.'

Then Bacchi told the professor his story, concluding with tears in his eyes:

'I am an old man now, you must please help me find an aquifer at Ghiaie before I die. It is not a question of money for me either: I created the Ghiaie! And, seeing the community like this, it's as if I have persevered all these years in raising a child only to find, at last, that he has lost the ability to walk.'

The professor sighed and said to himself: 'How can I deny consolation to an old man who has worked on this all his life?'

And finally he agreed:

'I will come.'

*

The professor arrived the following week and Bacchi, when he saw him, almost hugged him. The master diviner approached a nearby willow tree and cut a branch from it – all that he needed by way of a tool – and immediately set to work.

Bacchi could see at once that his was a more 'organic' method than that of the other water diviners: instinct as much as science informed his relationship with the terrain. It was also clear that he was a very educated man, refined, a true gentleman who, rather than putting on airs, inspired a certain awe.

The professor began by asking the people of Ghiaie, who had gathered to see what he would do, to show him the precise boundaries of the farm; then he questioned Peppone thoroughly.

Peppone had turned up because he'd been responsible for the earlier sampling of the well at Ghiaie and because he was the only person in the area with the machinery and expertise necessary to install an irrigation well.

Reporting the results of all his experiments at Ghiaie on the farms of the area, he concluded to the professor:

'I am as certain as my neck is as strong as a bull's, that *there is no water at Ghiaie*!'

The professor looked at Peppone's bull neck and shook his head:

'If you have the neck to bet that neck of yours against our ever finding an aquifer here you must surely be onto something. However, you never can be too sure in life.'

In truth, the facts did seem to prove Peppone right, because after hours and hours of divining, the professor gave up:

'For what my judgment is worth, I must conclude that there are no water veins of any significance.'

However, the sadness on Bacchi's face put such melancholy in the professor's heart that, on looking at him, he felt bound to give him a vestige of reassurance.

'Now I am tired and I cannot continue any longer. But we will resume our search tomorrow morning.'

*

The following morning Peppone was the first to arrive: his neck was at stake after all (if only symbolically). And if this made him somewhat passionately involved, then, too, the professor, that man of few words, had something special in his eyes that held this bull-necked mechanic in thrall.

His exploration of the terrain was resumed methodically, almost obsessively so. But when noon was about to strike in the bell tower, he had nothing more to show for his efforts than on the day before.

The sun was beating down like hell and, before returning to the farm, the professor felt a pressing need to rest for a while in the shade. The team had reached a dry canal (more of a stony ground than a canal), which marked the borderline of the western limit of the Ghiaie. Here, on the canal bank, an elm tree cast its centuries-old shadow over the ground and Bacchi and Peppone made for it, just ahead of the professor.

But the master diviner never did reach them, for at the very edge of that patch of shade, he came to a sudden halt, as if his feet had been nailed to the ground. To all appearances he was in the throes of an acute pain: with jaw clenched and muscles tense, the professor stared at the willow branch, held tightly in his hands as it came alive, jiggering uncontrollably down towards the dry earth.

He collected himself and walked away, before turning and retracing his steps, again stopping suddenly at the crucial point, his feet glued to the ground.

The master diviner repeated the test five or six times from different places and always, once he reached that crucial point, his brakes stuck fast and brought him to an abrupt halt.

He then marked the spot with a stone and made ever-increasing concentric circles around it: but the stick showed no sign of life at all, only moving again when the professor returned to the spot marked with the stone.

'There *is* water here,' he declared. 'It is right there and not very deep.'

Peppone shook his head:

'It's not possible: thirty diviners must have passed through here and they never detected anything at all!' he exclaimed.

'They came right here *at this point?*' enquired the professor, pointing to the stone for confirmation.

'I can't say exactly at that precise point,' replied Peppone, 'but they certainly passed close by. And if there had been a water vein, they would definitely have detected it. They were smart: I've seen them find water even in the most difficult places.'

The professor eyed the stone:

'My point is that there is no water vein around here: I scanned the whole area. But there, at that point only, there is water!'

Peppone spread his arms:

'In that case what we have is a miracle, because water doesn't come from the earth unless it flows through a water vein.'

'Here, at this point, there is water,' declared the professor. 'It may be that I don't detect a vein because it runs so deep. It may be that it is a rising vein of water, which here, at this point, has found porous soil and filtered upwards. Imagine, if you will, that an aqueduct pipe passes three or four hundred metres underground and here, at this point, they have inserted a tube that brings the water up, up to a few metres from the surface. But be that as it may, I can say categorically that down here, a few metres away, there *is* water.'

Bacchi, who until that moment had limited himself to gawking – now at the professor, now at Peppone – jumped up and began to shout:

'Water! Water! Any moment! Soon!'

Peppone calmed him down:

'If it is there, no one will take it away from you, so let's do things very calmly. There is no point in shouting that the water is there before we've even seen it. Today, around four o'clock, I will come with the hammer and we will begin drilling. We may continue all night. For the moment, keep quiet: if you start shouting that there's water and then you can't find it, you'll become an object of ridicule.'

Bacchi went away reluctantly, but before taking his leave he said they should put a taproot in place of the stone – a 'safer' way to mark the spot, but the professor would have none of it. In fact, he even threw the stone away.

'Later today, when I return, I will find the point again. If I don't find it again, it means I have made a mistake now.'

*

At four o'clock there were still several people hanging around the elm tree. Bacchi with his children, Peppone with his three assistants, a few farm workers, the tenants of nearby farms. When the professor appeared they retreated to the edge of the canal so as not to be in the way. The professor approached the elm tree, walking quickly, and suddenly there he was ... nailed to the earth again.

'It is right here,' he said. 'You may begin.'

The ground was rocky: large stones emerged beneath the surface and, before using a hydraulic hammer, this layer of stone had to be removed by hand. The men set to work and continued to quarry stone to a good metre and a half depth. Then they hit gravelly ground. But here the work was immediately interrupted.

'Let no one move! No one touches anything until the Marshal arrives,' Peppone thundered. And everyone retreated from the hole.

The Marshal arrived with two *carabinieri* and a doctor. A second later Don Camillo also arrived, along with the rest of the village.

The Marshal and the doctor went down into the hole.

'A small pile of bones with a few grey-green rags,' muttered the Marshal to Peppone and Don Camillo on his ascent.

'Hole in the back of the head,' added the doctor as he too reappeared. 'Stuff from 1945, probably.'

'Politics!' commented Don Camillo.

'War!' Peppone responded through gritted teeth.

There were a few moments of silence. Then Bacchi shook his head and said:

'Who knows who he is, poor guy!'

'We only found this on him,' replied the Marshal, presenting an ID tag on a thin gold chain. He rubbed the tag between his index finger and thumb to clear the dirt from it.

'It seems to have something engraved on it,' said the Marshal: "8 February 1929."

'Sixteen years ago!' exclaimed Don Camillo. 'Marshal, I think there's also a name on it.'

The Marshal took a small magnifying glass from his pocket and considered the tag:

'Cesare Deppi,' he read out. 'Who knows where he is from!'

'Borgodeste.'

It was the professor's voice. Everyone planted their eyes upon him.

'Sorry, how do you know that?' stammered the Marshal.

The professor spread his arms and shook his head sadly.

'I haven't forgotten my own son's name and place of birth,' he replied. 'He is all the more in memory since he was an only child. I was in the war and at the beginning of '45 the boy ran away from home to join the army. We never heard from him again. They sent him to the North and he never returned... His mother is still waiting for him.'

'I will need to interview her as part of my investigation,' said the Marshal to the professor.

'Investigation!' sighed the professor. 'He died. That's all. Now he will be able to rest in consecrated ground and his mother will know where to kneel to lament him.'

*

The professor remained in the village for a couple of days and, before leaving, he expressed a wish to visit the scene of disinterment once again.

Peppone and Bacchi accompanied him and looked on in silence.

'All the diviners passed through here without ever detecting anything,' the professor said all of a sudden. 'But I felt something because the land here was bathed in my son's blood.'

He shook his head sadly, then added:

'Blood is thicker than water.'

The idiom recalled him to Bacchi and the professor turned towards the old man.

'No matter, no matter,' Bacchi stammered.

'But it does matter,' replied the professor. And picking up his willow branch, he went down into the hole.

'I no longer feel what I felt before,' he explained. 'It wasn't the water, it was him that jiggered me...'

Peppone resisted a bullish Pavlovian response to blurt out: 'Was I right or was I right!'

And the professor continued:

'It was him that I felt so violently. But the water is there. Not a few metres away, as I was saying. The water is around 200 metres away... Whoever has faith will find it.'

*

Bacchi had faith: everyone told him he was a wild madman when he started sticking pipes into the ground near the elm tree.

He had faith and then understood that it was even more important to find the water source: not just for an irrigation system, but for something that he could not quite explain but which was very significant.

The water was found at 190 metres distant and, when Bacchi saw that tumultuous torrent coming out of the 20-cm diameter pipe, he developed a fever and took to his bed. The workers worked day and night and the well, with all its electronic controls, was ready ten days later in a small exposed brick house, which looked like a little fort. And the large pipe that came out of the wall at the foot of the concrete channel that would carry the water to the large ditch of the irrigation system looked like a cannon.

Bacchi wanted everyone to be present at the inauguration of the irrigation well and, above all, the professor.

The professor was accompanied by his wife, and it was the professor's wife who activated the system. The water came out violently – a torrent of clear, fresh water and, as soon as he saw it, the true significance of the find came to Bacchi as he made the inaugural speech:

'Behold the water that purifies everything, that washes the earth from the bloodstain of war and, together with the bloodstains of the earth, washes hatred clean from our souls... Amen!'

Don Camillo came forward and blessed the water. 'It is your water,' Don Camillo murmured. 'Holy water.'

Then the professor's wife wet the tips of the fingers of her right hand in the water flowing from the pipe and crossed herself. The professor also touched the water and crossed himself.

The people – the whole town had come out – stood there watching, holding their breath, and all you could hear was the roar of the water, but it sounded like music.

*

One afternoon in August, Don Camillo, arriving at the well, came upon a man sitting stock still on the bank of the concrete irrigation channel, gazing at the water.

He recognised him as one of Peppone's gang, a young man of twenty-five or so. He was transfixed by the water, and when Don Camillo appeared in front of him on the other side of the concrete conduit, he raised his gaze for a moment and immediately lowered it again.

But that moment was enough for Don Camillo to understand that his eyes were not the eyes of a normal person.

Don Camillo sat down on the edge of the conduit and waited.

You won't know the August afternoons of Bassa. There, in the middle of the deserted fields, in full sun, everything smells of a fairytale, and if the Devil should appear scarlet and grinning in the middle of a plain of burnt stubble the apparition would seem like the most natural thing in the world.

Don Camillo was waiting and, suddenly, the young man said, as if speaking to himself:

'Blood! This is not water, it's blood.'

'Water,' Don Camillo said in a low voice.

'Blood!' the young man repeated, still with his eyes lowered. 'I know it well because it is *his* blood...'

'Water,' Don Camillo whispered softly.

'Blood!' gasped the young man, looking in horror at the canal swollen with water. '*His* blood. I know this well because I touched him when that blood was still warm... I only followed an order... We thought he was a spy... I'm in the clear because I followed an order... I heard what his father said... I saw his mother... Blood. This isn't water, it is blood.'

'Water,' Don Camillo insisted gently. 'Touch it and see.'

The young man pulled back in horror. But Don Camillo insisted. And the young man, slowly, hesitantly, brought his hand to the water.

'Immerse your whole hand in it,' whispered Don Camillo. 'Bacchi was right: the water purifies, washes away bloodstains, erases hate.'

The young man dipped his hand into the freezing water. And all his nerves were jangling. Suddenly his eyes filled and two tears slipped down his cheeks and fell into the water.

The young man withdrew his hand and watched it drip.

Then, suddenly, he woke up as if he had emerged from a dream and looked at Don Camillo in amazement.

'Don't be worried,' Don Camillo reassured him. 'Only God knows what happened... If anything did happen.'

The young man got up and left. After taking a few steps he turned to look at the well pipe.

'Water,' Don Camillo told him. 'Not blood. Holy water.'

The young man continued on his journey, passed across the hot stone of the canal, and disappeared among the acacias. Don Camillo filled his usual water bottle with fresh water to wet the flowerbed under which the murdered boy now rested in peace. And, while he filled the bottle, something made him wonder where those two tears that fell into the water had ended up:

'Who knows where those two tears, now at one with the water, went!' he murmured.

God knew very well.

The Treasure (1957)

THERE WERE SO many foreign tourists to Italy in those days that a few big cars full of garishly dressed males and females even found their way into the heart of la Bassa.

In most cases they made only fleeting appearances: after a five minute stop in the village square they'd often be back on the road along the embankment in the blink of an eye. If you saw them you saw them and that was it.

People regarded them with complete indifference and were not impressed by the arrogant size or flashiness of their vehicles: the most you might hear was someone muttering:

'Better a beautiful local girl on a bicycle than an ugly furriner in a Chrysler.'

But then, famously, the two Germans arrived and no-one could deny them a certain curiosity. The first thing that grabbed those of the village who were in the piazza that afternoon was their car. With a crust of rust instead of chrome, tyres cracked and worn through to the canvas and with mudguards that looked like four wilted lettuce leaves, Peppone's battered and decrepit three-speed Balilla, looked like a top-end, custom-built, luxury car by comparison: they must surely have craned it out from a pile of scrap and delivered it 'as is' to the buyer.

In short, theirs was one of those cars which, left on the side of a public road, would have led any refuse worker to load it directly onto the rubbish cart without a second thought.

The other thing that struck us, as they emerged from this wreck, were the two Germans themselves. One of them in particular awakened the interest of those present because she was a young, beautiful woman dressed with unusual decency for a foreign tourist.

Her travelling companion was a boy of about fourteen or fifteen, blond and lean, with a face that seemed to be made in the same mould as the woman's, so much so that everyone immediately deduced: 'brother and sister'.

However, up close the woman looked more mature than at first she had seemed and the deference with which the boy treated her, plus a few words gleaned from one mumbling German, made it possible to clarify the actual degree of kinship between the two of them as mother and son.

The incomers sat at a coffee table in the arcade on the edge of the square and, after chatting with his mother, the boy asked for two glasses of beer. Then, when the barista returned with two bottles and glasses, the boy timidly asked, in rough Italian: 'Please, *signore*, may I take a few photographs? Would it be possible to climb the bell tower?'

'It depends on which side of the bed the priest got out of,' muttered Peppone, who was sitting at the next table and had heard the question.

The boy looked at him:

'Please *signore*,' he stammered, blushing. 'I don't understand too well...'

'The priest is in charge of the bell tower,' explained Peppone. 'And the priest is a nutcase.'

Evidently the adjective did not figure in the boy's vocabulary and Peppone realised this and clarified the conceptual picture he had been endeavouring to draw:

'*Priest nixt gut!*' he exclaimed with a grimace of disgust, and promptly left.

The boy stared into the barista's face with two eyes as big as headlights:

'Why did the gentleman say, "The priest is no good?"' he asked, gesturing to Peppone, who was on his way out.

The barista opened his arms wide:

'I don't know, but that gentleman is the Mayor and here the Mayor is always right.'

The boy seemed taken aback when he learned that he had spoken to the Mayor. He checked his pocket dictionary, then told his mother that he had listened to him with great interest and, in the end, declared the matter settled by tapping a coin on the bar tray.

Having paid for the beer, the two left and the spectacle of their departure of their rust-bucket was studied with extreme interest by all those present. Smilzo sneered and the German woman turned and gave him a terrible look. The old crock struggled up the embankment and disappeared. But the two Germans did not go to hell as Smilzo had wished out loud that they would.

In fact, towards evening the German boy reappeared in the village alone and on foot. He bought bread, fruit, cheese and a bottle of beer and disappeared without saying a word more than was strictly necessary. That evening at the café, someone spread the word that the two had set up camp beyond the embankment, half a kilometre from the village, under the colossal pylon from which the high voltage line made a great leap over the river and then hooked up to another identical pylon on the other side.

The Germans had erected a miserable, faded canvas tent there and seemed as calm as if they were in their own world at home.

'With tourists like this, the countryside will soon be awash with money!' commented Peppone.

And the matter ended there.

The following morning, Peppone had to cycle along the road to the embankment but he would never have entertained a thought of the two German tourists had he not discovered something too out of the ordinary to ignore. Some reckless person had climbed up the power line pylon and positioned himself a few metres from the top astride an iron bar, from which he was enjoying unrivalled views of the landscape and quantities of fresh air.

Peppone changed tack and, having reached the foot of the slope, found himself in front of the old crock and the tent belonging to the two Germans.

The woman, who was sitting on the ground preparing coffee on an oil stove, jumped when she saw Peppone appear, then immediately regained her composure and listened calmly to the verbal deluge that poured out of Peppone's mouth and down upon her.

When, short of breath, Peppone finally came to an end with it, the woman signalled that she hadn't understood a word and, raising her head, shouted something to the person up the pylon.

There had been no need, because the person in question was on his way down and was already some twenty metres from the ground. The boy, once he had arrived on the scene, explained the reason for his behaviour logically, naturally and with serenity:

'*Prego signore*: I wanted to take photographs from the bell tower. You said, "*Priest nicht gut!*" So I shinned up there.'

By now Peppone had said everything that could be said about wretches who climb high voltage pylons, and cut the boy short:

'*Verboten!*' he shouted.

The boy stammered that he hadn't done anything wrong, but Peppone was well on his way and furthermore didn't like the very fact of two foreigners setting up camp right there, under the pylon of a high voltage line.

'*Verboten!*' he repeated harshly. 'Forbidden to stay here!'

'It doesn't say, "Camping Prohibited",' the boy objected timidly.

'Listen to me!' Peppone shouted. 'Go and pitch your tent wherever you want, but not around here.'

The woman looked at him with hatred in her eyes, but Peppone was unmoved. 'If you came here for *verboten* purposes,' he thought to himself, 'morally you deserve no respect. But if you travel for the innocent purpose of tourism you deserve even less respect because a mother who lets her child climb up a high voltage pylon can only be a scoundrel!'

Returning after a couple of hours, Peppone saw that the two Germans had left: but still they hadn't followed Smilzo's advice. Late in the afternoon, the boy reappeared in town with a shopping bag, which meant that their new base was not that far away.

'I can't understand it,' Peppone thought on seeing the boy, 'with so many wonderful places in Italy, why have these two Krauts rained down upon us right here where, during the day, you're dying from the heat, and, at night, you can't sleep because of the mosquitoes.'

Then, that evening, even as Smilzo reported to him the most important events of the day, Peppone learned that the two foreigners had settled right next to the Church of the Ponte Vecchio, and he couldn't get the thought of it out of his brain.

*

Once upon a time, the road that led from the village to Altro Co' was little more than a cart track. A series of ancient farm lanes stitched together by trunks of municipal lanes and the old bridge across the Stivone, from bank to bank, and over it passed the Altro Co' road.

At the mouth of the bridge, beyond the Stivone, in a recess between the embankment and where the road ran down to the plain, stood a small decrepit church which originally served the inhabitants of Altro Co', but which, after a new road was built over half a kilometre from the old cart track, had been abandoned, along with the bridge, and Mass was now celebrated in the church only once a year, on November 11th, St Martin's Day.

Acacia bushes and nettles had invaded the little churchyard and vegetable garden attached to the solitary, ruined church, and it was right here that the two Germans had pitched their tent.

It was singly the worst place to set up camp and Peppone couldn't believe that a woman and her son had come from Germany to holiday in such a scrubland as this.

Even beneath the sheets Peppone continued to ruminate on that thought and, in the end, he believed he had found a comprehensive answer to his questioning:

'Germans are different from us.'

But then another consideration arose:

'Just because they are different from us it doesn't mean they are more stupid.'

If the two incomers were behaving like this they must be up to something.

Ten minutes later Peppone was dressed and heading towards the door. The night was already pitch black. Mounting his bicycle, he left the village and pedalled up to the old bridge. He then hid his bicycle in a bush, crossed the bridge on foot and set off along a path at the foot of the embankment, which would take him behind the small church of San Martino.

The path, which ran between tall shrubs, was little travelled and had a soft covering of grass and, fortuitously, a random wisp of wind tussled the leaves of some attendant poplar trees, sufficient to cover the advance of an entire division.

Having come to within a few steps of the church, Peppone stopped and surveyed what he could of the scene before him: both the old crock and the tent were there, side on to the church, and it seemed to him that the boy and his mother were sleeping soundly. But a few minutes later it fell clear that the two were, in fact, all too awake.

First came their whispering, then a small area of the church wall was illuminated and the light, though dim, was enough for Peppone to make out the faces of mother and son from the dense shadow.

The two were kneeling on the ground and, under cover of the car, the tent and the bushes and the light of a torch, were investigating a particular area of the church wall. They soon found the patch they were looking for and, after a short exchange, the boy started working the wall with a chisel. Ten minutes later he had the first stone out of the wall and set about the second. By then he had the measure of his task and cut the torch, continuing to work on in the dark.

Another handy gust of wind covering the sound of his retreat, Peppone found himself back at the bridge, where he recovered his bike and embarked upon the next step in the implementation of his plan.

*

By banging a make-do knocking-up pole against the shutters of a certain window in the presbytery, Peppone managed to waken Don Camillo and get him out of bed and to the window.

'Reverend,' he hissed, 'come down immediately, I need you.'

'Unless you're on the point of death and willing to renounce the entirety of your sinful life, I will not move – not even an inch.' Don Camillo hissed back.

Then, properly awake, he went downstairs and opened the front door to Peppone, who, very excited, told him the story of the Germans.

Don Camillo was unperturbed.

'I don't understand what they can hope to find in that hovel,' he muttered. 'There isn't anything to the value of two lire.'

'So you say!' replied Peppone. 'Why then did the boy want to climb the bell tower? Why, not being able to climb the bell tower, did he climb the high voltage pylon? He was looking for the church of San Martino and to avoid arousing suspicion didn't want to ask around. Then, as soon as he found it he pitched the tent there and now he's making a hole to gain entry. Twelve years ago a retreating German unit camped around that church of San Martino and was taken prisoner there by the Americans. It's not the first time a case like this has come up: someone has hidden money or some sort of stuff and now they've sent that woman and the boy to recover the loot.'

Don Camillo woke up completely:

'So what have you got in mind?' he asked suspiciously.

'Well, the situation is clear: the church is your business, but I'm the one who discovered the two Krauts. You need money for the nursery school, I need it for the seaside colony for my classmates' children; either we act in agreement and go halves or I go and call the Marshal and I lose everything and you lose too... The end justifies the means.'

'I don't make deals with the Devil,' Don Camillo replied. 'I'm going to advise the Marshal.'

'I'm coming with you then,' said Peppone. 'Just so that you don't, by chance, take a wrong turn and end up at the church of San Martino instead of at the police station...'

*

Once again the wind in the poplar trees collaborated as custodian of the operation and Don Camillo and Peppone arrived at the church just in time to see the last stone being pulled out of the breach in the wall.

The boy had clear ideas: he slipped into the gap and a few moments later the back door opened wide swallowing up the woman.

'Let them get on with it,' whispered Don Camillo. 'We'll intervene at the optimum moment.'

They hurried to spy at what was going on through a window and followed the action as if it were a piece of theatre.

After a quick session orientating herself, the woman pointed the flashlight at the altar and spoke excitedly with her son.

In front of the altar stood a sodden wooden dais and she needed to join forces with her son to move it. Once the obstacle was out of the way, the woman knelt on the ground and, taking a piece of paper from her breast, she studied it by the light of the torch. She then pointed to one of the large square stone flags on the floor and the boy attacked it determinedly with his chisel.

Having removed the flag and shattered the thin layer of mortar beneath it with the chisel, he began rummaging in the hole with his hands, digging out stones and dirt. 'The cadaver' lay about twenty centimetres below floor level and it didn't take long to pull it up because it was merely a steel tube about fifteen centimetres in diameter and just over half a metre long. The boy, after his mother had entered the church, had propped the back door from inside, but, with his shoulder, Peppone smashed his way in.

It happened in a flash: mother and son found themselves in front of the Mayor, as if he had emerged from the earth. The woman dropped their torch, but Peppone flicked on the one he had brought with him. Meantime, Don Camillo was busy lighting the altar candles and all the candles that he could find.

The boy, pale as death, held that large steel tube in his hands and stared wide-eyed at Peppone.

'Give me that thing!' Peppone ordered him, stretching out his hand towards the tube.

But the woman was quicker and more decisive than he: she snatched the tube from her son's hands and held it to her chest. Then she spoke quickly to the boy and the boy translated what she said:

'It is not yours. My father, an army officer, was taken prisoner here and his belongings were left here. We have come to take them back.'

Peppone turned towards Don Camillo:

'Reverend, these people take us for fools,' he chuckled.

The woman spoke excitedly with her son again, and again the boy translated:

'My father died three years after the war... Came back sick, very sick... My mother promised him to come take this and put it on his grave, inside a marble urn.'

Peppone pushed the boy aside and stretched out his hand to grab the tube, but the woman jumped away screaming.

'Don't touch! ...Don't you dare touch!' said the boy, standing between his mother and Peppone.

Don Camillo intervened:

'We don't want to touch,' he explained calmly. 'We just want to see what it is. That is our right and, indeed, it is our duty.'

The boy translated and the woman, after a moment's hesitation, unscrewed the lid of the tube and, taking out the contents, showed it to Don Camillo and Peppone.

The tube fell to the ground, rolling into a corner and it was as if a bell had rung.

'My father was a standard bearer,' explained the boy. 'My father is now very happy because the regimental flag has been reclaimed...'

'*Gut*,' replied Peppone.

It wasn't a long speech, but you have to take into consideration that it was improvised and that Peppone was pouring sweat.

As for Don Camillo, he simply said, 'Good night,' and if the two of them couldn't say four words, it was merely because they stopped at the third.

*

The old crock reappeared in the village around nine the following morning and came to a halt directly in front of Peppone's workshop.

The boy seemed especially surprised to find himself in the presence of the Mayor wearing a mechanic's overalls, and hesitated and then made up his mind to explain that something was wrong with his car's ignition. Peppone was what Peppone does and he knew exactly where to put his hands to work. He fixed the distributor, changed the coil, changed the spark plugs, adjusted the tappet clearance, cleaned the carburettor, adjusted the brakes, replaced two light bulbs and restored the oil level.

He worked quickly, furiously, and mother and son stared at him in dismay, thinking of the money all this would cost them.

'Please, *signore*, how much do we owe you?' stammered the boy when it seemed that Peppone had finished.

'Nixt! Nothing!' replied Peppone, unscrewing the tank cap and grabbing the hose and nozzle of a petrol pump.

'I'll pay for that,' chimed in Don Camillo, who had turned up quite some time ago and had been observing the mechanical and societal complexities of the whole operation unfolding.

Peppone having filled up the tank of the old crock, the boy tried to say something but Peppone bellowed over whatever it was:

'Get off with you!' he roared, pointing to the road that led to the embankment.

'Come, go!' added Don Camillo paradoxically, with an equally ferocious frown.

Then the lady smiled and, when the boy had put the car into gear and the car was moving, she turned and waved her handkerchief with another smile.

The Return of St Anthony (1957)

THE TREASURE WAS right there, where no one would have looked for it, and Don Camillo found it by rifling, without hope or expectation, through a pile of rubble and the minutiae of stuff – ancient vestments and documents – at the bottom of a chest.

Most of the papers were in bad shape and often indecipherable, but certain of them retained their integrity thanks to being wrapped in a bituminous laminated hessian cloth: they were just three clearly written sheets but contained things that had Don Camillo reaching out for something to hold onto lest he fall. Grasping the bell ropes to steady himself, he only let go when he found himself surrounded by people who were looking at him as if he were some kind of freak.

'I found the Saint Anthony documents!' he panted.

Those around him were many and sturdy enough, but they all backed away, as strong men and even bullies do when a furious madman runs loose.

'All right, Reverend,' Peppone responded politely from the front row. 'If you've found what you're looking for, everything is fine and there's no need to get upset.'

'And why not!' he shouted, grabbing the bell ropes once more. 'If a poet can make bells ring in celebration of finding a name for one of his characters[35], why shouldn't I who found the Saint Anthony archive?'

'Perhaps because it is two o'clock in the morning,' muttered Peppone.

Don Camillo let the bell ropes go. At eight that evening he had gone to put something away in the sacristy and, raising his eyes to the ceiling, he first discovered the stain: a tile must have cracked and, since the sky threatened rain, he had climbed up through a trapdoor that no one had touched for centuries, into the attic. There, after having identified the broken tile, he had also discovered the chest hidden behind a pile of scrap and rubble.

At first, the chest appeared to be full of old vestments gone to rags but, under the dusty junk, there was what Don Camillo had been looking for in vain for at least thirty years: the parish archive from 1750 to 1830.

Having lowered the coffin into the sacristy, Don Camillo had thrown himself avidly in amongst those ancient papers and had lost all notion of time.

Then, having found the package, he had lost his cool. Now, having regained the notion of time and a measure of self-control, he felt the tiredness of the long and agitated vigil weighing on his shoulders and went to collapse in his bed, after saying to the crowd staring at him in amazement: 'I'll see you again tomorrow morning at first Mass.'

Usually at six o'clock Mass, only a small group of old women was in attendance, but that morning the church was bursting with people because the matter of the night-time pealing and the archive of Sant'Antonio had both alarmed and, in equal measure, made everyone impatient to know the full story. But Don Camillo did not offer the spectacle that most had expected and, coming to his sermon, he began in a state of serene calm:

'Brothers... Brothers and cousins,' he pronounced, addressing the massive group of Reds gathered around Peppone, 'except for

---

[35] There is conjecture that this might refer to the Italian poet, Dino Campana, the veiled bell reference possibly resonating more from his name than a particular episode. Guareschi wrote: 'Se quel tal poeta ha fatto suonare le campane a festa perché aveva trovato il nome per un suo personaggio, perché non dovrei suonare a festa io che ho trovato le ricevute di Sant'Antonio?'

the young among you and especially those who have strayed from the path of righteousness to walk with those who deny God, you will all remember an ancient story linked strictly to this village and to this church. A fairytale, a mere legend, as defined by the experts when I wrote about it in the newspapers many years ago.

'At that time I stated that our parish church possessed a miraculous statue of Sant'Antonio Abate. In 1792, through the intercession of Bishop Ilario, the miraculous statue had been lent, for a solemn function, to the inhabitants of Torricella, a town in which a plague had been raging for some time and was depopulating the stables. The statue, a precious, coloured, wooden one from the 1400s, was never returned to us: the confusion that followed the French Revolution, the death of Bishop Ilario and that of our parish priest and the disappearance of the parish archive aided the plans of the dishonest people from Torricella. Every attempt to retrieve the statue was useless because the documents that could validate my and my predecessors' thesis were missing.

'Now we have found the documents: the letter with which the parish priest of Torricella declares that he has received the statue on loan and undertakes to return it within fifteen days. The letter, in which Bishop Ilario thanks the faithful of our parish for having loaned the statue to the people of Torricella... The letter with which the authorities and notables of Torricella *guarantee* the return of the image within the set deadline.

'I found these documents last night at two o'clock, a few moments before you heard the bells ringing.'

Don Camillo turned towards *il Cristo Crocifisso* on the altar and bowed:

'Lord,' he said aloud, 'forgive me if I am about to use language unsuitable for this sacred place, but in my ignorance I cannot find current terminology to express what I want to say any more effectively.'

Don Camillo resumed his speech to the faithful:

'Brothers,' he exclaimed, showing the three sheets found in the chest "*carta canta e villan dorme*" – "what's written down in black and white is incontestable": Sant'Antonio is ours and, whatever the cost, the people of Torricella will have to cough it up! Amen.'

'*Bene!*' commented Peppone, forgetting that he was a godless person in the House of God.

Later, at the People's Palace, he explained that he had spoken 'as Mayor':

'As Comrade Bottazzi,' he reassured his gang, 'I don't give a monkeys about any of the saints on the Christian calendar. San Antonio is only of compelling interest to me as first citizen and defender of Community Rights.'

'Sounds to me like he's interested in becoming a protégé of Sant'Antonio Abate,' commented Don Camillo when they told him.

*

The people of Torricella tried to wheedle out of it, but in the end they were forced to give in and one fine day they responded as follows:

'If you want Sant'Antonio back you can come and collect him. From today he is at your disposal in the sacristy of our parish church.'

It was then Don Camillo turned ugly:

'St Anthony is not a suitcase to be picked up at the left luggage office,' he remonstrated, 'and we are not people who allow ourselves to be treated like ragsdirt. Saint Anthony must return as he left.'

In the famous chest, in addition to the documents in the package, there was other stuff concerning Saint Anthony. For example, a brief but comprehensive chronicle of the original handover ceremony:

'The use of the Miraculous Image for fifteen days having been granted to the people of Torricella, through the intercession of the Monsignor Bishop and with the guarantees of the Notables, the people of Torricella came with a chariot richly decorated with precious drapes and flowers and pulled by two teams of horses with harnesses golden, up to the bridge over the Stivone and stopped there.

'The said bridge was admirably festooned with branches and flowers and there was a large triumphal arch also of branches and flowers. A richly decorated cart pulled by three pairs of oxen appeared at the opposite end of the bridge carrying the Miraculous Image of the Saint.

'After polite words from the Provost, the Holy Image was removed from the cart and, carried on a sedan chair to the middle of the bridge, it was handed over to the notables of Torricella, who then lifted it onto their cart. All this was accompanied by music, songs and great solemnity...'

The return of the Saint was now supposed to take place exactly like this on the bridge over the Stivone. But beyond the bridge something new was envisaged. Once over the bridge, the road that led to the village ran for a good kilometre through open fields and, to make the ceremony even more solemn and evocative, it was decided to line up the most comely cattle in the municipality along this green belt, on both sides of the road. Two leaders were to be provided by each farm and each beast had to have its horns adorned with ribbons and spikes of flowers.

Those from Torricella agreed to set up their cart but didn't want to do anything more than that. Don Camillo took an interest in decorating the bridge and personally directed a team to that end. On the Saturday afternoon the framework of the great triumphal arch was finished and the supports were ready to hang the lateral festoons along the parapets of the bridge.

To prevent the flowers and leaves from wilting under the burning sun of la Bassa, it was decided that the team would arrange the festoons and garlands from two in the morning on Sunday. The ceremony was set for nine and, since everything had, by then, been carefully prepared, there was plenty of time left over. Don Camillo, however, was not totally satisfied: to be complete, the lower part of the bridge could not be left bare.

There were kilometres of ready-made festoons: why not brighten up the arches and pillars with a bit of green too? The boys on the team agreed and immediately began hammering nails and laying wire along the arches and vertical supports. Naturally, in order to do this, the pillars needed to be cleared of brushwood and weeds, where the whole structure bedded into the embankment.

It was then, while scratching with hoes and rakes around the bridgehead on the village side, that the men discovered something that made them scream in horror.

Towards the end of the war, the English and Americans, who had time on their hands and ammo and petrol to waste, enjoyed hunting down civilians out on their own: scaring the cyclist, the little girl who brought milk to the dairy... They didn't hesitate to sacrifice bombs weighing quite a few hundred pounds in their adventures and for a bridge like the one over the Stivone they clearly found it perfect sense to waste 200 kilo bombs: like, in fact, the one that the boys of the team had discovered lying in the middle of the undergrowth around the base of the structure.

It had been there since 1944 and no one had noticed: it came to notice now, when everything was ready for the triumphal return of Saint Anthony.

The *carabinieri* Marshal responded immediately, sent everyone away and made the bridge secure.

'Until the bomb is removed, no one will pass through here,' he said.

'And Saint Anthony?' Don Camillo asked in dismay.

'If he can get through under his own steam, let him go ahead,' replied the Marshal. 'But if he has to be carried, he'll have to stay where he is.'

Don Camillo became agitated and insisted that the ceremony could not be postponed, but the Marshal shook his head:

'I have done all that I can do: I notified my superiors, explained the situation and asked them to send a bomb squad here as soon as possible. The bomb cannot be detonated because the bridge would collapse, and to transport it, it must be defused.'

Don Camillo replied that the bomb had remained quiet among the nettles for twelve years: why would it explode all of a sudden when Saint Anthony crossed the bridge?

'Equally, why should it not explode just then?' said the Marshal in turn. 'As long as I was unaware of the bomb's existence I could not intervene. Now that I am aware, I have a duty of care. If, suddenly, I discover that my best friend is a guy wanted by the police, I have to arrest him, even if I played cards with him every night for twelve years.'

*

Don Camillo had only had a drop of coffee and milk that morning and at midday he'd forgotten to eat and, now that it was already almost nine in the evening, he was walking up and down the church, still on an empty stomach ... if that can be said of a man who had a live cat in his stomach.

'Jesus,' he said finally, coming to a halt in front of the High Altar, 'if it weren't for Saint Anthony, this bomb would not have been discovered and would have remained nestling in the weeds, exploding, perhaps, in a day or a week, due to the imprudence of a boy or the chance fall of a stone. Saint Anthony has done so much for us, and we, as a reward, will have to say to him: "Tomorrow, we cannot receive you because we are madly afraid that the device that your return has made us discover will explode."'

'Do not worry, Don Camillo,' Christ replied. 'Saint Anthony is understanding.'

'Yes, Lord!' exclaimed Don Camillo desolately. 'The fact is, *I'm not!*'

'May Saint Anthony protect you,' Christ said in a sweet, if resigned, sort of voice.

Then, Don Camillo went out and, climbing through the garden hedge, took the path to the fields.

Twenty minutes later he appeared in front of Peppone, who was still at work on a tractor in his workshop until, on seeing the black ghost, he jumped.

'Damn you... Didn't they teach you in the seminary to knock when you enter someone else's house?'

'Yes, but I forgot. I need one of your tools. Immediately.'

Peppone looked at him amazed:

'What sort of tool?'

'Whatever it takes to unscrew the tip of ... that damned thing.'

The priest took a large wrench from his pocket and threw it on the ground:

'I tried with this, but it didn't work.'

The blood drained from Peppone's face:

'You tried to unscrew the fuse from the bomb?' he stammered.

'Of course: but you need a custom-made spanner that fits precisely. Here is a clay mould of the nut.'

Don Camillo placed a block of clay on the anvil:

'Pour a little plaster into the hole and you will have the exact mould of the fuse.'

Peppone shook his head:

'You are crazy and I cannot help crazy people in their deranged enterprises.'

'Are you afraid that the parish priest will show people that he has more guts than the Mayor?' asked Don Camillo.

Peppone made no reply. He threw some pieces of lead into a large iron ladle and, placing the ladle on the hot coals of the forge, began to turn the fan.

Then he poured the molten lead into the hole in the clay. At ten o'clock the iron tool was ready.

'Okay, Comrade,' approved Don Camillo, grabbing the long key. 'Send me an invoice tomorrow. If I don't come home, send it to my heirs.'

*

The key, made to measure, gripped the fuse perfectly, but the rust had locked the screw and Don Camillo, despite pulling like a pair of oxen, only managed to turn the bomb.

'You won't accomplish anything that way,' came a voice out of the darkness.

'I don't have the expertise in heavy weapons that an artilleryman, who is currently preparing the proletarian revolution, has,' replied Don Camillo.

'Instead of talking nonsense,' roared Peppone, 'try to hold this still while I work with the key…'

God knows how much they had to tussle with that obstinate beast, but in the end the fuse did come.

'It'd be less tiring to uncork a bottle of Lambrusco,' observed Peppone, who was dripping with sweat. But their efforts were not over:

'We can't leave the bomb here,' Don Camillo pointed out. 'It must be carried far away, out of the way, so that, whatever happens, there can be no danger to anyone passing over the bridge.'

A steel weapon weighing 200 or more kilos is heavy indeed and convincing the bomb to climb up the embankment slope was no easy matter.

It turned out to be easier to roll it down the bank on the other side.

Don Camillo threw himself onto the first row of vines:

'They are singed by frost anyway. All of them taken together won't yield a basket of grapes,' he muttered, starting to wind up the heavy wire that ran from pole to pole. Harnessing the bomb to it, the pair dragged it behind them until they reached the green centre of the plain, which, once upon a time, had been a rice paddy and earlier a swamp.

They found themselves walking for a long time in silence, side by side along the dark and lonely Molinetto road, when suddenly, Peppone observed:

'So, everything went well for me. I'm sorry for you.'

'Oh? And why's that?' muttered Don Camillo darkly.

'Because you can't tell people that the parish priest has more guts than the Mayor.'

But Don Camillo was unable to respond because he had turned pale and, had Peppone not caught him, he would have collapsed on the ground.

'What's the matter with you?' Peppone gasped when he managed to get Don Camillo back on his feet. 'Delayed-action terror?'

'Hunger!' roared Don Camillo. 'I can't see anymore! I haven't touched a crumb all day.'

'I may be godless, but not without conscience,' stated Peppone flatly. 'My house is just a stone's throw away: allow me to invite you to dinner.'

'If I have come thus far, I can manage it to the presbytery,' replied Don Camillo.

'Okay, but what will you find there? A piece of dry bread, a piece of cheese. At most a skimpy salami. In my house, however, there is a pan of tortelli with herbs and enough chicken to feed a seminar.'

Don Camillo swallowed a cubic metre of air.

'We will drink to the health of Saint Anthony,' insisted Peppone. 'I too, after all, did something for him.'

Indeed, in Peppone's house there was everything that he had promised, but Don Camillo had to put up with his furious hunger a little longer because Peppone wanted to do things properly and, having woken up his wife, he instructed her to prepare the table in the room, to reheat the tortelli and the cacciatora and to slice the famous culatello reserved for special occasions.

Peppone seemed to have become someone else and, if he was usually a curmudgeon of few words, now he behaved like those suffocating individuals who frantically look for any excuse to rabbit on.

He talked about the weather, the harvests, the works of Giuseppe Verdi, he even wanted Don Camillo to see his children's school notebooks.

And Don Camillo, with his brain numb from hunger, listened, thinking about tortelli, cacciatora, culatello and swallowing air. Cubic kilometres of it.

Time passed, but Peppone's damned wife still didn't appear to announce that everything was ready. When, finally, she did, Don Camillo entered the dining room almost in a faint. Culatello, tortelli, cacciatora: his mind was lost in a symphony of melodious aromas. He then sat down at the table and, when Peppone put the plate covered with a thick layer of slices of culatello under his nose, he had to make a huge effort not to grab a handful of the stuff.

'Help yourself, Reverend, if you'd like,' Peppone urged him cordially. 'And don't worry: it's already midnight and, when you leave, no one will see you.'

'Midnight?' stammered Don Camillo.

'Five minutes past, to be precise,' replied Peppone, taking his watch out of his waistcoat pocket. Don Camillo pushed away the plate of culatello and folded his napkin.

'Aren't you eating?' Peppone's wife worried. 'Is there something wrong?'

'Everything is fine,' replied Don Camillo. 'The fact is that I have to celebrate Mass tomorrow morning and, from midnight, I have to observe the rule of fasting.'

'I am sorry,' exclaimed the annoyed woman. 'I had no idea of the time and then he told me that there was no hurry and that I should let at least three quarters of an hour pass because he had to talk to you about important things...'

Don Camillo stood up, looked at "him", who was gorging himself on culatello, and said to him with hatred, through clenched teeth:

'*Maramaldo!*'

Peppone meanwhile attacked the tortelli without raising his head.

*

Nine hours later Sant'Antonio Abate arrived in the village with all the honours and it was such a beautiful celebration that it made Don Camillo forget all the troubles of the night before.

Now Sant'Antonio has returned to the small chapel of yesteryear, and if you happen to go there, look at the small votive offerings: first place in the row is given to a sort of notice board lined with red silk, and in the middle of it lies an aerial bomb fuse. Then, there are two signatures on the red silk, the first, cramped and almost indecipherable, one can imagine to have been inscribed by someone devoured by hunger; the other, languid and expansive, as clearly belongs to a certain Giuseppe Bottazzi.

An Arrival From The City (1958)

S UDDENLY A THOUGHT struck him that filled him with amazement: 'In three months, I will be fifty years old.'

He wanted to observe what a man who had reached the threshold of a half-century looked like and he moved his head to look at himself in the rear-view mirror.

He shaved every morning, never neglecting to touch up his moustache: but what he saw reflected in the bathroom mirror a thousand times was the official face of the industrialist who had made it in the world, not his *personal* face.

For at least twenty years, every morning he had shaved the Commendatore[36], served a cup of coffee to the Commendatore and driven the Commendatore to the factory. Here he took his place at the Commandatore's desk and, until after one o'clock, diligently carried out the Commendatore's orders.

The same thing happened in the afternoon, after a quick meal consumed in the restaurant, together with the Commendatore of course.

In the evening, he accompanied the Commendatore home and sat down at the table with the Commendatore's wife and children and listened to what the Commendatore and the Commendatore's wife and children had to say.

A truck darted towards him half a metre from the car's bonnet: he hadn't noticed the red light at the crossroads and was saved only because, naturally, the Commendatore's car had formidable brakes.

He took off again like a rocket and passed on his way without any trouble, but he was almost sorry that the Commendatore hadn't been crushed under the wheels of the truck.

'For twenty years I have been nothing but a slave to the Commendatore,' he pondered. 'Actually, thirty, because, even when I was just a youngster desperately struggling to make my way, I was already his stooge.'

In the mirror he had seen the face of the man who suddenly remembers his true self and discovers that he is old.

Here in the suburbs, the usual crossroads led one way to the factory, another into the countryside and took you God knows where. The man took the latter without hesitation.

He didn't know where he was going nor did he want to know: after a couple of hours he found himself in a large village and went down into the piazza to send a telegram to the Commendatore's wife:

'I have to be away for important business STOP I will notify you of my arrival. STOP Hugs Giuseppe.'

---

[36] The title '*Il commendatore*' was given by Mussolini to favoured captains of industry – industrialists who had made it in the world.

He continued his journey, content to travel south. At midday he dined with bread and salami in a small tavern. Half an hour later he was back on the road.

Whereupon, at a certain moment, a young woman with a large suitcase appeared across the bridge to a farmhouse and signalled him to stop.

Compliantly, he did stop.

'Are you going towards Castellino?' asked the woman, who was quite beautiful and had a fine head of red hair.

Giuseppe replied: 'Yes.'

Why shouldn't he have been going to Castellino? It was a place like any other.

The woman explained that she had to get to Castellino station by a certain time and waiting for the bus meant she could only catch the five o'clock train.

'It's lucky for both of us,' replied Giuseppe. 'I actually have to go to Castellino and I don't know the way.'

The red-haired woman knew the road perfectly and, at three, they arrived in front of the little station at Castellino. 'Thank you so much,' said the woman.

'Have a good trip' replied Giuseppe.

In the station square there was a café and Giuseppe took the opportunity to drink a couple of glasses of beer. On leaving the place he found twenty people in a state of ecstatic admiration around his car.

The damned Commendatore custom-built car! How he hated it now and decided to get rid of it.

He asked if there was a well-equipped workshop nearby and they explained to him that, to find such a place, he would have to go as far as Borgonuovo, on the State highway.

In three quarters of an hour he reached Borgonuovo, where he immediately found what he was looking for.

'Do you also do bodywork?' he asked the owner of the garage.

'We do it all.'

'Well, then dismantle the engine and completely overhaul it, then paint the car light grey, like the one there. I dislike her so black.'

The mechanic pointed out that it would take some time.

'No problem. Keep it for as long as you need. For the moment I have no use for it. I will happen by again in the future or I will write to you with instructions on the matter. I intend to pay up front.'

'Is it okay in a fortnight?'

'No. At least twenty days.'

'Agreed.'

The salami had made him exceedingly thirsty so he went for a beer at the first bar he came across on his way from the garage. A large mirror covered the wall next to the reception desk and Giuseppe found himself face to face with his public self once more.

The damned iron-grey double-breasted suit of the Commendatore! Giuseppe's bodywork clearly also needed to be changed.

Not far from the bar, there was a shop selling tailor-made clothes; he went in and immediately saw what he needed:

'A sturdy, loom woven work suit for a man of my size is what I need,' he explained to the sales assistant. 'Like that one over there, for example.'

The assistant explained that the suit indicated was the right size and sturdy, but defective, some stains, some small faults.

'It doesn't matter,' replied Giuseppe. 'It's for my driver. How much is it? Give me any old bag, I'll take it away myself now. I'm passing through.'

He went out with his working man's suit stuffed in the bag and immediately felt that people would find it strange that such an elegant gentleman as he would go around with such a crummy bag under his arm. He may have made a dramatic exit from his life as a captain of industry, but the figure in the slick iron-grey double-breasted suit was tyrannising him still.

'Not easy to get rid of the hateful Commendatore,' he mused.

He bought a cheap suitcase and bundled his now crumpled suit inside it, together with a toothbrush, a piece of soap and shaving gear.

Now the people who saw him pass surely found it strange that such an elegant man would go around with such a crumply fibre-cloth suitcase.

In the square, a half-empty bus was about to leave town. As Giuseppe got on it, the driver warned him:

'Hope you realise, the bus doesn't go as far as Torricella, it stops at the bridge.'

It was hot on the bus and, having paid for a ticket to Torricella, Giuseppe dozed off.

When the driver woke him up, it was already starting to get dark. He got out with his suitcase and found himself in the countryside, at the foot of the said bridge.

'The river damaged it,' the driver told him, seeing his uncertain demeanour. 'You will have to walk the kilometre into town.'

'Thank you, I was told...' replied Giuseppe. 'We have agreed that my people will pick me up in the car.'

He crossed the bridge on foot, having repaired it as best he could with a few boards, and let the other passengers set off ahead of him towards the town. Once the bus had reversed and moved away, Giuseppe left the road and made for the cover of a hedge.

In a few minutes the hated iron-grey double-breasted jacket of the Commandatore was inside the suitcase, together with his tie and hat. Giuseppe now had a rough new exterior.

What's more, returning to the road he even had a new face, because he had shaved away his moustache.

'Tomorrow I'll buy a shirt to match the suit, and a cap,' he thought as he walked towards Torricella.

Upon entering the town he noticed that no one cared about him anymore, and this filled him with pride. It was his first sensational victory against the Commendatore.

He found something to eat and a tavern to sleep and went to bed drunk.

*

The following morning he woke up in an excellent mood: for the first time, after many years, he didn't have to shave the Commandatore, serve coffee to the Commandatore and drive the Commandatore to the factory. He looked at himself in the wardrobe mirror and liked his new face, and while his rustic clothes made him less suave than the Commendatore, he did look much younger.

There was a market in the town and Giuseppe quickly picked up the shirt and cap he wanted and returned to the inn to remove the last of the Commendatore's encrustations from him. Along the way, someone came to the door of a shop and hailed him:

'Hey, you!'

He stopped in his tracks with a sinking heart.

'Wouldn't you like a second-hand bicycle, good as new?'

Damn, a bicycle would indeed be convenient. He went in and, after bartering with the mechanic for half an hour, went out with his bicycle. At ten o'clock, with the remains of the late Commander on the luggage rack, Giuseppe pedalled into the unknown.

He meandered along the dusty road between green hedges for almost two hours and, at the first village he came to, he stopped because he'd worked up a hunger. It was still too early to eat and he sat down at a table in front of the tavern he had chosen to have his dinner and the sound of the midday bell caught him there, while he was enjoying a large glass of dry white wine.

'It seems that the Reverend is left without a bell ringer!' someone chuckled.

At once it fell clear to Giuseppe that he had not arrived by chance in this village lost in the fields.

Three minutes later, coming out of the little door of the bell tower of the village church, Don Camillo found himself in front of Giuseppe.

'Reverend,' Giuseppe said to him, taking off his hat, 'is it true that you are in need of a bell ringer?'

'Yes, and so?'

'And so I would like to ask you if I could aspire to fill the position vacated by the bell ringer.'

Don Camillo looked at Giuseppe and the crumpled but new suit made him suspicious.

'Where do you come from? From prison?'

'Do I perhaps have the face of a scoundrel?' Giuseppe asked in turn.

'I couldn't say.'

'So, although it may seem unlikely, I am a gentleman. So unfortunate and such a gentleman that, rather than start being a rogue, I would like to be a bell ringer for you, even though I have never rung a bell in my life.'

'Ha!' Don Camillo laughed loudly. 'Beautiful! Someone who has never rung a bell would like to my bell ringer!'

'Bell ringers are not born,' Giuseppe replied calmly. 'After all, before becoming a priest you weren't a priest either.'

'But I spent my youth studying in the seminary!' exclaimed Don Camillo.

'Blessed be he who had a youth,' sighed Giuseppe. 'I, on the other hand, am one of those unhappy people who find themselves old without ever having been young. However, I know a little about music and, if someone wrote down the various peels as sheet music, I think I could manage. Even banging on the keys of a carillon ... I think.'[37]

'And while you're learning, what will I do?'

'You can watch how I eat.'

Don Camillo liked this rumpled man. And he liked him even more, a little later, seeing how he ate.

'Let's give you a go,' he said finally. 'If it doesn't work out, you get on your bike and skedaddle without making a fuss.'

A man who has the strength to create and manage a prosperous industrial unit employing 500 workers could not fail as a bell ringer. In fact, after a week, Giuseppe passed his exam with honours.

'Clear agreements make for long friendships,' muttered Don Camillo after the test. 'You've seen what it's all about. In addition to being a bell ringer, you must help me as a sacristan, take care of the vegetable garden, supervise the sharecropper, and in short do everything that can be used to help a poor and skinny country priest. As for the pay...'

'Give me food, sleep and some cigarettes,' Giuseppe interrupted him. 'It will be enough for me.'

A done deal: Giuseppe was hired and Don Camillo, more and more every day, came to believe that the Lord's own Office of Employment had sent the crumpled little man to him.

*

---

[37] Seasoned readers of Don Camillo will know that in the bell tower of the village church is a carillon, a pitched percussion instrument, its bells, cast in bronze, hung in fixed suspension, tuned in chromatic order and struck with clappers connected to a keyboard to create all manner of melodious harmony.

A month and a half passed like this and then, one afternoon, a light blue convertible stopped in front of the presbytery that seemed to be more a product of a jeweller than a car designer. A beautiful woman in her forties (or more) got out, decorated like a diva and with the authoritarian attitude of a great lady.

She was looking for Don Camillo, the archpriest, and as soon as she set foot in the presbytery dining room, she immediately got onto her subject of interest.

'Reverend, mine is a sad and distressing story. My husband has been missing from home for forty-five days. A telegram, sent by him, informed me that he was leaving on business and, since then, I have heard nothing more. Fifteen days ago a garage in Borgonuovo called our house to say that his car was ready. The gentleman who had left it had not returned, so the garage man looked for the owner's name in the car registration document and tracked down our address. I made for Borgonuovo.

'I went alone, without saying anything to anyone. You understand me, Reverend? Our position is delicate. We don't need any scandals. I recognised the disguised car and became something of a detective. I discovered that my husband had arrived in Borgonuovo after leaving a young red-haired lady in Castellino. Everyone had noticed them, because of the car and the woman, of course.

'In short: after questioning hundreds of people, I managed to ascertain that all traces of my husband's whereabouts were lost in a triangle encompassing Castellino, Borgonuovo and Torricella. I have searched the entire area, village by village, town by town, without finding anything, and now here I am asking you the question I have asked some fifty or more parish priests: are you aware of a stranger arriving in this village forty-five days ago from today?'

The lady took a photograph from her purse and handed it to Don Camillo:

'Have you ever seen this face?'

In truth Don Camillo had never seen that face, that of the Commendatore. He had seen another one. The face of a crumpled little man whose physiognomy had nothing in common with that of the moustachioed character in the photo.

He spread his arms wide:

'Of incomers recently, only my bell ringer…'

The lady had an impatient disposition:

'Who knows where he went! It is impossible that he disappeared just like that, as if swallowed up by the fog.'

At that moment Giuseppe, unawares, entered the room and found himself face to face with the Commendatore's wife.

The lady let out a scream, but Giuseppe plugged it:

'Paolina, I don't want a scene. You looked for me, you found me and you're about to tell me a lot of things that don't interest me. Save your breath. I'm fine where I am. You may keep the company, the house and everything I own, but leave me my freedom. I grabbed it just in time and I am keeping it. I will send you a power of attorney that will allow you to act in all respects on my behalf.'

The lady, who had been left breathless, rediscovered her voice: 'And the young red-haired girl?' she shouted. 'Why don't you talk about her?'

'Because I gave her a lift to Castellino where she boarded the train and I never saw her again. Women have nothing to do with my life here. The Reverend knows what I do and how I live. I haven't moved from here for forty-four days.'

The lady realised that it was useless to persist.

'Okay!' she exclaimed. 'I'm leaving, but you'll hear from me.'

'Have a good trip, Paolina,' Giuseppe replied.

The lady darted out of the presbytery and, a few seconds later, the blue convertible sped away.

Don Camillo looked at Giuseppe and shook his head:

'I'm not about to tell you anything,' he muttered. 'You'll see. Only you can be sure if you did the right thing or the wrong thing.'

'I did something right,' Giuseppe replied calmly.

It was, let me be precise for our story's sake, four in the afternoon. At eight, while Don Camillo was eating his meagre dinner, someone knocked on the presbytery door – a modestly dressed woman holding a fibre-cloth suitcase. Despite her scarf covering her hair and shadowing her face, Don Camillo recognised her immediately:

'Madam,' he stammered, 'I don't understand…'

'I am surprised,' the woman replied brusquely. 'I thought that the wife having to follow her husband was still common practice in the countryside, not just in the city.'

'Okay, however, your husband's position…'

'My husband's current position is that of a man who has suddenly gone mad. This means that my role must be that of the wife who does not abandon her husband in trouble.'

Don Camillo raised his eyes to heaven:

'Madam,' he said, 'if you want the party to be complete, make me mad too, so that there will be three mad people in this house.'

He steered the lady to the door:

'Behold, the bell ringer's house is there, on the first floor. When passing by the woodshed, be careful where you put your feet.'

*

The lady struggled a little to adapt: however, after four days, she was actively taking care of the vegetable garden and the chickens and had learned to make extraordinary omelettes with onions and to cook chickens, which were marvellous. After fifteen days, she felt ten years younger and trembled with pride when, passing through the village, she heard people whisper: 'She is the bell ringer's wife!'

Furthermore, her husband, without a moustache, without the Commandatore's uniform and with a face tanned by the sun, seemed to her to have once again rediscovered his long-lost youth. This halcyon life lasted a month before, one morning, a red Supersprint two-seater stopped in front of the presbytery and two youngsters jumped out – or rather, a young man and a young woman aged respectively twenty-four and twenty-two. As they entered the presbytery they pushed forcefully past Don Camillo and demanded:

'We know our parents are here and we insist on seeing them!'

Don Camillo felt an itch in his nose, but he controlled himself and went to call the bell ringer and his wife.

As they entered the presbytery, the young man and the young woman rushed towards them:

'Here you are! Here you are! *Feel the shame!*'

'Calm down,' Giuseppe admonished them. 'You're not at home here.'

'Neither are you. And neither is he! And it's time for you to stop playing the idiot and come home. People are gossiping. They say you ran away because the company is going bust.

'You can't just abandon your home and your business! You can't ridicule your children in this way!'

The lady intervened:

'We know very well what we are doing. We'll come back when it suits us.'

The young man gnashed his teeth:

'You will return at once! Or I will fill your house with journalists and photographers! There'll be an almighty scandal!'

'Be gone!' shouted Giuseppe.

'If you've gone mad, *we* don't have to suffer the consequences!' the girl shouted.

'We'll have you voted off the board,' the young man added ferociously. 'We'll take control of your affairs! We'll have you locked up in a nursing home...'

At that, Don Camillo fired a shot and the blow plastered the young man against the wall. A leaden silence fell in the room.

'You must go back home,' said Don Camillo to Giuseppe and the lady. 'You cannot leave two spoiled brats, so badly raised as these, on their own.'

Giuseppe turned towards them:

'Get out of here at once,' he ordered. 'We'll do the maths at home.'

The two youngsters left without saying a word.

*

'The bus for Borgonuovo leaves in half an hour,' said Don Camillo. 'You barely have time to get ready.'

After a few minutes, the couple – the Commendatore and the Commendatore's lady – returned to the presbytery.

'Father,' implored Giuseppe, 'may I have one last little fantasy with the carillon?'

'I don't see the point' replied Don Camillo. 'I do not understand where all this is coming from...'

'You do not understand anything: precisely because there is no plausible explanation, except that *one can do it*.'

The Commander went up to the belfry and began hammering on the keys of the carillon with his fists.

From far below, the lady listened *in éxtasis*. As she saw it, the Commendatore was playing for her and it seemed that she had never heard sweeter music.

An Unnecessary Detour (1960)

IN 1946, WHEN the Reds took over the municipality, Peppone immediately configured his brain to think about 'public works' – works to be carried out by the State for the people.

'For centuries,' he had pledged in electoral campaign rallies, 'in order to go to Solagna, which is in the south-east, the working man has had to travel north-west, then having arrived at Crocilone, he has to turn right and proceed in a north-easterly direction until reaching Stra' Lunga, where he must turn right again and, after fourteen kilometres, finally reach Solagna. Whereas, if instead he went south and, having reached the Ponte Nuovo, turned left along the Canalaccio, he would have found himself, after just two and a half kilometres, at the Molino Vecchio bridge, which is only eight kilometres away from Solagna. *In toto*, eleven and a half kilometres instead of twenty-two.

'In other words: the working man is forced to make an unnecessary detour that costs him ten and a half kilometres. And all this on account of the selfishness of one individual who, until yesterday, could do as he pleased, but for whom today the tune has changed!'

All maths aside, it was indeed a crazy affair: the provincial road past the village reached, after one kilometre, the bridge over the Canalaccio and the beginning of a small municipal road off to the left, which, running alongside the canal for two kilometres, ended up in the courtyard of the Molino Vecchio. From there to the Stra' Lunga the land belonged to the mill: a rectangle 100 metres wide by 500 metres long. The little road served only the mill and, to convert it for public use, it would need to be extended to the Stra' Lunga, knocking down the mill and cutting away a strip of the miller's land.

Peppone's project did not please the Bossi family who, for at least 300 years, had owned the Molino Vecchio, and had no intention of moving.

Shortly before the war, the Mayor had taken a stand and, having sent for old Bossi, had sung it to him plainly:

'I've been to Rome and the Boss is taking a personal interest in the matter. You're better off making a spontaneous gesture of good will to the people. We will compensate you, and you will install a modern cylinder mill in place of the old sort.[38] Loss of water rights will be compensated with a free supply of electricity. If, however, you intend to come down hard against us, then we will proceed against you in the courts and it will be the worse for you.'

Bossi replied that he would think about it and, while he was thinking about it, the war broke out: then he no longer thought about it and one day, meeting Peppone, he said to him:

'If I had listened to you, where would you find the electrical energy now to give me to run the mill?'

The project was forgotten but, once the war was over, Peppone brought it back to the surface again and, having become Mayor, he sent for Bossi and explained to him that if he had given up the mill quietly, generously, it would have been better for everyone.

'I am seventy years old,' Bossi replied. 'Let me die in my own house. You won't have long to wait.'

---

[38] In the old days, great stones crushed and ground the grain slowly at low temperatures, a process conducive to retaining valuable nutrients.

'I'll give you thirty days. Either you die in a month, or you will have to go somewhere else to die.'

'To kick me out you'll need a compulsory purchase order.'

'Of course. We live in a democracy and we'll do everything by the book – legally: complaints, appeals, reports, watermarked paper, stamps and so on. While the process is progressing, in exactly thirty days I will mobilise all the unemployed people of the municipality and deposit them on the little road beyond the Canalaccio bridge. So, when authorisation to begin the work arrives from Rome, it will already have been finished two years ago and everything will be done and dusted.'

These were difficult days. There was a bad atmosphere over it in that slice of land on the banks of the Great River: for better or worse the Reds, after thirty days, sent a band of wild men armed with spades, shovels and pickaxes to extend the little road beyond the Canalaccio, and Bossi broke out in a cold sweat.

Cutting across the fields, he went to ask Don Camillo for help and, together, they made haste into the city to plead their case at regional level.

The reply they received was that since the road was municipal property, the municipality could do all the work it wanted on it.

'And when the road is made and when it reaches my garden hedge…?' Bossi objected.

'Two kilometres will take them a long time,' they reassured him. 'However, if they enter your home, let us know.'

'What if they throw me into the canal?'

'We will come to fish you out.'

Work proceeded at the tempo of a unit of Bersaglieri[39] and, before long, the road gang solemnly celebrated the first 500 metres of its advance. 'In three weeks they will be at my house,' feared Bossi, who had once again gone to confide in Don Camillo. 'If you don't help me, how will I stop them?'

Don Camillo was willing to do anything to spite Peppone and the Reds, and he wracked his brain for an entire day in search of

---

[39] A 19th-century Italian military unit of sharpshooters always on the run from one place to another, the unit's tradition of running remains a feature in military parades and barracks duty even today.

an idea. He found it and, with Bossi's help, acted upon it. It was quite hard work and took three nights to implement, but no one noticed that anything was up.

In truth, Bossi was not wholly convinced of the plan and expressed his doubts about the effectiveness of the device at the centre of it.

'It's a mine,' muttered Don Camillo, 'but mines do not have to explode. In any case, as soon as the gang arrives in the mined area, I will be here with you to ensure that everything proceeds as it should.'

The enthusiasm of the brigade of volunteer sharpshooters, having reached its maximum intensity at 500 metres, began to fade. At 700 metres, the gang had reduced by a half, at 800 only Peppone's most trusted men were still holding out and, at 900, the undertaking was postponed to a later date.

Peppone spoke about the matter again five years later, during the rallies for the new administrative elections; then, after he found himself re-elected, the topic fell on deaf ears. Times had changed and, without the approval of a higher authority, it could not proceed.

Another five years passed, the Reds won again. Meanwhile old Bossi had died and the mill had ceased to work. The issue of the Canalaccio road was raised in the City Council by the opposition, who accused the Reds of beating around the bush.

Peppone replied that the administration had already made contact with the Bossi heirs:

'The mill isn't worth a penny and no one would buy it. We need it, but we better wait so we don't get caught by the neck. The taxpayer's money is precious and must be protected down to the last cent.'

Another three years passed and, suddenly, the bomb exploded: the Old Mill was bought by the municipality together with the strip of land required to complete the little road.

Within a week the work began, and the little road was the priority. It had to be made accessible to trucks before demolition could begin, because the Old Mill was a building without end, with massive walls, and a great deal of rubble would need to be swiftly removed.

Since the road ran along the edge of the canal, neither bulldozers nor excavators could be used: any excavation had to be undertaken by hand. Bigio, one of Peppone's top brass, directed the work, which went smoothly for the two kilometres of road before they came to digging up the Bossi family's garden, which was no longer packed earth like the little road. A far deeper cut into the bedrock had to be made. Having reached a depth of forty centimetres, Falchetto, a young linchpin of the Red action team, was finding the going hard.

The Old Mill was one of the oldest buildings in the village: it was said to have been built on the ruins of a castle (or something like that) and after having scratched around a bit with the tip of his spade, Falchetto began to conjure up a vision of hidden treasure with, as was logical, pots full of golden marenghi.[40] It was half past four in the afternoon: Falchetto fiddled around with his excavation works until five; then, as a disciplined comrade, he went to report to Brusco, another of Peppone's bigwigs.

Left alone, they enlarged the hole: they found no gold marenghi, but something much more interesting.

Il Falchetto ran to warn Peppone.

The hole was further enlarged: the exploration continued and all three were so intent on their work, lying face down on the ground, that they didn't notice the enemy coming up behind them.

After looking at them for a good while Don Camillo exclaimed: 'Have you found oil?'

They jumped to attention suddenly, as if they'd been caught stealing.

'If priests minded their own business,' remarked Peppone through gritted teeth, 'the world would be a much better place!'

'Things that take place on Municipal property are surely the business of all citizens,' replied Don Camillo.

There was one way only to prevent Don Camillo from looking into the hole: tie a millstone around his neck and throw him into the canal. But these were the days of 'détente' and the gesture

---

[40] The 20 lire Gold Coin referred to as the Marengo (pl. Marenghi) was currency during the reigns of the last three of Italy's kings.

would have been counterproductive. They let him look: Don Camillo knelt, looked, touched, scratched with his penknife, then jumped up very excited: 'We must inform the Prefect immediately!'[41]

'The Prefect?' roared Peppone. 'What does the Prefect have to do with it?'

'He has to do with it because, for me, this is an Etruscan tomb. Stuff from the 5th century BC or even earlier. However, the experts will decide.'[42]

'The experts won't want to bother with anything so random!' Peppone shouted. 'This is municipal property and *we* are in charge of it.'

'Comrade Mayor,' explained Don Camillo, 'an article of the penal code more or less decrees that anyone who destroys or tampers with a monument or other thing the cultural value of which is both significant and known to him – if the act causes damage to the national archaeological, historical or artistic heritage – he goes to jail.'

'For me that's a load of rubbish!'

'In front of two witnesses I told you that it is an Etruscan tomb. Your duty is to safeguard what you have discovered. Only experts sent by central government will be able to establish if and when the road works should continue.'

'My duty is to finish this damned road that serves our citizens!' Peppone shouted.

'*Fate vobis*,' muttered Don Camillo. 'You can do what you want. This very evening I will inform the director of the *Gazzetta* of the discovery so that he can send someone out and authenticate the discovery.'

'You may as well inform the Pope too!'

'Now, if I remember: the article of the penal code is No. 733!'

Don Camillo set off towards the town: he found his bicycle at the Ponte Nuovo and a short time later arrived home.

---

[41] The provincial administrator responsible for enforcing the orders of central Government.

[42] Etruscan tombs were elaborate affairs, often set out in a series of rooms. Among the most famous is the *Tomba dei tori* in the Necropolis of Monterozzi near Tarquinia, Lazio, in Italy.

After dinner he sat down to write a letter to the *Gazzetta*, but then he thought better of it:

'Let's give him until tomorrow.'

A couple of hours later, as Don Camillo was preparing to go to bed, Peppone turned up at the presbytery.

'Reverend,' he said, 'you know better than I that that road *is necessary*. We have been fighting for twelve years or more to be able to build it: now that we have managed to win the battle, the archaeological tomb emerges and, if those from antiquity and fine arts get involved, we will have to stop the work. It's just so much junk. We won't destroy it: we take the stuff out, piece by piece, package it all up and send it to the Prefect.'

Don Camillo laughed off the suggestion. Had Peppone not read the relevant article of the penal code?

'Reverend, the tomb is right in the middle of the road and we cannot make any detours around it: say we dig up the tomb, make another hole ten metres further on and bury it just as it was buried before. Then we inform the Prefect that we discovered it there and he sends the experts. Meanwhile, the work continues.'

They argued for a long time and, in the end, Don Camillo gave up: 'It's fine. I do not know anything. Do what you like. Dig up the tomb and move it.'

Peppone turned his hat in his hands, somewhat embarrassed:

'Reverend, you must be involved too. You know more about these things than we do... And then, the idea of rummaging around in a tomb... Disturbing the dead...'

Don Camillo rolled his eyes:

'Lord,' he exclaimed, 'this madman who, if the revolution broke out, would hang half the world without hesitating for a second, is afraid of a dead man from 5,000 years ago!'

'Time means nothing to the dead.'

*

Falchetto was placed on guard at the Ponte Nuovo and Don Camillo, Peppone and Brusco were able to deal calmly with the removal of the Etruscan tomb.

'Before touching it,' said Don Camillo, 'let's choose the right place to move it to and start digging.'

It was decided to move it north, ten metres from the road and two metres from the west wall of the mill.

'That way,' explained Don Camillo, 'the opportunity to find it can be said to have arisen during the demolition of the mill.'

While Don Camillo set apart items from the Etruscan tomb, Peppone and Brusco got digging.

Half an hour later, Brusco's pickaxe encountered something hard.

'We just reached some sort of foundation!' Peppone cursed.

'Let's see,' said Don Camillo carrying over a lantern.

Having widened the hole with a shovel and cleaned out the base of it, something glinted in the light of the lantern and it was a piece of mosaic floor. They widened the hole up to the wall and the mosaic continued all the way. They cleaned the base of the wall and all fell clear: the Old Mill had indeed been built upon the foundation of some previous construction.

Don Camillo remembered what he had read in the notebooks of the parish priest who'd preceded him:

'The story goes that where the Canalaccio Mill now stands there once stood an ancient church which was submerged and swept away by a flood. That church appears to have been built, as was so often the case, on the site of a pagan Roman temple.'

Don Camillo's predecessor had died at the ripe old age of ninety-five and, throughout his life, had been obsessed with the search for monuments to antiquity.

All three of them slouched and yawned alternately until dawn, by which time they had exposed at least twenty square metres of ancient pavement. All in excellently preserved mosaic, the floor ended one metre from the Etruscan tomb, completely covering the route of the road up to the west wall of the mill.

They cleaned it with buckets of water and watched the miracle emerging, glimmering under the rays of the first sun.

'Goodbye road!...' Peppone groaned disconsolately.

Don Camillo roused himself and, having reached the Etruscan tomb, knelt down and began digging out stones and scraps of earthenware.

'You can leave that where it is,' Peppone told him.

'There is no place for it here,' Don Camillo replied, continuing to fish for stuff.

Peppone became agitated:

'If there's a place for half a block of Roman pavement under the road why can't an Etruscan tomb find a place there too?'

'Find some boxes and some straw in the mill and help me pack up these pieces,' Don Camillo replied dryly.

'I won't pack anything!' roared Peppone. 'This stuff belongs to the municipality!'

'This stuff belongs to the parish,' replied Don Camillo, handing him a piece of terracotta vase.

On the shard was written in indelible ink: 'Torricella – Podere Roboni Anselmo – South-east corner – two metres from the end – 25 August 1879.'

'I'll take care of it now. I didn't realise it then,' Don Camillo explained.

Peppone shot him a wild, ferocious look.

'You didn't realise what when?'

'Twelve years ago. I saw this stuff in the attic of the presbytery. Collected by the old parish priest. Bossi was afraid that you would invade his garden and so he created a mock Etruscan tomb along the road, knowing that when you found it, the authorities would intervene to suspend the work on the road. Then you stopped, time passed...'

The veins in Peppone's neck swelled:

'Is there a scoundrel more scoundrel than a priest?,' he roared.

'No, comrade. A communist mayor, at most, is an equal scoundrel.'

Peppone went down into the hole in the ground and, kneeling down, carefully studied the mosaic more closely.

'Be assured,' Don Camillo said, 'I didn't have anything to do with that.'

Brusco hadn't noticed anything that passed between them, having passed out, shattered by fatigue.

'If my bones weren't broken,' declared Peppone, 'in a hundred years an Etruscan tomb would be discovered here with a priest inside!'

At which point Falchetto arrived:

'Everything okay there... Everything okay here?'

'Everything's fine!' shouted Peppone, pointing to the mosaic pavement.

Falchetto remained speechless for a good five minutes.

'Is it still the Etruscan tomb?' he stammered in the end.

'Always and a day!' shouted Peppone.

And even now experts continue to probe the archaeology of the Molino Vecchio, while working people who have to travel to Solagna are forced to take the usual 'unnecessary detour', of which Peppone had spoken back in 1946.

How time flies.

Il Terrone (1960)

CONCETTO IL TERRONE[43] was twenty-eight years old, but he barely seemed twenty-two because he was lean, small and, with his slim hips and his dancer's feet, he looked like a fashion model when dressed for a party.

Even in la Bassa, that strip of land lying along the Great River, the profession of peasant was going out of fashion. The Reds, despite the proletarian revolution not materialising, continued to write on the walls: 'No to the Government of Unemployment!' and 'We want bread and work!' But there was no agricultural labour to be found even at a black market price.

---

[43] A derogatory term used historically in Northern Italy to describe Southerners.

So, we had to resort to imported goods, to workers who came from southern Italy, who worked well because they really needed bread and work.

Concetto Delisanti had arrived in the village about a year since and as he brought with him a long letter from a Monsignor[44], Don Camillo had placed him with the Bozzoni, old-fashioned farmers who, having worked for about a century as sharecroppers, had bought il Ghiaione[45] with the idea of working it as landowners for at least the next thousand years.

The Bozzoni were very much on Don Camillo's side. They were polite as a spit in the eye, but clean and honest to the point of scruple. Soon enough, after less than a month's training, Terrone found himself fitting in fine.

Even too fine, if you take into account that, in so short a time, he actually became Bozzoni's most trusted man. Il Terrone was a good boy and straight with those he respected. Not a week went by when he didn't appear in front of Don Camillo with a basket of stuff or with some small problem for the priest to solve. He was open to advice, he didn't mix with townies and Don Camillo liked him a lot.

'He is a serious young man,' the archpriest would often say. 'I would bet my head on it that he will never do anything stupid.'

Then, suddenly, the bomb exploded and Don Camillo was happy that he hadn't had anything to do with it.

*

The Bozzoni tribe rested on seven pillars: the old man and his six children. Seven big creatures with hands the size of a dumpster's shovel and with a stubborn determination that would give you goose bumps. And the toughest among them was Desolina, made with the same material and out of the same mould as Bozzoni's other five children but, only God knows how it happened, female.

The Bozzoni annoyed a lot of people for their determination, for their unabashed rusticity, but above all because after a hundred-odd years of miserable, wild existence they had become owners of

---

[44] A priest honoured with the title by the Pope himself.

[45] Literally a 'scree', an unpromising stony plot.

Ghiaione and made it one of the biggest and most attractive plots in the area.

Peppone and his associates detested them and even when the air of la Bassa was hot as hell, no comrade Inspector had ever dared to stick his nose inside the Ghiaione farmyard looking to mark out a strikebreaking scab. Also they detested them because, when every Sunday morning the Bozzoni crossed the village square in a pack to go to Mass, people looked at the seven rude beasts with the wonder and respect normally reserved for the elephants in the Circus Krone[46]. Not even with the backup of all the communist sections in the province, would Peppone have managed to set up a team of elephants of the same tonnage, and this damned well annoyed the Reds. We want to say that quality counts, that Lenin and Napoleon, two little men, were heavyweights in a different sense, but sheer substance still has its value for the masses.

Naturally, since the Bozzoni led a very secluded life, caring exclusively for the land that they cultivated as skilled farmers, people who despised them didn't know where to hang their grappling hooks in order to laugh at them behind their backs. And in the end, that led to the singular Desolina becoming the scapegoat.

As the years passed and Desolina remained unmarried, people began to call her 'Desolata' and, at the time of our story, when she had reached the respectable age of thirty-five without even a fiancé's dog appearing at the Ghiaione gate, phrases such as 'So-and-so will get married when Desolina gets married!' had come into common use in the village and in the countryside round about.

So, that was the situation that appertained before the bomb exploded, and it is not difficult to imagine what sort of fall-out the bomb left behind when it did.

At first, everyone took the news as a joke, then, when they realised that the matter was dead serious, they became bitter about it.

Finally, when they learned who the betrothed was, they were able also to console themselves that the bad karma they'd created had

---

[46] One of the largest circuses in Europe, with lions, Asian and African elephants, a hippopotamus, a rhinoceros, horses, monkeys, pigs, porcupines, goats, zebras and parrots.

been justified all along: 'Concetto Delisanti!' they laughed. 'Only a skinny Southerner could have had the stomach to marry Desolata!'

Now this is not to say that Desolata was an ugly woman. She was simply a cuirassier dressed as a woman.[47] She could carry 130-kilo bags on her shoulders and when there was a famous bet with Filotti, and the seven Bozzoni yoked themselves to the plough and dug a twenty-five metre furrow, Desolina pulled so hard that she broke her piece of rope.

Don Camillo, upon hearing the extraordinary news was astonished because the idea that Desolina might get married had never crossed his mind and, imagining her decorated with white veils and orange blossoms ... well, it took his breath away.

So when he found himself in front of Concetto il Terrone, he went on the attack:

'Then you are to get married!'

'People run around talking of it, Reverend.'

'I wouldn't say so. I got the news from old Bozzoni.'

Il Terrone shrugged his shoulders:

'I need... Please understand me, when you live alone among foreigners you feel homesick for your family.'

'A wife, a father-in-law, five brothers-in-law, five sisters-in-law and twenty-four nephews: if you stay in the Bozzoni house,' exclaimed Don Camillo, 'you will find some family!'

*

Concetto surfaced fifteen days later. He did not arrive at the presbytery alone, as on his other visits, but accompanied by one of the Bozzoni, who, after greeting Don Camillo, left, saying:

'I'll be waiting outside.'

Il Terrone looked sad, like he'd aged:

'Father,' he exclaimed when they were alone: 'did you see? They don't let me out of their sight for a single minute and at night they lock me in my room.'

'What does this tell you, do you think?' Don Camillo made to wonder.

---

[47] A flashing cavalry soldier armed with sword and pistols and protected by a cuirass, a breast and back plate. Cuirassiers first appeared in the 16th century and continued into the 19th.

'They do not trust me.'

'There must be a reason.'

Il Terrone shrugged his shoulders:

'I panicked,' he explained. 'They want to move things along fast. But marriage is a serious thing, you have to think about it before getting married.'

'Of course: better sooner than later.'

Concetto seemed relieved:

'And then, Reverend, there are problems to solve. You understand me: special situations...'

'For example?'

The Southerner clasped his hands and groaned:

'Reverend, in my homeland I have ... an obligation to a woman. What must I do?'

'You're asking me?' Don Camillo exclaimed harshly. 'You know your business: consult your conscience.'

'Reverend, everything is dark in my brain. I am here so that you can enlighten me with your advice.'

The young man was pitiful and Don Camillo calmed down.

'Let's see. You say you have an obligation to a woman: obligation in what sense?'

'She is a thing from many years ago. I was still a boy... It's hot down there in the village and the heat makes your head spin...'

'I understand. And with Desolina, how are things?'

The Southerner opened his arms:

'Reverend, it's hot here too...'

Don Camillo jumped up in a fury: 'I cannot advise you to commit to one sinful liaison rather than another.'

'You can convince the Bozzonis to give me some breathing space so that I can sort things out. Someone from my town works in Torricella: he's mad to death at me and if the news of the impending marriage reaches his ears, God knows what trouble I'll get into...'

'That's nothing!' roared Don Camillo. 'You'll know about trouble when the Bozzoni find out how things are!'

'Father,' implored the Southerner, 'you cannot ruin me. I speak not to the man but to the confessor!'

'Of course, I know my duty,' replied Don Camillo through gritted teeth. 'But if you're not out of here within a minute, the man and the confessor will slap your face.'

Concetto skedaddled and Don Camillo went to vent his anger with Christ above the High Altar:

'Lord, I will never be able to forgive myself for having introduced that poisonous snake into the Bozzoni's house. Jesus, what can I do to prevent that poor girl from being dishonoured?'

'Don Camillo,' Christ replied, 'that poor girl is thirty-five years old and can uproot an oak tree with her arms. She did not miss any of your sermons and consequently knew the story of Eve and the serpent perfectly. The sin which that boy committed is not a sin that can be committed by one person alone. Do not place the burden of guilt solely on the shoulders of the weakest of the two. Each must bear his fair share of the burden.'

Don Camillo raised his eyes to heaven:

'God bless us all!' he begged.

*

Two days later there was a spectacle in the square: the ten o'clock bus arrived and a young woman got off. Small, robust, with rather unkempt black hair, she placed a battered fibre suitcase on the pavement and began shouting a list of names as if she were counting a battalion of soldiers.

The more she screamed the more little boys and girls were dumped off the bus and, when the bus had gone she had a herd of children around her.

The oldest girl was about ten and the youngest boy looked no more than two.

Suddenly the woman let out a heartbreaking scream:

'Ciccillo!'

She hurriedly reviewed the squadron, but Ciccillo was neither present nor correct.

The poor woman seemed to have gone mad and, seeing her sobbing, all the children began to shed tears and emit shrieks too. The sight was heartbreaking and the municipal guards rushed to take the woman to the Town Hall together with the whole herd.

No-one could calm her down and Peppone intervened: 'Try to control yourself. If you don't tell us what's happening to you, how can we help?'

'At the station, when I got off the train and got on the bus,' the woman finally explained, 'all eleven of them were there. Now there are only ten. Ciccillo is missing! Oh Ciccillo, my poor creature!'

At a nod from Peppone, Smilzo got on the phone and, ten minutes later, the case was solved: Ciccillo had remained on the bus, asleep under a seat. They had found him and would have him brought back immediately by public transport.

The poor woman wanted to kiss Peppone's hand at the very least and, as soon as she got her Ciccillo back, it seemed she would die of consolation.

'Eleven children,' exclaimed Peppone in amazement. 'And why do you travel with eleven children?'

'*Signore*,' replied the woman, 'children cannot be dumped in Left-Luggage.'

'Eleven children!' Peppone repeated.

'Eleven. And a husband who has been away from home for two years and no one knows where he is. He sends a few money orders, always from different places, without even a word of greeting. He hasn't seen his last child yet because it was born two days after he left. A family acquaintance who works in these parts wrote to me that my husband works in this municipality.'

'Impossible,' muttered Peppone. 'There is only one recent incomer here and he's a young man from the South.'

The woman took a mangy photograph from her bag and handed it to Peppone, explaining:

'I am Annunciata Capece and this is my husband, Concetto Delisanti.'

Peppone felt his heart sink:

'Yes, there is a resemblance to the young man who works here, but it is impossible that he is your husband: he is about to get married!'

*

Peppone did the right thing and straightway drove the woman to the threshing floor of the Bozzoni farm in Sputnik, the little pickup truck made by Peppone from a Fiat 514.[48] At the wheel, with Brusco at his side, Peppone had arranged Annunciata Capece on the open bed at the back of the truck, with her eleven children all around her.

It should be said that, before they got there, Peppone had navigated through all the main streets of the village *andante*, while Smilzo followed the pickup on a scooter, explaining to curious onlookers:

'Here are the wife and children of Concetto Delisanti, otherwise known as il Terroni – Desolata Bozzoni's fiancé – and they are here to wish them good luck for their wedding.'

It had struck midday and all the Bozzoni had just returned from the fields.

The old man and his five children became agitated, circling around Peppone who, together with Brusco and Smilzo, was helping Annunciata Capece and her children down from Sputnik.

'What's going on here?' old Bozzoni demanded of Peppone.

'One can hardly leave a poor woman with her eleven children in the middle of the village square,' explained Peppone.

'I wouldn't argue with that,' replied old Bozzoni. 'But why bring them here?'

Annunciata Capece stepped forward:

'Because my husband works here.'

She handed the old man the photograph of Concetto Delisanti, which was passed from one Bozzoni to another.

Meanwhile, Desolina had arrived at the scene and, unaware of what was going on, accepted the photo of her betrothed and exclaimed:

'So, what does this woman have to do with my fiancé?'

Annunciata Capece, wife of Delisanti, leapt forward like a tiger.

'She has something to do with it,' she shouted, 'because you are a bad woman who goes with married men and my Concetto Delisanti is the father of these creatures!'

Picture the scene: on the threshing floor stood the entire Bozzoni tribe, while the five daughters-in-law and their twenty-four children remained detached, in the background.

---

[48] Introduced earlier in 'The Law of '68' (*Don Camillo Takes the Devil by the Tail*).

Meanwhile, on the road close to the Ghiaione farmyard, people began to gather to enjoy the show.

Annunciata Capece, married to Delisanti, continued to scream and old Bozzoni strode forward:

'Get out of here, all you gypsies!' he ordered.

'For sure! I will! But not without my husband, the father of my creatures,' replied the woman.

'Be gone!' the old man ordered again and five beasts moved menacingly forward.

But a scream from the woman triggered a terrible counter-offensive: the eleven children crowded around their mother, clinging desperately to her clothes and began to yell as if they were being disembowelled, spurting great gusts of tears. While, between sobs, they implored: '*Papà! Papà!...*'

The Bozzoni retreated in terror.

'Enough!' roared old Bozzoni. 'Go get that scoundrel and send him off with all these gypsies!'

The eldest of his sons moved, but Annunciata Capece feared for the life of her husband, and started shouting:

'You mean to hurt him! You mean to beat him! *Aiuto! Aiuto!* They want to kill the father of my creatures!'

Peppone intervened:

'We must advise the Marshal!' he exclaimed. 'As Mayor, I cannot take responsibility for what may happen.'

'I'll take it,' growled old Bozzoni.

He called one of his five daughters-in-law:

'You accompany this woman to fetch that scoundrel. Get the key from your husband.'

Annunciata Capece crossed the large threshing floor, white with sunshine: the eleven creatures didn't let go and the woman looked like a battleship escorted by a swarm of cruisers. When the fleet reappeared, Concetto Delisanti was sailing alongside the battleship, head down. Seeing him, the Bozzoni jumped: but the battleship let out a howl of alarm and the escort closed ranks, opening furious fire with piercing screams.

Il Terrone, his wife and the flock of children, helped by Peppone and his comrades, climbed into Sputnik. Terrone, covered by a wife and eleven children, disappeared from sight and before getting behind the wheel, Peppone turned to old Bozzoni and said:

'Are we okay with the, let's say, the administrative issues? I mean wages, overtime, severance pay...'

'He'll be given everything he deserves. Even more! Just get him away or there'll be a slaughter!' roared old Bozzoni.

'No rush,' said Peppone. 'Do your accounts calmly and bring the money to the People's Palace: they will all remain guests of the municipality until tomorrow morning.'

Sputnik left, moaning, while Annunciata Capece married to Delisanti now changed her tone, blew kisses to old Bozzoni and sobbed:

'God bless you, *buoni signori*! God bless you who have given a father back to my creatures...'

*

That night Don Camillo didn't sleep, but in the early hours of the following day he made a decision and went to get Filotti's son out of bed:

'Follow that scoundrel: I want to know where he ends up. We have a score to settle, the two of us.'

'And what if he goes to Naples, Bari, Foggia or thereabouts?' replied the other.

'It'll never happen. Southerners who go up North never go back.'

*

At noon Filotti made his report: Peppone had taken them to Piacenza and left them at the station. There, il Terrone had had a long and animated discussion with his wife. He must have managed to convince her of something because the woman, when the train arrived, got on it with her whole gang and then looked out the window to wave to Terrone, who remained on the platform. The train departed, Terrone left the station and got on a bus. Then, about thirty kilometres away from Piacenza, he disembarked and headed directly towards the local parish church. End of story.

Don Camillo immediately set to work: he wrote to the parish priest of the village in question explaining that he was looking for a certain Concetto Delisanti to deliver a certain document personally to him. One week later, he received news of where his quarry had ended up, sent one of his trusted men to check it out and had the report confirmed. He had then written to the local parish priest, asking him to report any sign of Terrone's movement. Then, after hearing nothing for a month, he mobilised Filotti to pick him up.

*

Il Terrone suspected nothing: he was calmly digging a drainage ditch in a meadow of alfalfa, singing like a finch.

Don Camillo appeared in front of him like a ghost and, when the Southerner realised what was happening, he had already received two slaps of half a ton each. It was the vanguard of a storm of slaps and il Terrone took them all.

'And now,' concluded Don Camillo, 'take your suitcase and go back to your hometown.'

The Southerner looked at him in dismay:

'Reverend, I can't. I have a bond with a girl.'

'Well, I'll go straight away and tell people who you are.'

The Southerner had his eyes wide open with terror:

'Reverend, don't do that! I have to marry her!'.

'Like Desolina!'

'Don't ruin me... Desolina is another story. It was she who enticed me. I did it out of consideration for her age, her social position. But I really love this one and I swear that I will marry her.'

Don Camillo looked at him horrified:

'And your wife?'

The Terrone lowered his head:

'Reverend,' he muttered, 'in Milan there is an agency run by some smart women. Children are their commodity. All expenses are paid plus 10,000 lire for the mother and 1,000 lire for each child... I no longer knew where to turn and wrote to the agency. If it helps you, this is their address...'

He handed Don Camillo a card, which the priest rejected with a slap.

'Your intervention at the Bozzoni's cost me dearly...'

Considering that the obligation to marry Desolina had not brought about the unpleasant consequences that were feared, one might conclude that the cost was well spent, had the episode not been contrary to every moral principle.

Don Camillo considered il Terrone with disgust, then declared:

'Young man, your dirty game is over: either you marry the poor girl you have compromised or I will come and take you by the neck and make you marry Desolina'.

Il Terrone turned pale:

'I swear I shall!' he gasped.

Two months later, Don Camillo received Terrone's wedding invitation and, later, a letter from Naples:

'We are on our honeymoon and my wife greets you. I want you to know that I did not *have* to marry her. I told you that I did out of fear that you would make me marry Desolina. Unlike with the others there was no obligation, only the best reason to marry her? Your most devoted Concetto Delisanti, who implores your blessing as a wedding gift.'

Don Camillo replied to him with a one-liner: '*Va' a farti benedire!*'[49]

The Second Prize (1961)

WHENEVER MARTORELLO APPEARED it sure spelled trouble and Don Camillo, seeing him enter the parish lottery room, made ready.

[49] Literally 'Go and be blessed,' but equally, colloquially, 'Go suck on a lemon.'

Martorello was worse than a dry storm[50] and the Reds used him as an *agent provocateur* whenever they wanted to smash something up or bust some heads.

Slender, small and with graceful features, Martorello gave, more than anything, the appearance of a boy, but he was past twenty-three years of age. He belonged to the Falchetto squad and, seeing him in action, made one break out in a cold sweat.

'If that scoundrel is coming here to kick up a storm,' muttered Don Camillo to young Filotti, 'I'll kick him out of commission.'

But Martorello didn't seem to have the slightest intention of causing trouble and, after having browsed the wares on Don Camillo's counter, he bought ten tickets.

Unfolding the tickets, he looked at each number and put them in his pocket. Then he bought more tickets, never failing to unroll the rolls and clocking the numbers before sticking the tickets in his pocket. The story continued for some time and Don Camillo, who never took his eyes off Martorello for an instant, became ever more darkly suspicious because he couldn't understand what the young man was aiming for.

In the end, Martorello approached Don Camillo: 'I would like to speak with you,' he said.

'Speak.'

'To you alone.'

Don Camillo headed towards the small door that opened onto the entrance to the presbytery, with Martorello in train.

'We are alone,' he exclaimed when they were in the hallway.

Martorello took a handful of tickets out of his pocket:

'There are a hundred of them,' he announced. 'I know this because I had 5,000 lire and now I no longer have one. With these ninety-eight I won the usual charity fair rubbish, but with the other two I won the football and the record player. Check, see.'

He took two tickets from his jacket pocket which he handed to Don Camillo: the ball was the ninth prize, the record player the third, and Don Camillo remembered exactly the numbers of the

---

[50] Dry thunderstorms, in which rain evaporates before reaching the ground, are particularly dangerous because, when vegetation is dry, it more likely to catch fire from the lightning.

prizes from the first – a television – to the travel bag, which was the tenth.

'Congratulations,' he exclaimed, handing back the two tickets.

'I'll give you all 100 tickets if you let me take second prize. Come on, Reverend, that's good business.'

It was indeed a good deal because the second prize had the same value as the third. But Don Camillo shook his head:

'I cannot accept. The ticket that won the second prize may already be sold and the person who won it is entitled to have what they won. If your idea is to get me into trouble, you have not succeeded.

Martorello turned pale:

'My idea is only to win second prize because I want it,' he replied. 'These tickets cost me 5,000 lire: give me 2,000 worth of tickets and I'll give you all that I have.'

Don Camillo looked at him:

'Young man, the record player alone is worth 30,000 lire. Take it and sell it. Even if you give it away, you'll get 20,000 and can buy all the tickets you want.

'I'll sell you the record player for 15,000 lire,' exclaimed Martorello. 'I am no shark.'

They returned to the lottery hall and Martorello immediately realised that he had missed out. The second prize was no longer there. Someone had won it and taken it away. He collected the ball and the record player and left, ignoring Don Camillo and everything else.

'With what he won,' observed young Filotti, 'he shouldn't be so upset. What's his problem?'

'It seems that he was aiming to get me into trouble and the attempted coup went badly for him,' replied Don Camillo.

*

It was 1 pm and Don Camillo had just finished taking stock of the lottery when there was a knock at the door. He went to put the jar containing the lottery money inside the vegetable basket in the kitchen, removed his shotgun from the nail, loaded it and, crossed the passage on tiptoe, passing into the bell tower.

Juggling the bell ropes, he reached the peephole that permitted him a clear view of the front door of the presbytery.

'Who goes there?' demanded Don Camillo.

The man waiting in front of the door turned around with a start and the light of Don Camillo's torch illuminated his face.

It was Martorello, even paler than usual.

'I have to talk to you,' he exclaimed.

'Come closer and say your piece.'

'Let me in. I don't want to hurt you.'

'You couldn't, even if you wanted to.'

'Then why are you afraid?'

The young man clearly knew Don Camillo's little weakness[51] and, in fact, hearing talk of fear, Don Camillo left prudence behind and set off like a Panzer. A minute later the front door of the presbytery burst open with a crash.

'Walk backwards towards me and do nothing stupid or I'll liquidate you,' warned Don Camillo who, despite having left prudence behind, had not laid down his shotgun. Nor did he give up on her even when, having arrived in the dining room and after checking that his visitor wasn't carrying weapons, he ordered Martorello to turn around and sit down in front of his desk.

'Reverend: I'm here for the second prize.'

'Again?' roared Don Camillo. 'The second prize was won by a passer-by who took it away with him. *Finito!*'

'I know.'

'So what else are you interested in knowing?'

'Who made a gift of it to the lottery.'

'Nobody. I bought it personally, like I bought the television, the record player and the ball.'

Il Martorello chuckled:

'If so, the shop cheated you, Reverend. The second prize was handsome enough, but it had a manufacturing defect.

'I'm not as stupid as you Bolsheviks think!' replied Don Camillo.

He opened the desk drawer, took out a sheet of paper and read aloud:

---

[51] Reference here to 'The Fear Persists' in *The Little World of Don Camillo*: 'Fear is what you feel about dangers that you can sense but not understand where or what they are.'

'Complete porcelain service for twelve people, German made, very fine, value 40,000 lire reduced to 30,000 lire due to defective decoration on the bowls and fruit plates.'

Martorello stretched out his arm to grab the paper, but Don Camillo was alert and managed to put the invoice back in the drawer.

'I knew I wasn't wrong!' gasped Martorello. 'Reverend, you must tell me where you bought it.'

'You are not the one to whom I am duty bound to explain my actions,' Don Camillo replied harshly. 'Now go away. I've put up with you for long enough.'

'I'm not leaving here until I know where you bought it!' Martorello shouted, jumping up.

Don Camillo lost his cool and, dropping the gun, got up and grabbed Martorello by the lapels of his jacket. 'If you're crazy or drunk, I'll shake you out of it or give you a hangover,' he said, shaking him roughly.

'It's been eating away at my guts for fifteen years,' replied Martorello, 'and now that a glimmer of hope has appeared, I cannot not know.'

He said it in a certain way that made Don Camillo let him go:

'Explain yourself,' he muttered, sitting back down. 'And if there is a reason...'

'There are a thousand reasons.'

*

Martorello downed the glass of wine that Don Camillo placed before him and began to explain himself:

'I'm not from round here, as you well know. I've lived here for only eight years.'

'Would that you'd never come here!'

'I had to come. In 1945, when I was eight years old, we lived in a village near Reggio Emilia. My mother had died five years earlier and I was always with my father who used to sell crockery in the local markets. When the war ended, he loaded everything he could onto his wagon and cut out. As a young man he'd been a fascist: he hadn't harmed anyone, but someone had a grudge against him, he'd forsworn so and so to save his own skin. He had to leave the area.

'Having arrived at the Po River, he felt he was safe and began to peddle his wares around the markets of the Lower Plain. For a month everything went fine. To avoid recognition we never stayed or even ate at taverns along the way. The wagon became our home. During the day, when we moved from one place to another, I holed up in it. Then, when I came within sight of a village, my father made me get out and took down the bicycle, which was tied to the roof of the wagon. It was one of those wagons that maybe have their beginnings in the wagon time of Romanichal travellers. You can still see them around today. My father would continue on his way along the road and I would go my own way. He always gave me money to put my bicycle in storage and to buy me something to eat at midday and I wandered around markets and, perhaps, even stopped to browse my father's stall, as if I didn't know whose stall it was.'

"No one should know that you are my son," he would tell me. So, once the market was over, I would press on and we'd meet up again at some pre-arranged place. The bicycle was returned to its place on the roof of the wagon and I would be holed up inside.

'Pippo was a good horse, but old and weak and his pace was that of the old nags that pull third-class hearses: when evening came, my father would take a secondary road and, having reached some out of the way place, he would stop, unhitch the horse, tie him to a tree and then prepare dinner. Even if someone passed by, we didn't attract attention because they mistook us for gypsies.'

'We ate inside the wagon. Then, when night fell, my father would take the bicycle down, hide it behind a hedge, or in a ditch, and send me to sleep under the wagon, in the small rack where the hay for the horse was.'

"Whatever happens," he told me every evening, "you have to stay quiet, as if you weren't there. Give them nothing to let them even imagine you're there. If something happens to me, your duty is to keep quiet and, as soon as the opportunity presents itself, jump off, take your bicycle and pedal to your grandfather. Swear to me!" Every evening I swore.

'All went well for a month, then, one night, some voices woke me up: I parted the hay under which I was hiding a little and looked. The wagon shook just a little, then I saw my father walking towards the river with his hands raised and, behind him, there were two men armed with machine guns...'

Martorello's throat was dry and Don Camillo poured him a glass of wine, which he downed in one gulp.

'I had sworn,' he continued, 'and I didn't open my mouth. When they were a hundred yards away, I jumped off my hayrack and followed them at a distance, crawling behind a hedge. I saw my father fall struck down by a gunshot to the back. I saw the two dig a hole and throw my father into it. Maybe he was still alive. Then I saw them cover the hole with earth and stones and return to the wagon. They hitched the horse and, getting into the wagon, set off. I retrieved the bicycle from the hedge and followed them for ten or fifteen kilometres. When I came in sight of a dirty old town, the headlights of a truck dazzled me and I lost sight of the wagon.

'I was eight years old but I found the way to my grandfather. He was a poor lonely old man who lived more on air than bread and, for seven years, I remained with him. He died when I was fifteen: I picked up my bicycle and came back here. The hole where they buried my father was in the scree and it was the first thing I looked for. Nothing had changed: the land was covered in metre-high weeds. In those seven years my grandfather had explained everything to me, and when I arrived in the village I went straight to the People's Palace. I said that my mother had died in the bombings and my father had died in Germany, where the fascists had deported him. They found me a job and here I am. Have I made myself clear?'

Don Camillo shrugged: 'Up to a certain point. What does a china dinner service have to do with any of this?'

'It has something to do with it because, in the eight years I've been working to find out something about my father's murder, this is the first piece of evidence I've found. That dinner service was in my father's wagon. There were bowls, pots, plates and glasses, pans, but this service was something special. My father had given it to my mother when they got married, but my mother had never wanted to use it because it was too beautiful, even if the decoration had some flaws. As soon as I saw it at the lottery, I recognised it. You, Reverend, must tell me who sold it to you.

Only through knowing who did, can I find whoever killed my father and take him out. Do you understand now?'

'Yes,' replied Don Camillo. 'And all that being the case, I'll never tell you.'

'You don't want to tell me because he's one of yours!' Martorello shouted.

Don Camillo shook his head:

'You know very well that he is not one of mine. Otherwise, instead of going with Peppone, you would have come to me and would have made your investigations among my people. I won't tell you because Christianity does not sanction revenge.'

The young man panted:

'I've been waiting for this moment for fifteen years. I want to know who killed my father!'

'It doesn't matter at all,' stated Don Camillo. 'The *important* thing is that whoever killed him knows.'

'My father didn't hurt anyone: they killed him and, for fifteen years, he has been buried like a dog in a hole in the ground.'

'Take me there,' said Don Camillo.

*

The Ghiaione was three kilometres outside the village. They arrived there at midnight and Martorello, making his way through the undergrowth, found the place without hesitation.

'It's down here,' he exclaimed.

Don Camillo crossed himself and prayed for some time then turned his eyes to heaven:

'Blessed Lord, help your child's soul to free itself from the poison that makes it unworthy of your suffering. Speak to him, blessed Lord, tell him, as then, to take his bicycle and go back to whence he came.'

Don Camillo returned to the village alone because Martorello remained sitting on the cobblestones, among the undergrowth, talking to his father.

*

That same morning Don Camillo got on his bicycle and arrived at Torricella, which is seven kilometres beyond the village. In the piazza, under the portico, was Belocchio's shop and it was on this that Don Camillo set his sights.

'Everything okay, Reverend?' Belocchio asked him.

'Looks good,' Don Camillo replied. 'I need another dinner service – the same.'

The old man opened his arms:

'Can't help you, Reverend. It was the only one I had in stock.'

'Ask the factory to send you another one.'

'I got it years ago from a passing traveller who never showed up again. Where am I going to find one now?'

'Perhaps at the scree, in the hole under the split willow,' muttered Don Camillo.

'At the scree!' stammered Belocchio, turning pale. 'Which scree? I do not understand.'

'You'd better understand,' Don Camillo told him in a harsh voice. 'Be there tomorrow night with your van and a zinc box. He must be laid to rest in consecrated ground. Be there with the stooge who was with you that evening.'

Belocchio was dripping with sweat:

'I didn't shoot him,' he gasped. 'I swear to God. It was the other fellow. Someone who lived in the same town as the pedlar. We'd been in the mountains together. Once, when he came to visit me, he saw the pedlar in the square and recognised him. He organised everything. And he shot him. I took the wagon and the stuff and paid him his share. Nothing else.'

'Tell him. Tomorrow evening he must be there too.'

Belocchio shook his head: 'He's been dead these last ten years.'

'We'll see if that's true. In the meantime, get yourself to Ghiaione tomorrow night at midnight.'

'You want to ruin me to defame the Party, but you can't. You have nothing in your hand. No proof!'

'Be where I told you to be or I'll send the pedlar's son to get you. He's after you big time and if I tell him your name, he'll kill you like a dog.'

*

The following night, Belocchio was at Ghiaione with the van and the zinc box and, when he'd finished his work, he was deader than the pile of bones he'd dug out of the ground and placed in the box.

So it happened that the pedlar was laid to rest in consecrated ground and only Don Camillo and Martorello knew who lay asleep under the marble cross on which 'Unknown' was subsequently written.

Once the operation was over, Don Camillo went to kneel before Christ above the High Altar.

'I thank you, Lord, for having guided me while, in the darkness, I sought the right path.'

'It was not me behind the wheel of the van five nights ago, Don Camillo.'

'Lord,' exclaimed Don Camillo, 'I told you nothing because I didn't want to involve you in a matter that could cause us big trouble if it came to anyone's attention and the Court stuck its nose in.'

'Don't worry, Don Camillo,' Christ reassured him, smiling, 'it is forever a case that concerns only the tribunal of God.'

'Amen,' whispered Don Camillo.

People of la Bassa

The Young Master (1951)

Cino Faticati, at the age of seven, found himself alone as a stray dog. And since there is no better motivation than hunger, very soon Cino began to put his back into some work, albeit always choosing clean jobs, jobs that didn't get his hands too dirty, jobs that didn't force him to inhale a ton of stinking smoke in order to afford to eat a mere half kilo of bread.

He passed from being a pharmacist's delivery boy to tailor's boy, then, after a brief time in a barbershop, he threw himself with determination into electricity and, at eighteen, he was already skilled in the trade.

He was a tough, no-nonsense character, and it didn't take much to bring him to the boil, when he'd fire off a few big slaps that made people forget their home number. However, since he eschewed wine, liquor and tobacco and kept going on grenadine and peppermint candies, and since disorder of any kind riled him, even in his work clothes he retained a certain dignity, and the people of the village recognised this in the nickname they came to confer upon him, *Signorino* – the Young Master.

Signorino's one weakness was Iris Tollini and, to tell the truth, it was hardly a weakness to be ashamed of as she was a girl fashioned according to all the rules of true art.

The relationship between Cino and Iris aroused interest across the wider countryside. People shared the most flamboyant details of it: 'They're plucking the strings of a noble ideal, a type of courtly love! He gives her an authentic Swiss watch...', 'He brings her flowers...', 'He has a bottle of perfume sent from Paris for her...', 'When he speaks to her, he says: "Iris, please..." like in the movies...' His love for Iris was an almost heroic discipline of idolatry and ennoblement. It was a serious love, like il Signorino himself: a love without secretive escapades, without public scenes in the square and without gossip. This annoyed people.

It annoyed them the more because, except in the matter of politics, one could never – under the guise of a joke – give the Signorino one of those poisonous jibes that villagers like so much to share: the Signorino was not one to put his trust in people enough to make him vulnerable, and if anyone got angry with him, he'd cover it up with laughter and a few sharp slaps.

He was, in addition, one of Peppone's gang, none of whom ever trusted anyone with their secrets, did not accept jokes at their own expense and, just like Signorino, took everything seriously.

But if most people who didn't know him well only spoke to him about electrical systems and motors, those of 'the gang' did not spare him barbs in their company. Indeed they made such harsh comments at his expense that if it hadn't been for party discipline, self-criticism and suchlike, il Signorino would certainly not have taken the barbs on the chin.

'I would really like to know,' Peppone had once asked the young man, 'what difference there is between your behaviour and that of a spineless bourgeois.'

'There is this difference,' Signorino replied calmly. 'I conduct myself as I do because I am a good person, while the spineless bourgeois you speak of is not a good person. He only plays the part.'

This had Smilzo in stitches:

'Your romanticised principles and unfettered zeal will never make a successful revolution – as they saw in 1848!'[52]

---

[52] Smilzo is harking back 100 years to the Revolutionary Year of 1848, which set the First Italian War of Independence in motion in the north of a divided Italy, independence from the Austrian Empire. Especially relevant to il Signorino's case is that the insurrection brought a certain morally elevating, zealous pride to bear on the character of the suppressed people, expressed in a boycott on gambling and tobacco products (government monopolies that brought in over five million lire a year).

But the Young Master would not be aroused:

'When we have to take up the machine gun, we will see who shoots better: me, who is both idealistic and pragmatic, or you, who is a damnably rude person.'

No one had managed to make il Signorino lose his cool: certainly not those who counted for infinitely less in the gang than Peppone, Brusco and Smilzo: but now he received the call-up postcard for compulsory military service.[53]

*

That evening, the Molinetto tavern was packed, mostly with Reds, and Peppone held court. Il Signorino arrived and sat down and had his usual non-alcoholic beverage brought to him. But it was written in Destiny's ledger that this time he would not be able to drink it in peace.

Peppone, with a wink, gave the go-ahead to Smilzo, who immediately expelled a never-ending sigh from the pit of his stomach:

'And now who will bring perfumes from Paree? Who will bring her the flowers? Who will shower her with so many beautiful little words as sweet as honey?'

Il Signorino gave Smilzo a dirty look.

'Shut it or I'll make you shut it!' he said.

Then they all came upon him with their shouts and their laughter. They told him to stop acting like an idiot, to stop looking so desperate and not to think such stupid things and to drink wine along with everyone else.

'Now they'll send you off to be a *patatucco* in Sicily or Sardinia,' shouted Peppone.[54] 'And we all know what that will mean. Out of sight, out of mind. Your lady will remain here, easy meat for 2,000 lustful flies, who will do their best to take her away from you or to compromise her, leaving you there to gnaw at your soul! Let's be

---

[53] National service ('the sacred duty of the citizen'), established in 1861 with the unification of Italy (the Italian *Risorgimento*), appertained until 2005.

[54] Peppone had no time for Sardinia, where Antonio Gramsci, one of the founders of the Italian Communist Party, was arrested and, in 1937, had died in prison. In the war, both Sardinia and Sicily were considered crucial strategic locations. Post-war, Sardinia became a site for the proliferation of primarily NATO military installations, where il Signorino might well serve out his military duty.

frank, women everywhere are all the same. Then, when you come back, well, we will see!'

Peppone put a glass full of wine under his nose:

'Drink.'

The rest of the gathering began to sing 'La Trombettina'.[55]

'It will no longer be your beauty who wakes you up in the morning but the little trumpet...'

Il Signorino downed the glass of wine in one gulp, demanded another and then a third. He remained motionless for a few minutes, listening, then jumped up and shouted angrily:

'I will not go!'

What then transpired took only a few seconds: the young man grabbed the empty glass by its base, raised it with his right hand, stretching out his other hand on the greasy wood of the table and delivered it a beastly blow. The glass shattered against bones and tendons, leaving the affected left hand a mangled clot of blood.

There followed a moment of silence, then someone grabbed hold of the man's arm, tied a tourniquet around his wrist and emptied a jug of wine on what remained of the hand, before wrapping it in a napkin.

Peppone scanned the onlookers in the room, one by one:

'I know you all,' he said in a dark voice. 'And I have a faithful memory. Nobody saw anything here, nothing happened here tonight.'

They took this on board and sat back at their tables, resuming their card playing and drinking.

Il Signorino was transported to Peppone's workshop and the doctor sent for.

'He was helping me fix the engine block of that truck,' Peppone explained. 'The hoist chain broke and his hand was smashed, caught underneath it.'

---

[55] The song, based on a poem by Corrado Govoni, celebrates the joy, wonder and nostalgia of sweet memories. But their singing it is a mocking reference to 'Suona la tromba', the anthem composed by Verdi for the revolutionary year of 1848 from a text by the Italian poet and patriot Goffredo Mameli.

The doctor said that he could not guarantee anything very positive: he gave an injection against the infection and bandaged the hand:

'Youth works miracles and it may end well,' he conceded. 'But if this trouble had happened to a man in his forties, I assure you that he would never move his hand again. It would be good to get him to hospital.'

Left alone in the workshop, Peppone said to Signorino: 'You are a coward: it is irrelevant that it takes courage to smash your own hand, for you have to be a very great coward to show that much courage.'

The young man shook his head in dismay:

'I don't want to go!' he said. 'They will have to discharge me. In any case you can't tell me anything because you, of all people, have made a hundred speeches against military service. You said a hundred times that everyone should refuse.'

'You are even more of a coward than I thought,' replied Peppone. 'I never said that workers should kill themselves to prevent capitalists from exploiting them. If anything, I said that if capitalists continue to exploit the workers, the workers should defend themselves, if necessary killing the capitalists.'

Peppone wanted to spout a tsunami of words, but, in truth, his carburettor was blocked:

'When we say that we must fight for peace and against war, we are not saying that one must find a way to avoid going to war and leaving others in trouble. Anyone who does this is a selfish pig. He is a deserter, someone who runs away out of fear. So you did this to your hand simply because you're stupid, hiding behind the skirts of a stupid girl, and you don't have the strength to break away.'

He told Cino to get out of his sight and the Young Master left.

Walking alone through the deserted streets, time and again he passed and re-passed the house where the girl lived. At one in the morning he went to bed, but at two he was already up and, having thrown something into a briefcase, he went out and walked to the station.

He still had three days left before reporting to the military: he spent them in the city locked in a third-rate hotel room. Then, on the morning of the fourth, he showed up at the precinct and went to undress along with the other conscripts.

His hand hurt like hell.

*

When it was his turn to present his call-up card he was frozen in a cold sweat. He felt that something was about to happen, and something did. The NCO turned the card over in his hands, looked at a notebook, then spoke to a medical second lieutenant.

Cino saw them peering at his bandaged hand. They took him by the arm, walked him to an office and left him there, naked and raw, in front of a white-haired colonel.

'So you must be the young man who, according to what we have been informed, doesn't want to do military service...'

The boy gritted his teeth: some damned person had alerted the police.

'No sir,' he replied in a firm voice. 'I want to do military service like the others.'

'Good,' muttered the colonel. 'And that hand there?'

'Nothing,' replied the boy. 'It got hurt at work, but I'm fine now.'

The colonel nodded his head.

'Let's see,' he said.

'No need,' exclaimed the boy. 'I can move it well now.'

It was a terrible thing for him, but he did it to the end: there was a chair nearby, he grabbed it by the back with his bandaged hand and pulled it up, by sheer force of his wrist and with a firm arm.

The colonel looked at him for a long time, then got up and stood before him.

'Good,' he muttered. 'There's no need for me to look at it. Before you leave, however, get your bandages renewed. You're bleeding.'

The colonel lit a Tuscan and took a few puffs.

'Ever been sick when you were young?'

'No sir.'

'Ever been in any kind of trouble?'

'Never.'

The colonel sat down again and pressed a bell button. A soldier in a white medical gown appeared.

'This is Captain Franceschi. Let him look at it and report back immediately. Also x-ray him.'

The soldier motioned for the boy to follow him: but the boy shook his head.

'Signor Colonel,' he exclaimed in anguish, 'I have nothing wrong with me! If I had something I would have declared it! There's nothing to gain by becoming a soldier and if one can avoid it, one avoids it! I have done nothing wrong!'

The colonel told the soldier to get on with it and then the soldier grabbed Cino by the shoulder and pulled him along.

They took an x-ray right away, but then he had to wait God knows how long sitting in a small room before seeing the soldier in the white gown again.

Eventually Cino found himself in the colonel's office once more, where the colonel was holding a large black celluloid film in his hands.

'You have one lung completely gone and the other one going,' said the colonel.

'That can't be true!' the boy shouted.

'It is true and you must have known it for a while,' replied the colonel. 'Why didn't you get treatment?'

The Master lost his cool:

'And how can it be? I took care of myself, everyone in the village would have known about it, and she...'

He realised too late that he had said 'she'.

'Yes, "she",' muttered the colonel. 'If she finds out about this, she'll ditch you. While if she doesn't, you can marry her!'

'Not so! Not true!' the boy shouted. 'If I had wanted marriage she would have said yes last year, even the previous year! It's something else – something completely different!'

The boy had supported his words with gesticulations and the bandage on his hand had come loose again. The colonel looked at his wound then, going to a white cabinet, fetched some clean bandages and re-bound it.

'Why then did you smash your hand?' he asked. 'You knew they would discharge you for the lungs.'

'Because if I was discharged everyone would believe it was because of the hand.'

'What if instead of discharging you they sent you to prison for the hand, for deliberately avoiding conscription?'

The boy calmed down:

'In jail...' he said. 'It's fine in prison. She wouldn't have left me if I'd gone to prison for my hand... In prison, time passes like elsewhere. If I go to jail maybe I'll die before she leaves me.'

The boy had regained control of his nerves. The hard, cold Master was back.

'I am dying, Colonel,' he exclaimed. 'My sentence is already upon me. I want to die before she knows. Before her parents force her to leave me even if she doesn't want to leave me. I have no one in the world: I have never had anyone. I found the one soul there who became everything to me. I would never have married her: I know what I have, I know my sentence... It's enough for me that she doesn't leave me as long as I am alive. As long as I am alive I don't want her to know anything. Then, when I am dead, do whatever you want. I did nothing bad to her. Don't discharge me for what's going on inside me, discharge me for the hand...'

The colonel felt less and less like a colonel and the smoke from his Tuscan seemed to envelop him.

'Discharge me for the hand,' insisted the boy. 'Or let me die dressed as a soldier... You have seen how I am: you know that I still have little time. If there are landmines to clear, if there are difficult and dangerous things to do, I will always be the first to volunteer for them. Let me die as a soldier. The other lung is about to go too...'

The colonel threw away the cigar that was bothering him and cursed.

'But if I pass you for service and then you collapse... well, I'll take some ass kicking!'

'She knows nothing, I know that. And I will tell someone important what I did before I go on leave for ever.'

The colonel threw the negative and the diagnosis into the wastebasket.

'Pass,' he said.

The Doctor (1952)

'WELL, THAT'LL BE good for our calluses,' said the working folk of the village when they saw the little doctor arriving to replace the old doctor (who had left for a well-deserved rest).

To tell the truth, the new doctor looked more like a student on holiday who'd dropped in to amaze the village girls with his outlandish sports jackets, his patterned shirts and his Jean Marais[56] hairstyle. Then, three days later, when the doctor's mother joined him and moved into his apartment, attached to the clinic, people commented with evident satisfaction: 'That's fine: it seemed impossible that a little treasure like him be sent to us without his mother.'

There were many people in the village with problems to sort out in his surgery, but everyone hung back because no one wanted to be the first to fall under the hands of the new doctor. Then, inevitably, it fell to someone to resign himself to being the first, and Giacomo Macvò, known as Badile, was the one.

Almost fifty years old, Giacomo Macvò was a big man with the strength and mental agility of a caterpillar tractor, and his relationships with mankind were significantly hindered by the mistrust characteristic of a square-headed peasant. He had some sort of outburst on his face and one morning, seeing that it was spreading more and more, he jumped on his bicycle and made for the surgery.

---

[56] Screen actor, writer and, in the 1930s/40s, muse and lover of Jean Cocteau.

He found the doctor sitting with great dignity behind his desk, well combed and wearing a white cotton gown. The big man immediately got to the point:

'Doctor, this stuff has been coming out of my face for two days. Look at it, will you.'

The little doctor gave a quick and indifferent look at Giacomo Macvò's face, then replied calmly, pointing to a chair in front of the desk:

'Sit yourself down.'

He took a white folder and prepared himself to take notes:

'Name and surname?'

Giacomo Macvò, known as Badile, gave his name, surname, date and place of birth, occupation and residence. But this wasn't enough for the little doctor:

'What illnesses do you have? Try to be precise and not forget anything.'

The big man snorted:

'Doctor, I have no time to waste. I came here for the illness I have now, not for the ones I've had! Give me something for this rubbish that ruins my face.'

'To cure a disease, the cause and origin must be identified. If a tooth is decayed, the root must be healed before filling it. Filling a tooth while leaving the root diseased means making the disease worse.'

The little man brusquely reeled off all the ailments he had had during his life and still the little doctor was not satisfied because he wanted detailed information on the functioning of his liver, stomach, heart and so on. Then he asked:

'And your parents?'

Giacomo Macvò, known as Badile, widened his eyes:

'My parents?'

'Yes: what illnesses did your father and mother have?' the little man snorted:

'Doctor, forget about my parents! I'm the sick one. They're fine because they're both dead. Peace to their souls.'

'And what disease did they die from? At what age?'

Giacomo Macvò stood up:

'Look,' he said, 'are you the doctor or the police sergeant? My family's affairs concern me alone: don't worry about them and give me something to cure this outburst on my face. His tone was peremptory: the little doctor turned pale and, rising up out of his chair, he approached the big man and carefully studied his sick face.

'Have you ever had any illnesses, let's say...'

'Let's say *what?*'

The little doctor explained what diseases he was talking about and this outraged the big man:

'Hey, I say: what do you take me for?' he screamed. 'Do I perhaps have the face of a stinker? What do you think, that my house is a... Forget it, don't make me say bad things!'

The little doctor, who was pale, paled even more.

'A doctor has a duty to inform himself about everything,' he stammered. 'When you take your car to the workshop you have to say how many kilometres you have driven, if you have already had it serviced, if it consumes oil, if...'

'I don't have a car!' shouted the big man. 'I am someone who works like a beast from morning to night to get by as best I can!'

The little doctor let the big man unload himself, then he said:

'You need to focus on your liver.'

'In what sense?' the big man asked aggressively. 'You'd better believe that I don't bother anyone and I'm not liverish with anyone. As long as they leave me alone. We'll get liverish big time with the reactionary pigs in government...'

The little doctor shook his head:

'You misunderstand,' he protested. 'I simply wanted to say that that rash on your face is caused by a malfunctioning liver.'

'Let's not talk nonsense!' sneered the big man. 'I have a world-class liver! I'm capable of eating a kilo of salami and drinking eight bottles of wine as if they were peppermint candy! My liver is fine: give me something to treat my face.'

The little doctor filled out a prescription and handed it to the little man. 'Ointment,' he explained. 'A couple of times a day.'

The big man made to leave, but after taking a few steps, he stopped and returned to the doctor's desk.

'Please,' he said to the little man, 'I'll take my file.'

The little doctor looked at him astonished:

'This is for my information,' he stammered. 'Every patient must have a file.'

'I'd better hang on to it,' the man replied glumly, grabbing the folder. 'I don't like making my and my family's affairs public.'

*

The little doctor was full of good intentions, but little by little he had to renege on all his plans. So he contented himself with equipping the surgery a little better and made a long, detailed report to the Mayor, specifying everything he required. It was a very long note and Peppone couldn't even get to the halfway point of it. He immediately sent for the little doctor.

'I received your complaint,' said Peppone as soon as the little doctor appeared in front of him. 'You are new to the area and therefore do not know that everything regarding the surgery and healthcare was sorted out over a year ago with the purchase of a modern and fast ambulance service.'

The little doctor was amazed:

'The ambulance is an excellent thing,' he stammered, 'but the equipment of the surgery is a different matter altogether.'

'Not at all,' explained Peppone. 'The ambulance replaces all the equipment that is missing in the surgery because, when someone needs special care, they are taken by ambulance to the hospital in the city.'

'Right,' said the little doctor. 'But in some cases it is necessary to act immediately and the patient is not always in a condition that permits him to be taken to hospital.'

'Don't worry, doctor, we're fine on that one too. In cases of extreme emergency, the parish priest intervenes and prays to the Lord on behalf of the non-transportable patient.'

The little doctor spread his arms:

'This being the case, all I have to do is reach an agreement with the parish priest and the undertaker,' he stated.

The next day Peppone had the little doctor called in again and, this time, the entire general staff was with Peppone.

'Explain your concept to the gentlemen of the Council and illustrate your statement with examples,' said Peppone.

The little doctor explained his concept very clearly and, in the end, the gang concluded that theoretically everything was okay. But in practical terms many of the problems described would never have occurred to justify the large expense involved in updating the surgery.

The little doctor remained thoughtful for a moment, then said:

'It depends on the value you place on a human life. If you calculate the life of a human being, for example, at 1,000 lire, it is unlikely that the thousand cases necessary to justify the million lire that the updating of the surgery would cost will occur.

This might have floored the councillors with confusion had not Peppone immediately found an honourable way out:

'Human life is priceless!' he exclaimed. 'The trouble is that the municipality has no money. It's easy to write prescriptions when other people pay for the medicines. Try putting yourself in my position.'

'Gladly,' replied the little doctor. 'As long as you, in the meantime, look after the sick on my behalf!'

Peppone pounded a big fist on the table:

'Let's not throw this into the political arena!' he shouted. 'You were called here to be a doctor not an *agent provocateur*.'

The little doctor turned pale and left. But as fate would have it the matter didn't end there. Two days later, Peppone came to his doctor's office with a molar that was driving him crazy:

'Doctor,' he bellowed, 'pull out this damned tooth!'

The little doctor examined the tooth carefully, then shook his head:

'No,' he replied calmly, 'I won't take it out. You need to go to a dentist.'

'What kind of doctor are you?' Peppone shouted. 'Even the old doctor pulled teeth. Is it possible that you can't pull a tooth?'

'I am capable of it, yes,' explained the little doctor. 'But this isn't a tooth that needs to be pulled, it's a tooth that can be filled and saved.'

'The tooth is mine!' Peppone roared.

'But the professional conscience is mine,' replied the little doctor.

Peppone, enraged, grabbed the little doctor by his shirt:

'Either you'll pull out my tooth or I'll ring your neck!'

The little doctor turned pale but didn't answer.

Peppone loosened his grip:

'All right, young man,' he said, walking away. 'But you will pay for this – your funny business.'

*

Peppone reappeared in the surgery fifteen days later. He approached the little doctor and opened his mouth wide, pointing to a molar with his finger:

'It seems like a job very well done,' said the little doctor after having carefully studied the filled tooth.

Peppone closed his jaws and looked around. Then he launched an attack upon the little doctor:

'A million! Get on with you! Where do we find a million? Look again and pare down your claim as far as possible!'

The little doctor took a piece of paper out of the drawer and handed it to Peppone.

'One million one hundred thousand lire!' Peppone shouted. 'One hundred thousand lire more!'

'I had forgotten some essential things,' the little doctor explained calmly.

Peppone left shouting and there was discussion in the town hall for an entire night. However, in the end, the cost of one million and eighty thousand lire was allocated for surgery equipment with an adjoining room for very urgent operations and a recovery and observation room.

'Not because we have faith in you,' Peppone explained to the little doctor, 'but because we want to have a clear conscience. Tomorrow you won't be able to say: "If the municipality had done what I wanted, so-and-so wouldn't have died." See? Your manoeuvre failed!'

'I'm sorry I didn't pull out your tooth,' said the little doctor who, for once, instead of turning pale, blushed.

*

One day Cesarino Delpiò arrived to say that his mother was ill and the little doctor started his very battered Topolino and rushed off to see her.

Cesarino Delpiò was fourteen years old and lived with his mother in old Delpiò's house. Cesarino's father, the youngest of old Delpiò's three sons, had died six or seven years earlier, and the old man, together with his daughter-in-law, his nephew and two family members, ran the Piane farm, which he had rented for years and a day.

The little doctor didn't even know who the Delpiòs were, but as soon as he entered the farmyard he immediately realised that the old man was master of more than a shack.

'Doctor,' the old man said, 'if there's something serious, tell me.'

So, the little doctor visited this woman who, despite having such a big boy, was still very young. He told her to stay calm and take this and that medicine, then he went out and joined old Delpiò who was waiting for him in the kitchen. He explained to him exactly what her problem was about and concluded:

'The thing is very serious: either you have her operated on immediately or, at the first attack, she'll not recover.'

The old man shook his head:

'Operate!' he muttered. 'It's easy to take a knife to someone! We need to think about it carefully first.'

'There's little to think about,' replied the little doctor. 'Show her to whoever you want and they will all tell you what I am telling you. Naturally, since this is an extraordinarily difficult operation, to have guaranteed success all you have to do is have it carried out by the greatest specialist in the field. He is a man of conscience and, if he takes a knife to her, it is because he is sure of succeeding. I know him well because he was my professor.'

The old man shook his head and sighed:

'Who knows what it will cost!'

The little doctor looked around: he looked at that miserable house, at that thin, worn-out old man, dressed like a beggar, he thought of the woman lying in a bed that looked like a dog's kennel.

'If I recommend her, he will charge you as little as possible,' he said. 'He is a man of heart and he only gets paid well by the rich.'

The old man spread his arms:

'God have mercy on us. Since my youngest son died, my family and the rest eat up all that I earn.'

The little doctor appeared moved and left, promising to return the next day. He went straight to the People's Palace and went in asking for the Mayor.

Peppone welcomed him with great haughtiness and a similar amount of diffidence. The little doctor was not rattled:

'I believe it is my duty to point out a particularly pitiful case to you. A poor widowed woman with a child is sick and, if she doesn't have an operation, she will surely die. I can look after the professor who will operate on her, but for her stay in the surgery, some money will be needed. Can you tell me what can be done to save this poor girl's life?'

'And who would this woman be?' Peppone enquired.

The little doctor took his notebook out of his pocket:

'Maria Teresa Fraschini, widow Delpiò,' he replied.

Peppone looked at him for a long time without speaking, then went out and returned shortly thereafter with a register.

'Here,' he said, 'is how it stands. The poor woman is the daughter-in-law of old Carlo Delpiò, who runs the Piane farm as a tenant, but who is also the owner of the Casarossa farm of some forty biolche, of the Pioppa farm of fifty biolche, of the Giarile farm of seventy biolche, of the Cantone farm of thirty biolche. Delpiò, in addition to this little bit of stuff, has lots and lots of money to be able to operate not only his daughter-in-law but all the daughters-in-law in the province. So don't make a fool of me.'

The little doctor left and was not of a mind to go back to old Delpiò again: then he thought that the sick person might have been his own daughter-in-law and did return: he visited the woman and repeated to the old man what he had said the day before.

'Either you have her operated on immediately or, at the first attack, she dies. All you have to do is load her into a car and take her to the surgery. The cost won't be excessive: you'll get by with 200,000 lire.'

The old man opened his eyes wide:

'Two hundred thousand lire? This is crazy! Let's not even talk about it.'

'As you wish,' replied the little doctor harshly, 'the responsibility for everything that may happen is yours.'

'You are the doctor, not me,' objected the old man.

'I go as far as I can go. If I had the chance to do an operation like that I wouldn't be a doctor around here, I would be one of the top surgeons in Europe. I decline all responsibility: I'm telling you now and I will write the same to you today by registered letter.'

The little doctor went away and did what he had promised to do, keeping a copy of the letter; and he acted like this mostly to intimidate the old man. But the old man didn't show up. A month later the boy came again to say that his mother had had a downturn. The little doctor rushed in and managed to prevent the catastrophe with a few injections.

Coming out of the woman's room he attacked the old man rudely:

'What happened today is already one miracle,' he said. 'Take her to the surgery immediately. There's not a moment to waste if you don't want her to die.'

'Two hundred thousand lire!' replied the old man. 'Two hundred thousand lire! And where do I find it? Don't even think about it. In any case she's young and strong: we'll all die before she dies!'

The little doctor left, but when he returned to the surgery he couldn't sit still. He continually thought about that poor thing and that damnable old man. Something had to be done at all costs. He went to see Don Camillo, explained everything to him and concluded:

'Reverend, try talking to the old man. You must try to convince him. That woman's life is at stake. Do this and at one and the same time you save the black soul of that cursed man and the life of an innocent woman.

Don Camillo got on his bicycle and ran to find old Delpiò. He stopped him in the middle of the fields and immediately got to the point:

'There's no more time to waste: you have to take your daughter-in-law to the surgery. The reputation of the surgeon who will operate on her is a guarantee that everything will go well.'

The old man looked at him with hatred in his eyes, but contained himself. He was also smart enough not to even mention the money issue.

'Reverend,' he replied, 'if it were my flesh I could dispose of it, but it is her flesh, my daughter-in-law's. She needs to decide whether to be operated on or not. I can't take responsibility for her: she's not a minor! It's all up to her.'

Don Camillo could see no objection to that.

'If what you say is correct, try to convince your daughter-in-law to have the operation.'

'I'll try, Reverend. With all my heart, I'll try.'

Don Camillo returned to the village and told the little doctor what had occurred.

The little doctor was delighted: 'Maybe he saw the evil of his ways and wanted to save face. I'll go and listen to what he has to say tomorrow.'

And the next day, around ten in the morning, the little doctor stopped his car in the Piane farmyard. Old Delpiò was there waiting for him:

'Doctor,' he said, 'I explained to you how things stand. Now see it for yourself.'

The little doctor climbed the ladder and entered the woman's bedroom. 'How are you doing?'

'Better,' the woman replied.

'Did your father-in-law tell you that you need to be admitted to the surgery for a few days?'

'Yes,' the woman replied.

'Then cheer up because everything will be fine and you will be fine. You won't feel any pain. You'll feel like you're reborn.'

The woman looked at him with wide eyes, then she replied:

'No.'

'No what?'

'I don't want to have surgery. I don't want to go to the surgery. I'm fine here.'

The little doctor sat at the poor woman's bedside: he gently explained to her the extreme seriousness of her condition and concluded:

'Please, think about it: if you don't go, you will die. There is no escaping it!'

'I'm comfortable here,' the woman replied. 'I don't want to have surgery.'

The little doctor insisted, begged and begged again. The woman turned her head and looked at him with two eyes full of tears:

'Doctor, leave me alone,' she said frantically in a low voice. 'Let me die in peace! I have to die: the old man said that if I go to the surgery he will kick my son out of the house and won't leave him a penny of inheritance. You don't know the old man: I do. Doctor, go away and don't tell anyone. I am instructing you and you must obey me!'

The little doctor came down and the old man was on the threshing floor.

'So?' the old man asked.

'I can do no more, she doesn't want it,' replied the little doctor through gritted teeth.

'This is a serious problem,' sighed the old man. 'We can't operate on her against her wishes.'

The little doctor headed towards the Topolino and, as he was about to get in, the old man's grandson arrived.

'Leave my grandfather alone,' the boy told him in a threatening voice. 'If you want to make money on my mother's flesh, you're barking up the wrong tree.'

The little doctor looked at him in amazement.

'Yes,' continued the boy. 'You get in a huddle with the city doctors. You send us people to do the cut and then you take half.'

'Who told you that?' asked the little doctor.

'I know,' replied the boy. 'If it weren't so, you would do the operation yourself.'

'It's not a common case, we need a specialist,' said the little doctor.

'You won't cut my mother up,' the boy stated. 'If you take advantage of my grandfather because he is old, I'll make life very difficult for you!'

The little doctor left and his heart was full of anguish. He felt the need to speak, to tell someone this horrible story.

But he heard the woman's voice again: 'Don't speak to anyone. I order you!'

*

Another week passed. Then, one night, the boy came again and woke him up.

The woman was sick. Worse than the other times, so much so that the poor thing had also sent for the priest. Don Camillo arrived shortly afterwards and found her asleep.

'I gave her some injections,' explained the little doctor. 'I fear she won't wake up this time.'

The boy was there too and stepped forward:

'We must save her,' he said.

'Too late,' replied the little doctor. 'Even if you wanted to, you could never take her all the way to Milan. She would die along the way.'

The old man entered.

'Poor woman, she's done suffering!' he sighed. And his voice sounded so false, so horribly false that the doctor and Don Camillo turned towards the old man at the same time and both felt a mad desire to break his bones.

The woman sighed very slightly. She was still clinging to life, desperately, but soon all her strength would abandon her.

'You cannot let her die like this without trying something,' stammered Don Camillo.

Then the little doctor turned pale and looked at Don Camillo with wild eyes.

'God be with you,' said Don Camillo, touching his sweat-soaked forehead.

'When the ambulance comes, take the woman to the surgery immediately!' the little doctor shouted madly, rushing down the stairs.

The battered Topolino flew along the dark streets. The little doctor, having alerted the ambulance workers, had entered the surgery and got on the phone.

'Very urgent, *signorina*, it's a matter of life or death: quickly, in the name of God!'

When the ambulance nurses entered the surgery with the woman lying as if dead on the stretcher, Milan came through on the telephone.

'Put her there and everyone away!' the little doctor shouted, covering the telephone mouthpiece for a moment.

The woman was laid down on the table and everyone left while the little doctor said in a frantic voice:

'Professor, professor, it's me. Mario Parelli! Yes, Mario Parelli!'.

The little doctor explained the woman's situation and concluded:

'Professor, if I don't operate on her immediately she will die, assuming she is even now still alive. I assisted you during three of your operations, professor, do you remember? I remember everything and, in recent days, I have been studying your book. If you can help me and assist me here on the telephone, I will operate on that woman.'

The little doctor had by now regained his calm and resolute voice.

'Parelli,' replied the distant professor's voice, 'this is madness. It's impossible!'

'God is with me,' stated the little doctor.

'I'll be with you too then,' replied the professor's voice. Meanwhile the doctor's mother had come down to the surgery.

'You hold the receiver for me!' ordered the little doctor, putting on his scrubs and putting on his gloves.

And then one of those extraordinary tales of modern remote surgery – the difficult operation carried out inside the cabin of a ship on the high seas under the control of the famous surgeon a thousand miles away, connected to the scalpel only by the invisible thread of radio – commenced.

The little doctor remembered everything from his own experience perfectly and described the various operations he was about to perform.

'Okay,' the remote voice replied.

Then he described the diseased part when it had been discovered by his scalpel, and the distant professor closed his eyes and saw that painful flesh and followed the tip of the scalpel with extreme precision, as if he were there, looking over the little doctor's shoulders...

Meanwhile, Don Camillo, kneeling on the hard cobblestones in front of the surgery building, continued to speak to the black sky of the night and every now and then repeated:

'Jesus, assist him! I have pledged your word!'

And the archpriest suffered as if the scalpel were digging not into the woman's anaesthetised flesh, but into his own conscious flesh.

Then, suddenly, the door of the building opened and the little doctor appeared.

'God was with me,' said the little doctor in a distant voice. 'Now I have to help that poor thing as best I can.'

*

The woman remained in recovery and observation for two days, then the ambulance was able to take her back home.

A Milan newspaper published a half-page on the extraordinary story of the highly challenging operation performed by the young doctor, conducted with the telephone assistance of the great surgeon: Peppone was as proud as if he had done the operation himself.

It took the little doctor a week to restore order completely to the inside of his brain. Then, one fine morning, he went to visit the woman to see if everything was going well.

'Everything is fine,' he said as he went out to old Delpiò and the boy, who were chatting in the farmyard with Don Camillo, who had just arrived.

'I am pleased,' replied old Delpiò. 'Now we will have to settle the accounts, doctor. How much do I owe you?'

The little doctor smiled:

'Simply the reimbursement of all units of the telephone call with Milan: 2,835 lire.'

The old man took his greasy wallet out of his waistcoat and counted 2,835 lire.

'Damn phone calls are expensive,' he commented, handing the money over.

The boy chuckled and muttered:

'Less than if the famous specialist had been involved, grandfather! Now they will have to settle for 1,400 lire each, instead of 100,000!'

The little doctor heard and threw himself at the boy: but, in reality, he didn't move an inch because Don Camillo's big hand had hooked him by the shoulder.

'Good morning everyone,' Don Camillo said, smiling, pulling the little doctor after him.

They got into the Topolino and Don Camillo filled every crevice of the tiny vehicle.

'Yesterday I received a letter from Milan,' said the little doctor suddenly. 'They want me at my professor's surgery. I'm leaving this dreadful place.'

'After all the expense you made the municipality run to? You have a moral commitment…' replied Don Camillo. 'And the city, it's something else. God is in the city like everywhere, but there is less confusion here, less of the hurly-burly, and one soon realises that God hears one's voice better in la Bassa.'

The little doctor was silent for a few minutes, then exclaimed ferociously:

'I tell you, the first time I get the Mayor in my clutches, I'll not pass up the opportunity to pull a tooth or two!'

'That is a source of satisfaction which would never be available to you in Milan,' said Don Camillo. 'And satisfaction is never so available as to be bought.'

'All too true,' muttered the little doctor.

Christ in the Dresser (1958)

D ON CAMILLO, WHO was surveying the square from the dining room window, went out to collar the doctor as soon as he spotted him:

'What news?'

'Bad,' replied the doctor. 'It's getting worse by the hour. I don't even know which saint to turn to anymore and I have recommended a referral.'

'Has it come to that?' Don Camillo said with surprise.

'It has,' confirmed the doctor.

'Well then, I'm going to him!' exclaimed Don Camillo. 'We go back a long way: he won't send me away.'

The doctor shook his head:

'Reverend, what he says counts for little, his entire staff is gathered in the kitchen and they won't even let you in.'

Don Camillo left the doctor and hurried into church to let off steam with Christ above the High Altar.

'Lord,' he said. 'Peppone is ill and I need to speak to him *at once*. Tonight could be his last.'

'If he has called you, Don Camillo, make haste,' replied Christ. 'Let no-one knock in vain at the door of the Lord.'

'He didn't call me,' explained Don Camillo humbly, 'but I have to talk to him anyway, whatever anyone does to stop me. Lord, in order to save a soul one can surely bruise a few heads...'

'No, Don Camillo,' Christ established. 'There is no such thing as evil for good purposes; evil is the antithesis of good – always.'

Don Camillo bowed his head:

'Forgive me, Lord,' he whispered. 'I will go to Peppone's house and, if his men forbid me to see him, I will throw myself on my knees and beg them to let me go up to his room.'

'What if they mock your prayers and your humility?'

Don Camillo crossed himself and left without reply.

It was half past eight in the evening. At nine o'clock Don Camillo was still angrily walking up and down the presbytery corridor:

'Okay,' he concluded, coming finally to a halt. 'I admit I'm dead wrong, but I'm going anyway.'

He didn't have time to remove his cloak from the coat rack in the hallway before there was a knock on the front door. It was Peppone's youngest boy. He entered, scared and panting:

'Father wants to see you,' he explained. 'He told me in my ear. Nobody else knows. Not even mother, not even Smilzo, Bigio and the others. Now they're all in the kitchen and think I've gone to bed. You must come in half an hour, Reverend. I will leave the garden door open and wait for you. Let no one see you.'

Don Camillo clenched his fists:

'I am a priest, not a thief in the night!' he exclaimed indignantly. 'And I intend to behave like a priest!'

The boy looked at him with fear in his eyes:

'Father is very ill,' he stammered.

Don Camillo had no answer to that and the boy left.

Twenty minutes later Don Camillo was preparing to take his cloak down from the coat rack again when he heard a knock at the front door and, this time, it was a woman wrapped up in a large black shawl.

'My husband is ill,' explained the woman, who was very agitated. 'No one knows that I have come here: I acted on my own initiative. Politics is one thing, conscience another and I don't want to have anything on my conscience. I want you to see my husband and to speak with him.'

'Does your husband agree to this?' Don Camillo enquired.

'No. I told you he knows nothing. This is my idea.'

'What if your husband won't see me?'

'You will return home and it will end there. Of course, I will pay for your trouble.'

'It's not a question of payment or inconvenience,' Don Camillo said. 'You have to be aware that if Peppone starts ranting and raving, a damned ruckus will break out.'

'He won't,' the woman reassured him. 'He needs all his strength just to take a breath.'

'He'll be fine then,' muttered Don Camillo, taking up his cloak. 'Let's go.'

'Not now!' the woman exclaimed. 'All the team members are in the kitchen and they must not see you at any cost. I'll go back home and keep them at bay: in about twenty minutes, come to the house on the garden side and go straight up. You know the way.'

Peppone's wife, wrapped in her shawl, left the presbytery post-haste and Don Camillo began to wait calmly for time to pass.

When, for the third time, he stretched out his hand towards the cloak in the hall, for the third time he withdrew his hand without the cloak: there was a knock at the door and, on opening it, Don Camillo found himself in the presence of Smilzo.

'The boss is in trouble,' said Peppone's lieutenant, getting directly to the point. 'We have reason to believe that the clergy has been informed. Well, I also come to you on behalf of the others to point out that it wouldn't be bad if you, on your own initiative, went to have a look at him. Let's clarify the situation: we know the boss and we know that he is tough and he would never have called a priest; we know that a priest is of no use, much less so at the bedside of a sick person; however, given that the boss risks losing his life, *transeat*. One only dies once and, when one is about to drown, one may cling even to a chicken coop stick. I don't know if I have explained myself...'

'You explain yourself so well that you deserve to be kicked into kingdom come. Lucky for you there's no time to waste. Let's be off.'

'Not right away,' Smilzo warned. 'Peppone's wife is still up and we don't want her to see you. We will keep her at bay in the kitchen and in ten minutes, on your own initiative, you will arrive at the boss's house: enter through the garden, go up and make yourself known. Make sure you hurry and try not to make political capital out of this.'

*

When Don Camillo ventured forth, as instructed, Peppone's boy was waiting, hidden in the garden.

'I thought you weren't coming,' he said to Don Camillo in a faint voice. 'Everyone is talking in the kitchen now, even my Mum. You go up and I'll stand guard on the stairs. If anyone comes, I'll knock three times on the door of father's room and you will hide in the closet.'

To get to the staircase, Don Camillo had to pass in front of the glass in the door of the kitchen. He saw them all gathered around the table. They spoke loudly and whenever Peppone's wife saw an empty glass, she would fill it with red wine.

'Walk on tiptoe otherwise someone will hear you,' the terrified boy whispered.

Once they reached the first floor landing the boy pointed to the door into Peppone's room and retreated to his station on the stairs.

Don Camillo hesitated for a few moments in front of the closed door, then crossed himself and turned the handle. The room was very hot, half-lit, and the smell of medicines hung in the air.

Don Camillo gasped: he didn't imagine finding himself in the presence of a Peppone so profoundly different from usual. A long beard made him look gaunt and accentuated his ill-health, while his heavy eyelids made his eyes look hopelessly dull.

Don Camillo sat down next to his bed and looked at the bottles that cluttered the bedside table, then shook his head:

'Comrade,' he said to Peppone, 'you are seriously ill. The doctor didn't tell you, but he told me. However, your biggest problem is that you are afraid to die.'

Peppone grimaced.

'I'm not afraid of anything or anyone,' he replied, speaking with difficulty.

'You're hopelessly afraid of dying,' insisted Don Camillo.

'I'm sorry I'm dying because I can't see your lot taking a dive in the elections,' explained Peppone.

'If that's all there is to it, you may yet die peacefully. But even if you live for 200 years, you'll never have the satisfaction you crave.'

'I am sorry for the children, too,' whispered Peppone. 'They're still so small.'

'Why worry about them? The Party will raise them for you.'

Peppone shook his head:

'For the children, the most broken-down father is better than the most efficient substitute,' he stated with a sigh.

'If you care about the future of your children, why let fear overcome you?'

Peppone gave a start and opened his eyes:

'*I'm not afraid!*' he exclaimed, for an instant rediscovering his characteristic aggression. 'If I die it's because I cannot resist it!'

Don Camillo looked around him, then opened his arms wide:

'Don't be angry: I believe you. Alone, you cannot resist death. You should have known that you needed someone to help you and not sent the only one who could help you away.'

Peppone looked at his friend – the enemy – deeply concerned and then Don Camillo pointed to a nail stuck in the wall above the headboard of Peppone's bed:

'There was something hung here once,' he said in a wooden voice. 'Who took it down?'

'I had it removed,' explained Peppone, his eyelids lowered. 'It remained there until after my wife and I were the only ones who entered this room. Then, with the illness, there was a constant coming and going of people here... I had it removed when the Secretary of the Provincial Federation came to visit me...'

'Nothing less!'

'Father, understand me,' Peppone protested. 'I didn't do it as an insult, but for the people. I couldn't let my superiors and comrades see me with *him* above the bed... It's a question of ... dignity...'

'You scoundrel!' shouted Don Camillo. 'Do you, even now, have the strength to blaspheme? Where is he now?'

'In the top drawer of the dresser,' replied Peppone.

Don Camillo got up and went to open the top drawer of the dresser. Wrapped in tissue paper, he found Christ and hung the crucifix back up on the nail above Peppone's headboard:

'Is there anything else?' he asked gruffly.

'You know how it is, Reverend: we are men and I too, in life, have done my stupid things. But all light stuff.'

'Except, of course, for the stupidity of actively joining a party of excommunicated scoundrels.'

'It wasn't the party of the excommunicated when I joined it,' protested Peppone. 'There would normally be some discussion here... I hope you won't take advantage of my condition to bring politics into it.'

'I hear you. In short, you would say that, apart from being a soldier in the Communist Party, you haven't done any other major dirty things.'

'Yes, Reverend. Unless it was a majore dirty thing to hide Christ in the dresser.'

'Which of course it was!'

'I atone for it now. I thought about it day and night, but I couldn't get up and I didn't have the courage to tell someone to put it back.'

'I absolve you. As penance you will recite 5,000 Our Fathers, Hail Marys and Glorias.'

Peppone smiled sadly:

'If only I had time!'

'Time will be found!' Don Camillo asserted.

Don Camillo stood up and, turning his gaze to the Crucified Christ, prayed:

'Into thy hands oh Lord I commend his spirit, although I don't know what you can make out of this rag of a man.'

'He will make me beautiful!'

Don Camillo simply looked at Peppone with contempt and, getting up, left without looking back.

The staircase was dark and after descending the first flight, Don Camillo tripped over something. It was Peppone's boy, who was sleeping like a log on the bare wooden floorboards.

Don Camillo took off his cloak and wrapped it around the child.

'Sleep peacefully, little bundle of rags,' he muttered.

Passing in front of the kitchen he saw that everyone was sleeping, abandoned at the table.

'Sleep, sleep, people,' said the priest. 'There is someone who was hiding in the top drawer of the dresser and he has now returned to watch over your chieftain.'

It was a damnable night in the craziest April in history, and outside it was snowing. Without his cloak, Don Camillo should have felt bitterly cold: but no.

For Don Camillo it was a very sweet, warm spring night, alive to every possibility of a new day.

The Sins of Our Fathers (1960)

SIGNORA CLEMENTINA WAS a woman with a good head on her shoulders. With her, you could discuss anything … except Carletto.

When Carletto, at the age of ten, got into big trouble, Boraschi, a rude man, painted two slaps on his face. However, they were the first and last so placed because la signora Clementina fainted, remained in bed for two days with a fever and, for an entire month, acted as if she were deaf and dumb, simply looking at her husband with such hatred it gave rise to goose bumps.

Carletto was a son of fear, an only child who arrived at the last minute after twelve years of marriage, just as Boraschi was about to go to war, and Clementina – left to manage things on her own – had clung desperately to the child, willing to defend him to the last shot.

The Boraschis lived at Ghiare, a large out-of-the-way estate, and here, once Carletto had finished primary school, the problem of continuing his studies arose. Boraschi himself proposed putting the boy in the best boarding school in town, but Clementina wouldn't hear of it.

'He will do what so many other children do,' she decided. 'We will send him by car to the station every morning and collect him when he returns. As long as he's a child I want to keep an eye on him always.'

However, when Carletto entered high school, Clementina had to give in and agree that the boy could stay in town to study. The choice of where he would board was not a simple matter because Clementina wanted to take care of it personally and that required time and effort.

It was agreed that the boy would spend Sundays at Ghiare and, for the entire first year, every Saturday evening Carletto returned to town punctually. In the second year, given the increased difficulty of his studies, the boy had to spend most of his Sundays in town, then, once the third year had begun, he made it clear that he could only dedicate the Christmas and Easter holidays to Ghiare.

It was precisely after the first months of the third year of high school that one evening Boraschi took stock of the situation:

'Once the boy has obtained his high school diploma,' he said, 'he will have to start thinking about joining the family business.'

Signora Clementina raised her head sharply:

'Once he has obtained his high school diploma,' she made very clear, 'the boy will simply be thinking about matriculating at university.'

'I have turned fifty-six,' Boraschi responded, 'and I am tired of struggling with spiralling costs, sharecroppers and troubles of all kinds. Having him on board would help me a lot.'

'Don't I help you enough already?' asked Clementina. 'And then, who's stopping you from hiring a manager?'

Boraschi jumped:

'A manager!' he shouted. 'My father left this business to me to manage, and I have kept the estate, enlarged it and improved it to pass it on to my son! Now he is eighteen years old: if we wait any longer, city habits will inure him to life on the land and all that it means.'

'Carletto must get his degree!' Clementina insisted categorically.

'Here we have no need for a lawyer or a professor of fine literature, but for a farmer and the land is itself a farmer's university.'

'Carletto will get his degree,' Clementina insisted stubbornly. 'If you don't pay for his studies, I will pay for them. At the cost of selling all the farms in my dowry. I will never allow your agrarian selfishness to prevent my son from following *his* inclination and following *his* path. It is up to him to decide what he wants to do. However, it's still early to talk about it: we'll talk about it again when he finishes high school.'

Boraschi did not insist, because Clementina's voice had become harsh and her eyes menacing.

*

Carletto arrived home a week later: he had come to collect some books he needed, and intended to leave the following morning.

Coming in from the fields for dinner, his father found him sitting in front of him and responded to his greeting with a disgruntled muttering.

'Are you sorry that your son is back?' Clementina asked aggressively.

'He has nothing to do with it,' replied Boraschi. 'Others are making me liverish.'

'What's happened?' urged Clementina.

'Follini is leaving,' muttered Boraschi. 'After thirty-five years he is leaving us to go and do I don't know what job in the city.'

'That's logical enough,' observed Carletto.

The father raised his head and looked at him in amazement: 'What's logical?'

'It is logical that, after having been a servant for thirty-five years, one tries to live as a free man,' Carletto replied calmly enough.

'He wasn't a servant with us,' his father clarified. 'He was a sharecropper on the best farm and treated with due respect. I renovated his house, gave him machines and tools, set up his stable with carefully selected animals...'

Carletto shrugged:

'We should have thought about this happening earlier. A long time ago. It is pointless to lighten the load of the cart when the horse is exhausted. The landowners have pushed their tenants too hard.'

The young man spoke slowly, in a gentle manner, without gesticulating, and Boraschi felt intimidated.

'I,' he stammered, 'I am not a landowner. I am a farmer.'

'Of course,' Carletto admitted, 'many landowners are farmers: unfortunately, in their relationships with their workers they don't think like true agrarians. When they sponsored fascism, for example. In 1922, Mussolini's action squads wore the farmers' black shirt, but used the landowners' coercion methods. You know what I mean.'[57]

'In 1922,' Carletto's father replied resentfully, 'I was eighteen years old, as you are now, and, together with my father, I defended our land and our work. The Boraschis acquired their land piece by piece by their own toil and by using their brains. My father's father was a small tenant farmer, but he knew how to make the value of land double that of others. In 1922 the Reds did not want the workers to feed or milk the cows during the strikes.[58] Should we have let the animals die in the stables? It was necessary

---

[57] Agrarian ideas were supposed to cultivate moral character and to develop a full and responsible person. Carletto is insinuating that in fact Italian landowners, particularly in la Bassa, where the class struggle was so intense after the First War, sponsored fascism and Mussolini's rise to power in 1922 in order to keep the workers down.

[58] As in 'Men and Beasts' in *The Little World of Don Camillo* (Pilot, 2013).

to recruit scabs and then defend them from the strikers' reprisals. The Reds were besieging our farmyards: should we have let them in to destroy everything?'

Carletto lit a cigarette with studied deliberation:

'The situation,' he explained, 'although it presents itself in a diametrically opposite way, is, essentially, the same today. Back then the serfs wanted to occupy the threshing floors, today they want to abandon them. Then they were looking to defend their rights inside the farms, now they are looking to their rights beyond the fields. Then the landowners paid the price for what they hadn't done for the workers before 1922, today they must pay for the good things they didn't do after 1922. And, of course, now they must also pay for the violent oppression of the workers by the fascists they sponsored from 1922.'

Boraschi looked at his son full of amazement. And that was how Don Camillo found him when he arrived for the usual evening game of cards. Still seeing the table set for dinner, the priest was embarrassed:

'I am too early,' he apologised.

'No, you are too late,' replied Boraschi, recovering his composure. 'If you had arrived a few moments earlier, you might have heard a son prosecuting his father.'

'I didn't put anyone on trial,' Carletto clarified icily. 'I limited myself to making a logical analysis of a phenomenon. You were surprised that Follini wants to abandon his job on the farm and I tried to spell out the reasons why he does. I didn't invent the history of Italy, and fascism is part of the history of Italy, so much so that it is studied in schools.'

'Isn't it a little too early?' Don Camillo enquired cautiously. 'Wouldn't a little more distance in time enable young people a truly objective picture of events?'

'It's never too early to focus on the truth,' Carletto asserted. 'It would be, among other things, stupid and dishonest to keep historical truth hidden from children so as not to offend the susceptibilities of their fathers. Indeed, it should be every honest father who says: "My son, I made such and such a mistake and I want to explain it to you well so as to avoid you falling into the same mire as I did."'

Don Camillo turned towards Boraschi:

'The boy is right,' he stated flatly. 'Frankly acknowledging one's mistakes is the healthiest of principles.'

'Okay,' admitted Boraschi. 'The trouble is that I don't know what mistakes this farmer has ever made in the political field. I have always been a farmer and I have never gone out to upset anyone: I defended myself when they threatened me, I went to war when they called me up, I only demanded from others what I was entitled to and I gave others all that was their due. I have never held political office, I have never dealt in slavery, I have always behaved as a good Christian, a good citizen and a good family man. I have no great merit, but I don't think I have any great faults either.'

Carletto shook his head: 'Reduced like this, the history of fascism is as innocent as a toffee. What of the twenty years of tyranny? And the imprisonment of opponents of the regime? What of racial persecution? What about imperialist colonialism? And the Nazi war that shocked the world? And the civil war? Suffering, violence, deaths, blood, ruins, destruction... Who should we blame? Do we heap blame on a hypothetical devil or a hypothetical destiny?'

Don Camillo spread his arms:

'Let us consider a hypothetical humanity that has lost any sense of Christian charity,' he suggested.

'Too simple and convenient,' Carletto retorted. 'Those responsible for the evils of humanity are actual men actually guilty of having imposed, with violence, certain ideas for their personal gain. We need to identify those men and make them face their responsibilities and atone, before we can turn the corner.'

'Right,' Don Camillo admitted politely. 'But, in my opinion, knowing your father's life pretty well myself, it doesn't seem to me that he can be blamed for imperialism, colonialism, racial persecution, the Nazi war and so on.'

'Reverend,' replied Carletto 'you teach that Christian morality does not allow that evil can effect good. There is no such thing as evil for good purposes; the end can never justify the means. What is evil remains evil, what is good remains good, while evil can never arise from good, good can never arise from evil. Cause and effect are in that sense one. Evil is on one shore, good on the opposite. Whoever walks on the shore of evil walks on the path of the Devil. On one side we fight for a just cause, on the other for an unjust cause. To be entitled to God's forgiveness, those who fought the unjust war must recognise it and repent. Even if a man did so in good faith. And in war both the General and the toy soldier bear responsibility, both the pilot who drops the atomic bomb on a city and the clerk at the Depot. This is what children ask of their fathers: the honest recognition of having fought for an unjust war.'

'The unjust war would be the one lost?' Don Camillo enquired cautiously.

Carletto smiled: 'This is what the technicians call "clerico-fascist collusion",' he said.

The only advantage that Don Camillo had gained from fascism was represented by the glass of castor oil that Camoni had made him drink in 1922[59]: he felt his hands itch for action, but Clementina was there and admiring her Carletto in ecstasy, ready to tear apart anyone who dared to touch a hair of his head.

He therefore stood up and said:

'It's getting late for cards. And then, tomorrow morning, I have a lot of things to take care of...'

'Tomorrow morning I'll have a lot to do too, if the workers vote to strike,' muttered Boraschi.

At that moment the leader of the men came in to announce that the workers had decided to go on an all-out strike starting at midnight and, since the topic didn't interest him, Carletto withdrew to choose his books to take to the city.

'Tomorrow morning I would like to leave on the first train,' he said to his mother.

'I'll wake you,' Clementina reassured him.

*

At four o'clock it was old Filomena who woke him and told him that Signora Clementina was waiting for him in the yard with something important to say. Carletto, having downed a bowl

---

[59] Reference is made to the Fascist signature practice of forcing political enemies to drink castor oil. See 'The American Indian', *Don Camillo and Peppone* (Pilot, 2016).

of coffee, went out and found his mother in the cowshed with a dirty handkerchief on her head and boots on her feet. While Boraschi and two old men were setting up the milking machine, Clementina, helped by the women of the house, was filling the mangers with hay.

When she saw Carletto, she took a pitchfork from a corner of the shed and placed it in his hands, telling him:

'You take care to clear the piles of manure. The wheelbarrow is there.'

'Mom,' protested Carletto, 'the train leaves in half an hour.'

'You're not leaving,' his mother replied brusquely.

'But today I have a test in class,' exclaimed Carletto.

'Your homework here is more urgent,' the mother stated flatly.

'It's an important module for the quarterly average. I want to go to the State exams with good grades.'

'You take your State exam here!' Clementina shouted impatiently. 'Your studies are over: you've already learned too much.'

Carletto couldn't believe that his mother was serious, but Clementina cleared his mind. Seeing him so perplexed, she grabbed him by the arm and pushed him between the shafts of the muck barrow. Then, to get him going, she gave him a slap in the face that sounded like a gunshot.

Straight out of a pedagogy manual, it was one of those precise, perfect punches that only old country teachers know how to give and which had the power to bring back, into an eighteen-year-old pumpkin, the fresh thoughts of a twelve-year-old.

The slap was music to Boraschi's ears:

'Verdi is great,' he enthused, 'but Clementina beats him every time.'

Carletto took up the pitchfork and began to spike the manure from the floor, muttering:

'Such is the *Fascisti* way!'

'Appeal to the Chamber of Labour,' advised Clementina.

But that was the end of it and it and it turned out to be good for everyone.

Public Opinion (1960)

THAT PESCAROLO WAS on people's lips is hardly surprising, because that is where the trouble occurred. Yet Pescarolo is, at bottom, not greatly different to any of the villages in la Bassa. You plant one leg of a compass in the middle of a little square, with the other you draw a circle of seventy or 100 metres radius and inside the circle you find everything: the church, the cemetery, the school, the communist cooperative store, the tavern – which also sells cigarettes and food – the bus station, the bakery, the mill, the weighbridge, the monument, the barber – who maybe also works as a tailor and, between cutting a beard and a jacket, finds a way to trade chemical fertilizers and cattle feed – the doctor's surgery, the garage with adjoining petrol station, the nursery, the blacksmith, the carpenter and the electricity line pole powering twenty-five lights, which constitute the urban illumination plan.

All this within a relatively small radius because, even if, as in Pescarolo, village population amounts to some 2,000 souls, the built-up area is minimal, as many of the village houses are scattered across the plain, one for each farm.

Once upon a time, where the bus stops now, there was a station for a steam tram with a weighbridge adjacent, along with a wooden shed, which had an important function: it belonged to the sugar factory and received the beets brought by local farmers on carts pulled by oxen for onward shipment by tram.

Naturally, they had a post office as close as possible to the tram station and, again as in Pescarolo, no-one would ever have thought of moving it had the old postman not retired.

*

The postman from Pescarolo had important connections in the city and few challenged his authority, even as his methods changed with time, not always to the advantage of his customers. The old men of Pescarolo would tell you that, as a young man, he did not hesitate, even if the wind blew or the sky threatened rain, to go his rounds. Then, as the years went by, he became less reckless and only set out when he had sufficient guarantees of not becoming embroiled in unpleasant meteorological adventures. Later still, when he reached a certain maturity, he adopted a system of seasonal mail distribution. That is, he accumulated the incoming correspondence and took it to its destination when the weather was good. This did cause some bitterness because not everyone appreciated a system which, while undeniably rational, was not geared to satisfying the real craving for news that tends to arouse those with distant children or important business.

Meanwhile, beyond the post office, progress was progressing and the distressing plague of illiteracy was rapidly being overcome: the number of children attending the school was consistently increasing and, since the school building was but five or six metres from the post office, the postman was able to establish a new system of mail distribution, entrusting the delivery of letters, postcards and packages to children returning home after their lessons were over.

Here was a fine example of effective collaboration between School and State, and the new generations of Pescarolesi grew up with a sharp sense of duty towards the community.

Only in cases of particular importance, that is, when the postman sensed that a letter was awaited with a measure of impatience, would he intervene personally, organising the service in such a way that it would arrive at the recipient's house at dinnertime, be it winter or summer.

What's more, to dispel that shadow of discomfort which contact with state officialdom usually causes citizens accustomed to a secluded and, in a certain sense, independent life (as in the case of small landowners or wealthy tenants), the postman did not hesitate to sit at table with the recipients of the "special" correspondence, willingly accepting to participate – as an equal – in their meal.

The worst service that any bureaucrat can render to the State and to the citizen is to assume a 'state' mentality, which detaches him from real life and makes him, instead of an intermediary who brings the citizen closer to the State, a dry instrument good only for having the opposite effect. The postman of Pescarolo understood this fundamental principle and paid no attention to sacrifice in order to put it into practice: so much so that he bought a small motorcycle to reach the most distant farmyards of the district and thus was able to benefit, in a single day, as many as three families, reaching the first at lunch time, the second at tea time and the third at dinner time.

With the spread of rapid communications and the advent of radio, cinema and eventually television, curiosity made its way through the tenacious curtain of fog which, for centuries and centuries, had isolated la Bassa from the rest of the world. In addition to the usual letters, postcards, registered letters and money orders, daily newspapers and illustrated magazines began to reach the people of Pescarolo.

Then a healthy thirst for knowledge took possession of the old postman, who took to reading with such admirable application that he never happened to deliver any newspapers or weeklies which he had not diligently read earlier – even at the cost of stealing hours of sleep.

He did not interrupt his reading even during his frugal meals, and many of the most sensitive Pescarolesi were, more than once, moved by receiving magazines and newspapers that bore humble traces of soup or the unmistakable circle left by the fried egg pan.

*

By now, the postman had reached the final stage of his long career, a few years separating him from retirement. Back then the post office itself was the simplest and most essential workspace one could think of: a room on the ground floor with a door to the street. Inside the room, two wooden partitions isolated the north-east corner, leaving four-by-four metres available to the public, three metres from ceiling to ground. In each of the two partitions, an opening served as a door. It might seem like a poor thing, but the presence of the old postman gave the environment such dignity as to make it almost magisterial.

Pescarolo was a long way from the city, but the building fever that raged there spread its deadly bacilli far and wide. And so in Pescarolo, after 100 years of complete indifference, a feverish anxiety gripped its people.

Locally, it was the municipal administration controlled by Peppone's Reds that forged the new era and it did so, naturally, with the violence and rudeness typical of all communists.

One morning, two cars full of people arrived at Pescarolo.

They were technicians and municipal bigwigs who approached the school building, took measurements, consulted each other and discussed at length the projects they had in mind.

Fifteen days later, a truck with various pieces of equipment stopped in front of the school: a bricklayer and a labourer got out and, having set up their scaffolding, attacked the east wall of the building. They stayed there for ten days and, when they left, the school had, instead of just one window on the east side, two. And the two new windows were equipped with shutters and retractable security grilles.

It was a new and unprecedented thing and the people of Pescaro became disconcerted, then they slowly recovered and, a week later, the barber refashioned the pavement in front of his shop... The blacksmith repaired the roof of his workshop... The carpenter removed a window and doubled the width of his front door.

So it was that the 'building disease' quickly spread through the village. Someone went so far as to start building a house from scratch. His example was followed.

The old postman could not distance himself from the constructive fervour: he represented the State in Pescarolo and the State must always support every praiseworthy initiative of its citizens. He began, therefore, systematically to inspect all the works in progress, taking a deep interest in the projects, discussing them, making all his long and precious experience available to the developers, supporting them with solidarity, generously sharing their worries.

But, while the building renaissance of Pescarolo had some highly beneficial effects, the postal service suffered.

The proliferation of comics, cinema, television had had a negative impact on the new generation. The ideals of boys had been profoundly changed: boys were unspeakably rude to the postman when he asked them to deliver the mail or, worse, pretended willingly to consent, then, having received the letters, opened them surreptitiously, deftly and with a criminality of mission removing the letter from one envelope and putting it into another envelope, closing both with infernal skill and only then delivering the manipulated missives.

The building works increased in number and significance and the postman could not abandon them. While waiting for his pension, he hired the owner of the house that housed the post office.

From then on, Pescarolo, thanks to the personal sacrifice of its postman, finally had a postal service.

Then the old postman had to interrupt his service: his pension caught up with him. Reluctantly, he left the post office. Then, once the ongoing building work, for which he felt responsible, was finished, he left the village.

But he was a faithful servant of the State to the last: before leaving, he researched and compiled a detailed report on the miserable conditions in which the Pescarolo post office found itself, on the need to create a new post office and to normalise the service by hiring new staff who could offer greater professional, moral and political guarantees than the current one.

Which is really where our story begins, because, after all, the story so far is not yet a story but rather a trifling description of how life in the village went on, a trifle in which the message that would make it a story (and a particularly appropriate one, given that a 'message' is itself a postal topic) is concealed.

So, the message now needs to be run down.

*

Don Camillo was hoeing the garden of the presbytery when one day the parish priest of Pescarolo appeared before him.

'Don Camillo,' said the parish priest of Pescarolo, 'there is a village in a predicament and, if you don't intervene, it won't be able to get out of it.'

He explained that someone had thrown a spanner in the works by managing to convince the municipality to move the post office to a new building under construction.

'Moving the post office from the centre of the village to the suburbs!' he exclaimed indignantly. 'The owner of the building where the post office is presently located is willing to carry out all the necessary expansion and improvement works to obviate the move, but they won't listen to him. They want to team up with the Devil to the benefit of the owner of the new house under construction, who is anticipating I don't know how many years of rent. He is someone who "knows a thing or two".'

Don Camillo looked at him curiously:

'I understand what you're saying,' the priest muttered, 'but what am I supposed to do about it? I'm not the Postmaster General.'

'We have sent a complaint to the Mayor,' replied the parish priest of Pescarolo. 'All the heads of our families have signed it. But the letter has fallen on deaf ears. Instead of recommending the will of the people, the Mayor has covered it up, buried the protest. Don Camillo, only you can force Peppone to see sense.'

'I will try,' Don Camillo decided.

*

Smilzo, as soon as he saw Don Camillo appear, formally advised him: 'The Mayor receives the public on Wednesdays and Saturdays from nine to twelve.'

'I am not the public,' replied Don Camillo. 'I come on a private mission.'

Smilzo remained uncertain for a few moments: 'Who should I say is here?'

'A priest who wears size 45 shoes.'

'Now you may think they have a purpose,' Smilzo admitted through gritted teeth. 'But they'll be no use to you the day you make the Big Exit.'

Don Camillo dodged his tempter and barged into the Mayor's office without knocking.

'We need to ask a question in Council to propose that good manners be included among the subjects taught in seminaries,' exclaimed Peppone as he looked up to find Don Camillo standing in front of his desk.

Don Camillo had a personal score to settle with Peppone and didn't even bother to listen to him. He sat down, ignited his Tuscan vehicle and announced:

'Let's talk about *public opinion*.'

'If you find some unfortunate person who will listen to you, go ahead,' Peppone replied disinterestedly.

'You listen to me, Mr Mayor,' continued Don Camillo. 'Public opinion is what politicians need when elections are at stake. Once the elections are over, public opinion is no longer of interest. Public opinion represents the opinion of all the citizens who pay taxes and the salaries of our public servants. It should be considered the most important thing, but, when our public servants are Bolshevik agents, public opinion is worth nothing because the so-called "dictatorship of the proletariat" ends up as no more than the dictatorship of proletarian Comrade X.'

'Fine,' approved Peppone. 'So much for the theory. Basically, who are you upset with?'

'With Comrade Peppone, who doesn't care about public opinion and sweeps it under the carpet.'

'The undersigned Mayor Giuseppe Bottazzi is not sweeping up anything!'

'Why then didn't he forward the Pescarolesi's petition to Post Office HQ? Every family has signed it: isn't this petition the true expression of public opinion in Pescarolo? If the people of Pescaro, without exception, except the guy who would like the post office in his house in the suburbs, want the post office to remain where it is, why doesn't the Mayor forward their petition with a recommendation to implement it?'

Peppone pounded a large fist on the desk:

'Because the people of Pescaro, without exception, except the guy who would still like to keep the post office in his house in the village, want the post office to be moved to the new house!'

Peppone opened a drawer and took out two foolscap sheets of paper, which he placed in front of Don Camillo:

'Petition A requesting that the Post Office stay where it is. Signatures of all the people of Pescaro, including the parish priest. Petition B requesting that the Post Office be moved to the new headquarters. Signatures of all the people of Pescaro, including the parish priest.'

Don Camillo checked carefully and everything matched.

'When things are like this,' shouted Peppone, 'the Mayor puts public opinion in Pescarolo *here.*'

He indicated where he intended to accommodate public opinion in Pescarolo and, considering the particular location, it was not a bad choice.

The Reverend was served right: Don Camillo stood up and, having bowed slightly, left.

Once he reached the presbytery, he jumped on his bicycle and took off towards Pescarolo.

The parish priest of Pescarolo turned pale when he heard what Don Camillo told him; in the end he spread his arms wide and said:

'I couldn't choose between my parishioners. The one in the new house is also a good Christian. Indeed, better than the other, because the owner of the house where the post office is now located is quite Red. He came with his petition and I had to sign it. And so did the other side. You can't create hatred when you live in a village.'

'However, the two petitions cancel each other out. We looked for and found a middle ground that would fix everything: we proposed putting the post office in the nursery school building attached to the presbytery. Proceeds from the rent benefit the kindergarten children, who belong to all social classes. The people in charge are going around collecting signatures.'

'Good,' roared Don Camillo, getting back on his bicycle. 'But I don't want to hear any more about this nonsense.'

But it was written in Destiny that he would hear about it again and a week later, he did.

'Does the Reverend receive...?' Peppone enquired aggressively of the village priest, who was pruning the pergola vine in the presbytery garden.

'There are no office hours in the House of God.'

'Even in the garden of God?'

'Yes, even in the vineyard of the Lord.'

Peppone took a sheet of foolscap paper out of his pocket and handed it to Don Camillo:

'Petition C,' he explained, 'comes with a request to have the best of both worlds[60], and move the Post Office to a suitable room in the nursery school, attached to the presbytery. Signature of all Pescarolesi.'

Don Camillo checked and returned the paper with a shrug.

'That being the case,' he muttered, 'it seems to me that everything is in order.'

'No!' Peppone shouted, shoving a second piece of foolscap out of his pocket. 'Petition D, with a request that the post office be moved to suitable premises of the consumer cooperative annexed to the People's Palace. Signatures of all the heads of Pescarolese families. This is the best of all worlds, because if the priest from Pescarolo wants control of the post office, we want it too!'

Don Camillo returned the sheet of paper and resumed pruning his pergola vine. Peppone watched him for a while then stated baldly:

'I suppose you know that if you prune it like that, it'll produce the most disgusting wine in the entire area.'

The provocation cut deeply and Don Camillo couldn't let it go. He put his secateurs away and walked with a determined step towards the door into the presbytery. Peppone followed him and they came to a halt in the dining room. 'This,' explained Don Camillo as he opened the corner cabinet, 'is, by lucky chance, a bottle of the wine I made from that vineyard another year.'

The wine was good and the one from the second bottle even better. The good *idea*, however, lay in the third bottle and it was Peppone who found it:

'Clearly, to fix things, we need a fifth petition – Petition E – to be sent to the Minister of Posts telling him what the situation is and beseeching him to intervene and resolve the issue *with authority*.'

'Approved!' replied Don Camillo. 'You draw up your earnest request and send it to the Minister.'

---

[60] The Italian idiom, 'salvare capra e cavoli', comes into its own, meaning literally 'to save both the goats and the cabbages'.

'Me?' Peppone chuckled. 'I cannot: the Minister is a Christian Democrat. You do it: he's one of yours.'

'I can't,' stated Don Camillo. 'He's a left-wing Christian Democrat.'

'Let us both sign it,' concluded Peppone. 'You represent the clerical part and I represent the left.'

Don Camillo muttered that certain alliances between the Devil and Holy Water are not going to work.

'It is not an alliance,' replied Peppone. 'The point here is simply that when public opinion doesn't work, then private opinion must step in.'

That is what he said, and let it be the 'message' of my story.

The Vendetta (1961)

'LORD,' SAID DON Camillo to Christ above the High Altar, 'they have called again. This time I really have to go.'

'For two months I have been hearing you say that,' replied Christ.

'You will never hear from me again. I am leaving today... More's the pity.'

'Pity?' Christ was amazed. 'Are you not happy?'

Don Camillo spread his arms desolately:

'Lord, how can a poor shepherd be happy when his flock has been taken from him?'

Christ's voice became severe:

'Don Camillo! Is this, then, the measure of your gratitude to those who have shown that they hold you in such high esteem?'

Don Camillo felt a lump in his throat and he vented it before *il Cristo*:

'Jesus, you gave me a horse and I am grateful. But if I, riding that horse, fall, is it ungrateful to be sorry that in falling I broke my leg?'

'Don Camillo, it was not I who gave you the horse.'

'I know, you would never have been so wayward as to promote the last infantryman in Christ's army to cavalry officer.'

'Do not worry, Don Camillo,' Christ comforted him, smiling. 'You will soon learn to ride your horse.'

Don Camillo lifted his cassock a little and pointed to his enormous feet:

'Lord,' he exclaimed, 'I doubt it. I was born too ... pedestrian.'

Don Camillo was profoundly unhappy. Incredible things happen in this most deranged world, it can even happen that a man is recognised for his merits. Thus, one singularly fine moment, did the old Bishop communicate to Don Camillo news of his distinguished promotion:

'It's crazy, my son, but now we've made you Monsignor and, what's worse, we've decided that you will leave your parish to come and create confusion here with us.'[61]

A treacherous course of action indeed, with only ten days to move lock, stock and baggage from the village to the city.

After two months, Don Camillo was still *in situ*, but now he could no longer find fresh excuses to postpone his departure. This was the situation and we may understand his unhappiness.

Filotti arrived in the church bringing the morning's news:

'All is well, Monsignor.'

'And the Senator? Has he left for Rome again?'

'Not yet. And you? ...What did you decide?'

'God's will be done. As soon as the new parish priest arrives, I will leave.'

---

[61] Readers of *Comrade Don Camillo* (Pilot, 2017) will already know the extraordinary context in which the archpriest's promotion took place, as well as the election of Peppone to the Senate in Rome.

After Filotti left, Don Camillo remained alone, walking up and down, stopping, every now and then, to look at the things that he had already seen a hundred thousand times.

'Why are you sighing, Don Camillo?' Christ asked.

'Lord: it is sad to leave your homeland, to go far away...'

'Don Camillo, it is only thirty kilometres away.'

'Thirty from here to there,' specified Don Camillo. 'But 3,000 from there back to here... Distance is a relative thing.'

'Except for the distance between God and man: that always remains the same.'

'I don't know. I believe that, in the city, God seems further away than in the countryside. Lord, when I am there, will I feel as close to you as I feel you are to me here?'

'That will depend on you, Don Camillo.'

*

The time had come to pack his bags and Don Camillo went to the presbytery and began to gather the most urgently necessary stuff: he would have the rest sent on to him later. The furniture, crockery and all the other household goods would be left to the new parish priest, who was young and needy.

The words of the Crucified Christ had consoled him and he suddenly felt more serene than he had ever been. He had decided to take the leap and no one would be able to change his mind. There was a knock at the door, he went to open it and found himself in front of the last person he could ever have imagined – that famous Gisella who, although she was a very respectable piece of work as woman, was to be considered one of the wildest men of Peppone's gang.[62]

There was an old disagreement between Gisella and Don Camillo due to a certain 'painting' that she spoke about at the time, and now the woman had every appearance of wanting to lock horns in a fight.

'Are you that monsignor who was the rector of this parish?'

Don Camillo replied in kind:

---

[62] Gisella, the revolutionary who had her hind quarters painted red in 'The Painter', in *The Little World of Don Camillo* (Pilot, 2013).

'And are you that girl who, before becoming a scoundrel, was Gigi Marasca's wife?'

'Still am, unfortunately!'

'So why, instead of staying at home doing your wifely duty, are you always out looking for trouble?'

'Because, when the husband is a dirty reactionary who consorts with priests, the wife has a duty to work for the good of the people.'

Gisella reached into her décolletage and took out a large white envelope, which she handed to Don Camillo.

'Here!' she said. She then turned her back on him and, getting on her bicycle - which was a man's bike – her husband's – she meandered away.

Don Camillo left the image of her where it had been and returned to the dining room holding the envelope between the tips of his thumb and forefinger, as is done with things of dubious origin: and, if we take into account the particular place from which the envelope had come, we must admit that such mistrust may have been justified.

His brief conversation with the wild woman had not disturbed him. On the contrary, it had given him good reason for satisfaction:

'If I were not fully aware of the high responsibilities my new status entails,' he considered, 'what would have stopped me from slapping that scoundrel?'

The large envelope contained a luxurious leaflet, which bore a few neatly printed lines:

> *Maria and Sen. Giuseppe Bottazzi*
> *are honoured to announce the*
> *marriage of their son Athos*
> *to the young lady Rosetta Graspa.*
> *The wedding ceremony will take place*
> *IN THE TOWN HALL*
> *at 10 a.m. on the 15th of this month.*

The words 'IN THE TOWN HALL' were printed so clearly as to make them legible from fifteen metres away and Don Camillo suddenly lost sight of the lofty responsibilities that his new status entailed.

*

Il Cristo above the High Altar watched him reappear before him, his face congested and the veins in his neck swollen to bursting.

'Lord,' shouted Don Camillo, showing him the wedding invitation, 'no one has ever dared to perpetrate a civil marriage in my parish!... And he not only dares to do it, but wants me to know about it... Sacrilegious criminal, I won't be able to stop him, but I will boil him on fire. I will pulverize him!... Lord, why don't you electrocute him?'

'Don Camillo, even if I wanted to, how could I do it if you do not tell me who he is?'

'Lord,' shouted Don Camillo, 'who could have such impudence but *Peppone*?'

'Peppone?' Christ was amazed. 'And how can an already married man become married?'

'He doesn't get married, it's his son.'

'Don Camillo,' Christ reproached him, 'why do you make the sins of the son fall upon the father, who is innocent?'

'The innocent is the son, Lord. It's Peppone who wants it like this... He does it to take revenge for the last beating he took... He's the one... Miserable, because he was made a senator and has to wear a tie, he thinks he can take it out on God!... I'll say things that will take his breath away... I'll have them printed this big for him... And if he has the courage to show me his filthy face, I'll beat him.'

'No, Don Camillo,' Christ chided him sweetly, 'once your anger has cooled you will remember that you are a minister of God and you will not beat Peppone.'

Don Camillo thought about it for a few moments and admitted in a calmer voice:

'Yes, Lord, I fear it will end like this... But what a shame...'

The hours struck.

'Don Camillo, it's getting late and you haven't packed your bags yet,' warned Christ.

'I have already telephoned Don Cesare not to come yet to take over the reins,' replied Don Camillo. 'Until further notice *I cannot leave my post.*'

'Until further notice … from whom?' Christ asked.

'You, Lord,' Don Camillo explained in a firm voice.

Faced with such a precise and certain statement, Christ found nothing to object to and remained silent.

*

That night Don Camillo struggled to sleep because he had a live cat in his stomach. But, worse, Peppone struggled because he had a wife in bed who was even more alive than Don Camillo's cat, so much so that, at three after midnight, he was going over his story for the third time:

'You behaved like a coward! You did everything in secret and you faced me with a *fait accompli*… But a wedding invitation is not *a fait accompli*, it's a piece of paper and I mean to use it…'

An explanation then followed as to what use his wife intended to put the wedding invitation.

Peppone wearily pointed out that the idea didn't seem a happy one given that it was a very thick piece of cardboard, and once again the woman reiterated her basic concept:

'My son will get married like his mother and father got married.'

'He will marry as *I* have arranged!' replied Peppone.

'You haven't arranged anything. Your bosses decided on it!'

'Nonsense,' muttered Peppone.

'Yes, your bosses who, when they get tired of their wives, fire them and get a younger one. And, since for them marriage is a joke, it must become one for others too. So, first of all, we are expected to ditch the Eternal Father along the way.'

'God has nothing to do with it. God doesn't bother you at all. We need to get rid of the priests! Yet you defend them!'

'I don't defend priests, I defend marriage. And I will not allow my son to become a public concubine to spite the priests.'

'There you are! Behold, before us are the consequences of damned clerical propaganda!' Peppone shouted, shaking in bed.

At five o'clock the discussion was still going on, then, suddenly, tiredness overcame Peppone and his wife and they fell into a deep sleep.

At the exact same time, Don Camillo, who had fallen asleep with a nail stuck in his brain, woke up with a start. While Don Camillo slept, his subconscious had kept watch to find the key to the problem. And it was the key that Don Camillo kept in a drawer in his desk. He jumped out of bed and, just as he was, in his nightgown and without even putting his feet in his slippers, he went down to the dining room, retrieved the key, grabbed an electric torch and went up to the attic.

He immediately dug out the box, found the field altar and all the other old things, among them the photographs that he had searched for in vain for hours and hours. All three were there: yellowed but still clear. In one you could see a very young military chaplain in the act of presenting arms with the famous 75 mm cannon, in the second the same military chaplain intent on celebrating a Mass in the camp, assisted by the bold artilleryman who acted as altar boy. And he, Don Camillo, was the very young military chaplain.

Don Camillo held the old, dear photographs he had found close to his heart and lost himself in the fascinating, sweet vision of a large newspaper page bearing a large photograph accompanied by a caption – something like:

'Who, then, would have imagined that this altar boy, photographed here while – thoughtful and pious – he waves a thurible to and fro with his little hand, would become Comrade Senator Giuseppe Bottazzi, acolyte of Stalin and Khrushchev?...'

Coming down very excited, Don Camillo didn't even think about going back to bed.

*

At eight o'clock, while he was having breakfast, he saw a woman appear in front of him and struggled to recognise her as Peppone's wife, so pale and haggard was she.

'I come about the wedding,' she said.

'What wedding?'

'That one there,' explained the woman pointing to the invitation card that was lying on the table.

'You have the wrong door, then. The Town Hall is on the other side of the square.'

The woman shook her head:

'The couple will marry as Christians... Naturally this marriage will have to remain a secret between you and us.'

Don Camillo snapped:

'A secret? For you, getting married in church is something to be ashamed of in front of people?'

'Reverend...'

'Monsignor!' Don Camillo specified.

'Reverend!' the woman insisted, 'as a priest it must be enough for you that these two young people set things right with God.'

Don Camillo picked up the invitation and showed it to Peppone's wife:

'Here it appears that Maria and Giuseppe Bottazzi are honoured to announce that their son will be married in front of the Mayor. Either you are honoured to announce publicly also that the boy will, in addition, get married before God or nothing happens. I cannot allow God to be considered less than a Mayor.'

The woman was tired:

'You know, my husband is in a delicate position. He gave his word and can't now take it back. We need to save face.'

'I save nothing for him,' shouted Don Camillo, '...and I don't like arguing with women. Tell him to come here and we will talk.'

'And how can I tell him?' the woman exclaimed. 'He doesn't know I've come here. It's something the couple and I together decided...'

Don Camillo jumped up:

'I only like things done in broad daylight. If you want us to talk about it again, everyone must come here: you, your husband and the betrothed. No subterfuge!'

The woman left and Don Camillo heard nothing more about the matter for the whole day.

At eight in the evening there was a knock at the door and it was the second wave. A meagre wave because they were simply two young people and, what's more, in less than a happy condition. She was pale with red eyes and he had a wrinkled and bruised face. Once arrived in the dining room they stood in front of Don Camillo's desk like two frozen codfish.

'So?' muttered Don Camillo.

'We're getting married,' said the boy. 'We're here to do what needs to be done.'

'And your father?' Don Camillo enquired.

'My father has nothing to do with it. This woman and I are getting married. I'm an adult and I do what I want... I can, can't I?'

Don Camillo struggled to find the right words.

'Of course,' he replied. 'Anyway, you know ... it will take regular banns and so on. You can't do things secretly... So your father will find out...'

'He already knows,' said the boy and he could easily do without saying it because he had it written all over his face.

The girl burst into tears:

'He gave him a lot of beatings,' she sobbed. 'He swore he would take away his workshop and kick him out of the house...'

'I don't care,' exclaimed the boy. 'I know my job and we will manage very well.'

Don Camillo intervened:

'Okay, I agree. Now it is late. We will sort it all out tomorrow. Come whenever you want ... in the afternoon ... even late. Better later.'

The couple left and Don Camillo ran to give the news to Christ.

'Lord,' he asked after he had explained in detail how things had happened, 'this is a great victory, don't you think?'

'How can you say so without knowing the extent of what has been lost along the way?' replied Christ.

Don Camillo thought about this for a long time, weighed the pros and cons and honestly admitted:

'Lord, the bill doesn't add up, does it.'

'Don Camillo,' whispered Christ, 'if to create a family we have to destroy another, I believe that it does not add up.'

*

If, the night before, Peppone hadn't been able to sleep a wink because his wife had spent it peppering him without respite with accusations and recriminations, he spent this night sleepless for the opposite reason.

A woman who never lets up is terrible, but a woman who doesn't want to speak at all is downright terrible.

Peppone had insulted his son, he had beaten him, he had threatened to kick him out of the house and, with this weighing heavily on him, he wasn't even allowed the relief of arguing, of yelling, of letting off steam.

His wife was awake, she was sighing, but not a word passed her lips.

At first light Peppone got up, shaved and went down to the kitchen: but, even so cleansed, even with his beard despatched to the ground floor, the situation knew no change.

As soon as he heard his son open up the workshop, he rushed in. The boy was putting stuff from the workbench in a box:

'What are you doing?' Peppone asked him darkly.

'These are tools that I bought with my own money and I'm taking them away with me,' the boy replied without turning around.

'So you've decided to leave!' Peppone roared.

'I didn't decide it, you decided it,' the boy explained, turning around. He had a black eye and a face full of bruises and Peppone felt a shiver run down his spine.

'What's the point, you turning a regrettable scene into a tragedy,' exclaimed Peppone aggressively. 'Now that the trouble is over, you may stay here.'

The boy shook his head and resumed picking up his tools from the bench.

'Then go!' Peppone shouted. 'Since you and your mother have conspired against me, why don't you take her away with you?'

'I will do as soon as I get a house,' the boy replied calmly. 'We already agreed.'

Once things reached this point Peppone found himself, quite logically, in a situation that allowed him only one way to go. He couldn't beat his son because he had already beaten him, he couldn't beat his wife because he had never hit her and, furthermore, they weren't speaking. All he had left was to beat up the parish priest.

To be honest, Don Camillo did have something to do with it up to a certain point, albeit very indirectly; but Peppone was freed from all doubts as to his next move by the wisdom of one of the basic principles of communist party doctrine:

'The priest is at the root of all suffering by the working people.'

*

The root of the working people's suffering locally was in fact making himself a latte when the sudden appearance of Peppone caught him unprepared.

'Monsignor,' Peppone growled in threatening manner, 'my son will get married in church, but it won't be you marrying him.'

Don Camillo looked at him in amazement.

'And why?' he asked.

'Because, at a wedding, a priest with a face swollen with slaps would stand out like a sore thumb.'

'In this case you are wrong, Senator,' replied Don Camillo. 'For a start he would have a face very much in keeping with that of the groom.'

'I feel a need to stand on your face!' Peppone shouted, clenching his fists, ready to spring.

Don Camillo didn't move an inch. Instead, he took out his half Tuscan and turned it on.

'Reverend,' roared Peppone, 'defend yourself or I'll shoot you down!'

'Have a seat, Senator.'

'Don't be so polite!' Peppone sneered. 'Remember that my youngest son was a tearaway and it was you who tamed him! You were more up for it then.'[63]

'I was a parish priest then, not a monsignor.'

'I'm no longer a mayor, but a senator!'

'Exactly,' Don Camillo calmly concluded. 'A parish priest may put himself on a par with a mayor, but a monsignor cannot stoop to the level of a communist senator.'

Peppone saw red, but his ignition failed because a scream exploded behind him:

'Wretched man, is the trouble you've caused not enough?'

---

[63] Reference here to Michelle, known as Venom, the youngest of Peppone's children and described as a 'capellone', literally a long-haired hippy, whose strength was drained from him, Samson-style, by Don Camillo in *Don Camillo and Don Chichi* (Pilot, 2021).

It was Peppone's wife and she collapsed on a chair.

'Your son is leaving home!' the woman gasped.

'Good luck to him!' Peppone shouted.

'If he goes, I go!'

'Happy travels then to you too!'

Peppone's wife turned towards Don Camillo:

'Reverend,' she exclaimed, 'an honourable family is ruined because of you!'

'A family headed by a man like him is not an honourable family,' Don Camillo specified. 'If you've run into trouble, it'll have been his fault.'

'It is *your* fault,' the woman insisted. 'Everything would have been fine if things were done as I said.'

'And how is that?' Peppone asked aggressively.

Don Camillo stepped forward:

'Tizio is a fierce opponent of yours and he prides himself on it. Supposing one evening he came to you secretly and said: "I remain what I am, but you should give me your Communist Party membership card without anyone knowing, so that, if unfortunately Khrushchev wins, I find myself with all the cards in order." Senator: how would you behave?'

'I would kick ass,' replied Peppone.

Don Camillo opened his arms: 'So why would I have agreed to marry your son in secret?'

'What?' Peppone shouted.

Don Camillo turned towards his wife:

'Didn't you come to ask me exactly this?'

Peppone looked at his wife, who lowered her head.

'But I...,' she shouted, 'I don't know anything about this...'

'Senator,' objected Don Camillo, shrugging his shoulders, 'how could I have imagined it?'

Peppone stood with his legs apart in front of Don Camillo:

'Monsignor, I see what you're up to,' he insinuated. 'According to you, I am the sort of individual who, to save face in front of the people and preserve peace in his family, would come to propose a compromise of this kind!'

'In my opinion, yes,' Don Camillo agreed quietly.

'So,' shouted Peppone, agitated, 'you think I'm an imbecile!'

'No. An idiot would leave things as they are. So he would bust up his family without even saving face, because his son is getting married in church and not just in a town hall as his father had decreed. Instead, your wife comes here to seek an agreement that will allow her to have it both ways – to save both the goat and the cabbage.'

Peppone jumped up:

'Ah! I would have come here for this!'

'I hope so.'

Peppone's wife, having remained silent for an entire night, had a formidable reserve of words at her disposal and she let them go in a torrent of abuse. Peppone tried to resist it but the avalanche of words overwhelmed him and, crouching on the sofa and holding his head in his hands, he waited for the deluge to end.

During which, Don Camillo had plenty of time to finish preparing his latte.

When, after a century, the woman did fall silent and Peppone re-emerged from the ensuing silence, he stated with resolute determination:

'I don't want to take back anything, publically!'

'Okay,' Don Camillo reassured him. 'The public will know nothing. I'll settle for a private u-turn.'

'What would that involve?'

'At the wedding, none of my lot will attend. But all the militants from your section must be there.'

Peppone jumped up and down:

'I will never give you that satisfaction!' he shouted.

'Senator,' Don Camillo replied, 'I don't want satisfaction, but the Eternal Father must be given at least a little.'

Peppone ran off swearing that, rather than accept blackmail, he would have himself disembowelled. And Don Camillo went to make his report to Christ above the High Altar:

'Lord,' he said 'if the couple get married before God and no family were to be put asunder, could we then speak of victory?'

'We are still at the same point as before, Don Camillo,' replied Christ. 'How can you say this if you do not know for sure the cost of the whole operation?'

'Lord,' argued Don Camillo, 'it would be a good opportunity for a bit of publicity. Now, of course God doesn't need advertising, but I think...'

'*I* think too,' Christ interrupted, smiling.

*

In the late afternoon, Brusco arrived to negotiate and said immediately and clearly that the conditions imposed by Don Camillo were unacceptable.

But Brusco was a positive man, and exemplified his positivity with well measured words:

'Things are not as they may seem, seen from the outside looking in,' he explained. 'The communist organisation is efficient, but not perfect. We, like the other parties, have treacherous elements in our ranks, whose sole aim is to make up the numbers. The dignity of the Section is at stake here and we must act with great caution. Only safe elements may be present at the ceremony: people who know how to keep shtum.'

He handed Don Camillo a piece of paper:

'Twenty-five people in all?' Don Camillo was surprised.

'Yes, Monsignor,' muttered Brusco, 'and it should be twenty-four because, if we are honest, I still don't know how I'll manage not to say anything to my wife.'

'I lose out, but I accept' said Don Camillo.

They discussed the other details and quickly reached an agreement.

*

Nestling at the foot of the floodplain, on the river side, was the decrepit church of San Lucio; an even more rural saint than Sant'Antonio Abate because he was the patron saint of cheese makers and personally dealt only with butter and parmesan.

The little church stood in the most deserted part of the shore and Mass was celebrated there but once a year when floodwater allowed it. It was agreed that on a certain morning, after the first Mass had been celebrated, Don Camillo would be taken by Brusco and, stowed with weapons and baggage inside a van, transported to the Porto Vecchio. From there, having embarked upon a boat, he would, by river, reach the little church, which was a hundred steps from the water.

Everything went according to pre-established plans and, when Don Camillo arrived at the church of San Lucio, the entire gang of infidels was waiting for him. They had arrived one by one in roundabout ways, protected by an invisible but highly efficient surveillance service located at key points along the way.

Nobody showed any signs of noticing, let alone recognising, him.

The little church was squalid, bare, with large damp stains on the walls and it smelt of mould. Don Camillo began to prepare the altar and, every now and then, he peered behind him: they were all there impaled upright like cod on sticks, with hard and impenetrable cod-like faces.

He had brought a chest of candles and candelabras and arranged them all around. The flowers were plastic but, once all the candles had been lit, they would make a fine impression.

While he struggled with all this, the militants watched him with extreme indifference as if he were busy with things that didn't interest them in the slightest. They didn't even get upset when he began to unfurl the red velvet runner from the altar to the door of the church. No one offered to lend him a hand. He checked that everything was in order, then turned decisively to a Red in the front row:

'You,' he instructed, 'stand there with the accordion and, when I signal, play.'

'And where do I find an accordion?' Red muttered.

'I have brought you one and I have brought you the music that you will play too.'

Red Rosso shrugged his shoulders and couldn't even object that he didn't feel like playing sight unseen because all that he knew of music had been taught to him, *temporibus illis*, by Don Camillo, and everyone knew that Rosso was the best player of the accordion in the area.

Meanwhile, Peppone was becoming impatient:

'Monsignor,' he demanded in an aggravated sort of voice, 'are we there yet?'

'Almost. The altar boy is missing. I couldn't bring one of my own, so you'll have to take care of it.'

'I'm sorry, but the communist section does not include an altar boy department.'

'Then tell some of your young men to come forward and refresh them with *your* boyhood memories.'

Peppone chuckled:

'I have to disillusion you: none of my men have ever been altar boys.'

Don Camillo took a photograph from his pocket and showed it to Peppone:

'Not so,' Don Camillo concluded. 'And if this young man doesn't help me during Mass, I will not only leave everything and depart, but I will publish this large photo in an important newspaper and write what I know about it underneath. However, if the young man in it helps me, I will, at the end of the Mass, give him the photo as a reward!'

Peppone had turned pale:

'It's filthy blackmail,' he exclaimed through gritted teeth.

'Not so,' Don Camillo replied, handing him the photograph. 'God does not want an unwilling performance.'

He gave the photograph to him there and then, and having lit all the candles, issued instructions for the wedding to begin:

'Let the father of the bride go find the bride and, give her his arm, and accompany her up the aisle...'

The bride's father was Tognone, the most rustic and ill-conceived Bolshevik in the universe:

'Me?' Tognone asked.

'I said the father of the bride. If you're the father, go.'

Then he explained what the groom had to do and what the others had to do, and then he disappeared behind the altar, reappearing shortly afterwards dressed as he should be, and everything unfolded as planned.

When Tognone entered, giving his arm to the bride, suddenly it seemed that the little dilapidated church came completely alive – lit up and shining a mysterious gold. Behind the church Peppone's son, without the others knowing, had worked through the night like a damned man and had managed to build a hut made of branches, whence his girl, who had arrived there in a little proletarian jacket, had emerged dressed in every girl's dream of a bride's dress.

Tognone walked alongside his daughter as if he were afraid of touching her and ruining her dazzling fluorescence. Those in Peppone's gang were no longer as immobile as codfish and all the hard faces softened. From that moment on, everything worked with extraordinary naturalness. Without anyone realising it had happened, Peppone suddenly found himself intent on assisting Don Camillo in his celebration of Mass, the mysterious Latin words that he thought he had forgotten a century ago coming back to his lips as if his time as an altar boy had been yesterday.

And the others didn't even think, let alone blink for a second, that the altar boy was a senator. Everything seemed natural and logical and Don Camillo himself was so caught up in the drama that, when Peppone made a mistake in moving the missal, he surreptitiously gave him a kick with the same spirit, the same spontaneity and detachment, as when any distracted altar boy might do the same.

And then, at just the right moment, a ray of sunlight exploded from the window above the High Altar and, when Rosso began the wedding march, it seemed that the notes were coming not from Don Camillo's accordion, but from the pipes of the organ of San Pietro.[64]

---

[64] Guareschi's reference may be to St Peter's Basilica in the Vatican or to the organ at the Basilica of San Pietro in Venice, the work of the superb Dalmatian 18th-century organ builder Pietro Nachini.